Whispers VI

Whispers VI

Edited By
STUART DAVID SCHIFF

DOUBLEDAY & COMPANY, INC.

GARDEN CITY, NEW YORK

1987

This book is dedicated to:
CAMP ECHO LARK
Love will pervade us till death separate us,
We're friends, friends, friends.

All the characters in this book
are fictitious, and any resemblance
to actual persons, living or dead,
is purely coincidental

Acknowledgments

Introduction copyright © 1987 by Stuart David Schiff
"The Bones Wizard" copyright © 1984 by Stuart David Schiff for *Whispers* #21–22. Reprinted by permission of the author.
"Leaks" copyright © 1987 by Steve Rasnic Tem. By permission of the author.
"Everything to Live For" copyright © 1987 by Charles L. Grant. By permission of the author.
"Bogy" copyright © 1987 by Al Sarrantonio. By permission of the author.
"The Fool" copyright © 1987 by David Drake. By permission of the author.
"Repossession" copyright © 1987 by David Campton. By permission of the author.
"The Years the Music Died" copyright © 1987 by F. Paul Wilson. By permission of the author.
"The Woman in Black" copyright © 1984 by Dennis Etchison for *Whispers* #21–22. Reprinted by permission of the author.
"My Name Is Dolly" copyright © 1987 by William F. Nolan. By permission of the author.
"Toad, Singular" copyright © 1987 by Juleen Brantingham. By permission of the author.
"Sleeping Booty" copyright © 1986 by Richard Wilson. By permission of the author.
"Privacy Rights" copyright © 1987 by J. N. Williamson. By permission of the author.
"One for the Horrors" copyright © 1983 by Stuart David Schiff for *Whispers* #19–20. Reprinted by permission of the author.
"The Black Clay Boy" copyright © 1987 by Lucius Shepard. By permission of the author.
"Where Did She Wander?" copyright © 1987 by Stuart David Schiff for *Whispers* #23–24. Reprinted by permission of the author's literary executor, Karl Edward Wagner.

Library of Congress Cataloging-in-Publication Data
Whispers VI.
Stories originally published in Whispers magazine.
1. Horror tales, American.   2. Fantastic fiction, American.   I. Schiff, Stuart David.   II. Whispers (Fayetteville, N.C.)
PS648.H6W484   1987   813'.0872'08   86-32978
ISBN 0-385-19927-9
Copyright © 1987 by Stuart David Schiff
All Rights Reserved.
Printed in the United States of America.
First Edition.

Contents

Introduction

Time is short. Truly. We are put here for a scant amount of rotations of our sun. In the allotted span, we must make our mark. We tend, for the most part, to group. By this I mean that we associate with our own kind (people of the same country, family, religion, vocation, avocation, and the like), a gathering of like souls, of friends. Horror and fantasy readers, writers, and artists are no exception.

About fifteen years ago I graduated from school and left the comradeship of my New York group of horror and fantasy friends (Frank Belknap Long, David Hartwell, Gerry de la Ree, Lee Brown Coye, Virgil Finlay, and the like) for the fellowship of the 82nd Airborne Division of Fort Bragg, North Carolina. Despite the forced closeness that soldiers jumping from moving aircraft obtain, I greatly missed the kindred souls in the *Weird Tales* tradition. By some quirk I cannot recall, I found out about a gathering of horror-fantasy types in the Durham, North Carolina, home of Edwin Murray. It was probably the most important contact I ever made in the field. From it grew personal friendships with David Drake, Karl Edward Wagner, Manly Wade Wellman, Frances Garfield, Richard Minter, John Squires, Ed Hoffmann Price, and others. All of these people I have mentioned made great contributions to my magazine and anthologies. We all "grouped" and gained strength from our friendships.

Time is short, though. The band is beginning to thin. Time has taken Lee, Virgil, and, recently, Manly. With death it is appropriate to think back upon one's associations and see what fruit they gathered. Fortunately, it was a bountiful harvest. My journal has, irregularly, spanned fourteen years. Many awards have come the way of it, our contributors, and our anthologies. More importantly, though, lasting friendships blossomed, major art and fiction contributions to the field were created. The cover artist to this volume, Anatoly Ivanov, says it all in his remarkable cover painting, "Life Goes On." Even in death, there is life. There is a continual thread linking the groups of the past with the groups of the present and the groups of the future. My *Whispers* anthologies follow that pattern.

Looking back over my previous five books in this series, I find that six of the fifteen contributors to this volume are new to the series. That leaves nine previous contributors, among whom only one, David Drake, is a member of all six books. Like Anatoly's painting, there is change, but life goes on. I hope all of you readers will enjoy life to the fullest, cherish the few moments we have with the people and things we like the most. Time is short. Truly.

Stuart David Schiff
70 Highland Avenue
Binghamton, New York 13905

Whispers VI

I was greatly pleased to have Alan Ryan accept for me my fourth World Fantasy Award. Our friendship goes back several years, including a time when he did not (openly) laugh at me when at a convention I opened my car trunk to find that I had left all of my clothes home. I also recall rejecting his first couple of submissions to Whispers, *but I knew his enormous talent would overcome my editorial blindness. "The Bones Wizard" proved me right, as it won 1985's World Fantasy Award for best short fiction after it appeared in my* Whispers *magazine. It is a moving and passionate gem.*

THE BONES WIZARD

by Alan Ryan

THE BONES WIZARD is sitting on a straight chair on the stage of the Bottom Line on West 4th Street in Greenwich Village. He is rightmost on the stage, on your left as you sip your Bud or Bass and blow smoke that drifts upward, clouding the spotlight beam. On the far side of the stage sits a woman of about thirty, plain, black hair cut short, knees carefully crossed, wearing a sun dress bought on sale at Clery's in O'Connell Street in Dublin. She is the band's girl singer, and when she sings her voice soars high, but she is quiet now, smiling slightly and secretly as the five boys make the music. Next to her is the youngest member of the band, a plain-faced boy, his features without expression, who plays the guitar. His eyes are open as he plays and he is staring, unseeing, at the cloud of smoke in the golden beams of light. Next to him is the bouzouki player, older than the others, tall, gray hair tousled, hunched forward on his chair, lips pressed tight, eyes squeezed shut, fingers flying on the strings. Next to him the player of the button accordion twists his body with the rollicking music, his right foot bounces madly from the floor and his left, in a muddy blue sneaker, taps and taps to keep up the pace. Next to him the fiddler, leader of them all, is lost in his music and only his fingers and arms and his eyes are alive, watching other fingers flying on the keys and buttons of the accordion, leading the way through the twisting hills and wandering lanes of the tune. And next to him is the bones wizard. His bodhran is silent on the floor, leaning against the leg of his chair. Now he plays the bones, the white slivers flashing in his flying right hand, the left hand clenched in a fist on his knee, and his eyes never leave the fiddler's fingers. The bones are a blur and their music rattles faster and faster, challenging the other players with the clatter of his speed. The fiddler glances over at him and grins, nodding, as the music rushes headlong, ancient music from the headlong Irish hills, but the bones wizard only drops his eyes and ducks his head. The bones wizard is playing at his best tonight and nothing can stop him now.

"Haven't you the sense to come in from the rain?" his mother scolded on so many wet afternoons of his youth. He would come in from the barn, smelling of the cows, or from the field where he'd crouched beneath a spindly, lonely tree and his boots would be thick with the mud and his wool coat smelling of the wet, and there she'd be, hands planted on hips and the creases deep in her forehead. Those creases themselves, so permanent a part of her face, had grown as dear to him as her eyes, and when she scolded like this he could do nothing but hang his head.

"Is that it then?" she'd insist.

"I suppose it is," he'd mutter, because it was a proper question, requiring an answer, that was clear from her tone, and he had to be saying something no matter how stupid it sounded.

"You suppose it is," she'd invariably reply, and the rhythm of the exchange was dear to him too.

"I do suppose it," he'd say, with the grin starting at the corners of his lips though his gaze was still set on the floor.

"And it's the music as well, I don't doubt."

The phrases came as regular as responses in the Sunday Mass.

"Aye," he'd say, and press his chin against his throat, for she was not to see the smile coming on him. If she saw the smile, the rhythm of the thing would be broken.

"It'll be the death of you, that music, Sean," and she'd put her hand on the back of his head. "Your head is as wet as the lambs themselves, the poor dumb beasts. Now be peeling off them wet clothes, and not a step more inside the house with them filthy boots on you. Off with them where you stand, I've enough to be doing with your dad and the big ones and their muddy feet all over. That's it, and the sweater as well. Now be off, and don't be coming to the table till you look like the son God intended me to raise. I'll have one at least that can keep his hands clean for an hour at a time."

And when he'd come back, his face and hands scrubbed pink—not for the cleanliness of it but for her small pleasure alone—the tea would be ready and fresh brown bread besides.

"Must it always be the music?" she'd ask as he took the first bite and licked butter from his lip.

His mouth full, he could only nod.

And she'd sigh. "It's a killing virus in your blood," she'd say. "All the rest is satisfied with the listening or to make a bit of music at the weekend, but you must have it every day of your life. Is that so, Sean?"

And he'd nod in reply, his eyes meeting hers straight on this time, not because his mouth was full but because he was incapable of thinking the thought fully in mere words.

The bodhran was on the shelf above his bed. She'd bought the goatskin-covered drum for him on a long-remembered trip to Galway. He could still so clearly see the shop filled with musical instruments, a dusty little shop just round from Eyre Square, with the drums hanging from the ceiling like so many chickens in the poulterer's shop. The Celtic design painted in red on the skin was faded now, worn with constant use from the pounding of the two-headed beater. She'd been feeling flush at the time—she'd told him that afterwards so as not to let him think this could happen all the time—and she'd asked if there was anything else he'd enjoy. The clerk had suggested the bones if the boy liked the rhythm of the music more than the melody, and they were cheap besides, being only plastic. Two curved pieces of plastic, mottled gray and white, and the clerk arranged his clumsy fingers on them and showed him a little what to do. He loved the primitive clacking sound they made, though on that day in the shop he could get no sound from them at all and the clerk only a little and that not much like music. He'd have them as well, he'd told her in a whisper, eyes wide and pleading, if they weren't too dear. Now the bodhran remained at home—you couldn't be carrying it through the hills when you went to fetch home the cows—but the bones were always in his pocket, always within reach of his fingers, dirty or clean.

They were coming near the end of the ritual now.

"The bodhran or the bones?" she'd say.

Now the smile could be brought out from hiding into the warm yellow light of the kitchen. She'd see it and smile and return and put her hand on the softness of his cheek.

"The bones," he'd say every time.

The fiddler beams out at the clapping and whistling of the crowd. They are close to the stage and he can see their faces and thinks he recognizes some of them from previous visits to New York. Maybe he saw them here at the Bottom Line or perhaps at Town Hall—that was always a good gig and plenty of free drinks after—or at Shanachie Records across the river in New Jersey where they played in the old converted railway station and sometimes a freight rattled past in the middle of a set of reels.

Slowly the audience grows quiet.

"God, it's grand to be in New York again," the fiddler says, and the audience yells a bit at that. "It's a fact, you know, there's more Irishmen here in New York than there are at home." More yelling.

It goes on for a few minutes, the chatting with the audience, while the bouzouki player holds the instrument up to his ear till he's satisfied with the tuning.

The fiddler is boyish-looking, with a light that dances in his eyes. The strangers in the audience have all become his friends. They could look him up if they're ever in his town back home and they could sit and drink happily together, and he knows it and knows that they know it too.

"We're going to do a couple of jigs for you now," he says. "Three, to be exact, which as you all know is more than a couple, but what the hell. The first one, I don't know what it's called, but we got it from Sean here, and there's no telling who taught it to him."

Sean smiles at the audience and bobs his head while flexing the fingers of his right hand.

"The second one," the fiddler continues, "is called 'O'Malley's,' and don't be asking me who the hell O'Malley was because I'm damned if I can tell you, and the third is called 'Pat Flynn's,' and I don't know that gentleman neither. Are you ready?" he asks, and looks left to the other players and right to the bones wizard.

"Are you ready, Sean?" the fiddler asks, and turns his head to wink broadly at the crowd.

"Ready," Sean answers, suddenly straightfaced, solemn, and the audience laughs.

"It's hard to tell with that one," the fiddler tells them. He looks up and down the line again.

"One, two, three, *four!*"

And in the very same instant the bones snap together and the bow bites hard at the strings and the music is singing again.

It was raining hard in Dublin and the River Liffey was churning with the dark brown mud the day Sean met the fiddler.

They ducked at the same instant into the doorway of Bewley's to escape the downpour, the fiddler hugging his case to his chest, and banged their heads together so hard they were both dizzy for a full five minutes after.

So for recompense, and since the rain showed no sign of letting up, they went inside and stood each other three hot cups of tea.

"You're a fiddler, are you?" Sean asked, avoiding the other's eyes.

"I am," the fiddler replied, "or it's a bloody strange knockwurst I'm carrying about here with me," and he tapped the case that rested against his leg.

"Have you a band?" Sean asked after a while, his voice as casual as a breeze across a lough on a sunny summer's day.

"After a manner of speaking," said the other slowly. "Are you a musician?"

"After a manner of speaking," said Sean, and the words were like a code or a secret handshake and then they could get down to it.

No country-and-western, nothing of the sort. That they could leave to all the rest and let them be welcome to it. The old music, played strictly in the old way, that was the ticket, the genuine article, and nothing else would do.

All around them in Bewley's, conversation ran high as people went back for more tea and waited out the rain. The place smelled warm and snug, the smell of wet wool only adding to the flavor of the air.

"It's my band, you see," said the fiddler, "me and the two others at the moment, but I expect we'll be ready for bookings in no time at all. I don't suppose it's the pipes you play, I could use a man quick at the pipes."

"No," said Sean, "not the pipes. I can do it a bit in a pinch, but not so's people would pay."

"That's honest, at least," said the fiddler. "Don't tell me the bodhran."

"The bodhran," said Sean. "And the bones. Mostly the bones, for preference."

"I'll listen to you, then, if you tell me you're good."

Sean looked at him.

"All right, then. Well, the rain be damned, I say, when you can have music. Are you for it?"

"I am."

And they dashed from Bewley's through the puddle-filled streets of Dublin and back to the fiddler's tiny room. There was a bodhran lying on the unmade bed, but Sean ignored it and took the bones from his pocket.

It was a dark and narrow room with only a small desk beside the bed and a wardrobe with a door that would not close. They sat on straight chairs, facing each other. Sean could feel the wetness of his hair at the back of his head.

"Do you know this one?" said the fiddler and played a bit of a tune.

Before he'd played even enough for a sample, Sean was in it with him and the fiddler knew at once he'd met his match.

"Is it plastic they are?" said the fiddler when they'd finished a set of three numbers. "Yes, I see. You'll have to be getting the genuine article, you know. The tone is just a bit different, but you know yourself that it's worth it. I know a man in Dundrum who makes them."

"Yes," Sean said. "Now I have the occasion, I can do it. Real bone he uses?"

"The genuine article. Horses and whatever, and maybe ivory."

"I'm in, then?"

"You're in. You're a wizard at it, a bloody wizard. Are you as good at the bodhran?"

"Nearly."

"But it's the bones you prefer."

"The bones," said Sean. "Will you have another tune?"

"I'm going to let Sean introduce this one," says the fiddler. "And if you can make heads or tails out of what he tells you, would you be kind enough to let me in on it?"

When the laughter subsides, Sean leans down to the microphone set near his knee to go inside the open back of the bodhran. He does not touch the microphone to move it, so he is bent nearly double on the chair. The audience chuckles again. They know him from other concerts in the past.

The spotlight grows brighter on Sean and dims on the rest of the stage. He angles his neck upward so he can look at the audience.

"This next one," he says quietly, "is one I learned from a priest I knew when I was a boy. He was a very musical sort of a priest, you see." No one laughs, because his voice is so low and so serious. "He told me the name of it's 'Katie O'Connor's Gone Off For to Marry,' but I don't think that's it. Once we were playing it in a pub in Castlebar, in County Mayo"—"Up Mayo!" shouts a woman in the audience—"and there a fellow told me he knew it as 'The Goat on the Side of the Hill' and his father had taught it to him by that name. I think it's confusing a bit, because I don't see what a goat could have in common with Katie O'Connor, but—"

"There's a lot our Sean doesn't see," the fiddler says into the microphone, and the audience chuckles warmly.

Sean, still bent double on the chair, angles his head now toward the fiddler, and the audience, loving it all, laughs at the look of him.

"Best you just play and don't be talking," says the fiddler.

Slowly Sean straightens up and, without another word, settles the bodhran on his knee, left hand stroking the inside of the skin. He does a run with the beater across the surface and rattles it sharply at the wooden frame of the drum.

"Are you ready, Sean?" the fiddler asks solemnly.

"Ready," says Sean in the same tone of voice.

"Can you keep up the killing pace?"

"I'll try," says Sean.

"All right, then," says the fiddler. He nods twice to the others and their fingers go leaping through a hornpipe.

Sean lays a groundwork with the bodhran, its hollow pounding reminiscent of the primitive hills and the blue-painted warriors that walked them, but when the first tune ends and they slide together into the second of the set, he lays down the drum and picks up the bones, settles them in his hand, clacks them once or twice, and then takes over the lead and sets the pace himself.

At a farmhouse near Spiddal in County Galway, Sean sat on the broken front steps with the father of the lady of the house. The old fellow was trembly and unsteady and Sean had to help him to a seat on the topmost step. In the distance was Galway Bay but you had to make an act of faith that it was truly there, for water and sky made one great blur of gray. The air had been soft all day but now, with the evening coming on, it was sure to rain again. Sean was worried about the car he'd borrowed from a fellow he'd met at the pub in Salthill where they'd played last night. "The godforsaken thing don't run in the rain," the fellow had said, "like many a horse my father, God rest his soul, put a pound on in his day."

"You make them, then, do you?" Sean asked when the old fellow was settled at last.

The man reached one trembling hand into the pocket of his jacket and drew out a crumpled packet of cigarettes. It took ages for him to extract one of the three that remained, get the rest back into his pocket, fish out the smudged box of wooden matches, and—hardest of all with fingers that defied his stubborn will—get the thing lighted and going. Sean knew from the old fellow's mute determination that he must not offer to help, so he silently waited it out.

With the cigarette at last firmly attached at the corner of his lips, the old fellow said, in a voice as gray as the sky, "I do."

Sean leaped into action, wanting not to waste a moment that was in his own control. He pulled the bones from the breast pocket of his flannel shirt and held them out to the old man.

"These are what I play," he said. "But I'm wanting something better. They tell me all over Ireland, and in America as well, that it's you that makes the best."

The old man handled them for a long time, turning them in his twisted fingers, as if the music they held trapped within could enter his brain through the white skin of bloodless fingers.

"My father taught me the trick of it," he said at last around the cigarette in his mouth and the smoke that made him squint one eye. The ash on the cigarette was an inch in length. It dropped off now with the motion of his lips, but he took no notice of it.

"These are good," he said. "But I'll make you better. If you've an ear, you'll hear the difference."

"I have," Sean said quietly. "I'll hear it in the bones."

The woman is standing now, her lips close to the microphone. She smooths the front of her dress. Her speech is shy and hesitant as the lights fade elsewhere and focus on only her and at the other side of the stage on the bones wizard. They are alone on the stage, the others having slipped away in silence.

"This is a song I had from an old woman in Ballyconneely, in Galway," she says, her voice soft and a little smoky. "It's about a pretty young girl, the prettiest in her town, who marries a fellow who goes off to sea and then . . . Well, you'll hear what happens after." She glances to her right. The bones wizard is watching her, left hand on his knee, right hand poised and ready. "It's only me and Sean for this one," she says into the microphone.

And the bones wizard moves his right hand, the movement almost invisible, and the bones are making a terrible ancient sound, going at twice the pace of the singer's slow soprano which glides atop the rhythm in a sobbing lament, all the sadder for the contrast with the bones. But after a bit, the voice and the bones come together as one in their sadness, twisting around each other, as if for comfort, and the song they make sounds as old as the stones of the earth.

Some rich London swell had wanted the privilege of feeding them after the concert, and they had all gone off with him except for Sean. Sean had spent an hour walking by himself, working out the intricacies of a new tune in his head, and when at last he thought to look around, he saw a sign above an Italian restaurant that told him he was in Frith Street, so he knew he was still in Soho. He must have been walking pretty much the same streets for the whole hour. The pubs were closed, but he thought vaguely that he might be a bit hungry when he saw the bright light of the Pizza Express in Soho Square.

He got talking with the girl at about the time his pizza was set before him. She was by herself at the next table and, after a while, when he seemed too shy to invite her to join him, she made the suggestion herself.

She'd come to London from Portsmouth, she told him. She was young and chubby, with great pillowy breasts that shifted invitingly beneath her thin sweater, and her skin was pink, nearly glowing with its own soft light. After a while, he thought to ask her what she did.

"Well," she said, "I work in this kind of a private club. I'm a kind of a hostess, if you see what I mean. It's in Great Windmill Street," she added, as if that explained it all. She was leaning forward, her breasts dented by the edge of the table. "I have my eye out for model work, you know, anything in that line. I've done a bit of it, but only for, well, rude pictures and that sort of thing, the kind you can't show your mum. It's not really what I'm after, of course, but it'll do till the better sort comes along."

He listened but said nothing, not looking at her breasts where the table pressed against them or at her smooth and glowing skin, but watching the vision that danced in her eyes.

"And who are you?" she wanted to know, and it struck Sean as odd that this pink and plump girl would be as interested in hearing about him as she was in talking about herself. "I've told you about me," she said in a matter-of-fact voice, "so it's only fair you should tell me about yourself."

"I'm a musician," he said. "I play the bones." He took them from his pocket where the heat of his body had warmed them. He held them out for her to see—she had been, after all, so open about herself with him—but it was clear from the angle of his arm and hand that she was not to touch them.

"It's these I play," he said. "I've had a lot, you know, and these are good, but they're not the best. I've an eye out for the best."

Suddenly embarrassed, he hid them away again in his pocket. When he looked up, he was dazzled and surprised to see his frankness rewarded with a lovely smile.

The others are back on the stage now, the girl sitting silent, slapping hands on knees, while the five boys sail on the music. Button accordion, bouzouki, guitar, and fiddle course the swelling tune on the dance rhythm of the bones.

The bones wizard is playing with his eyes closed tight. His left hand is a fist so hard that the flesh has turned white and bloodless. His right hand, with the gleaming white bones, flashes in the brilliant spotlight, a blur, an ivory sliver, and the music seems to issue from the very air itself.

The bones wizard is deep within himself, breathing not air but rhythm and music and percussion as primitive as the pacing of human breath. He is playing the bones he always wanted. Somewhere in the misty depths of his mind, somewhere far beyond the music, he remembers a plump and pretty girl in Soho who did not know that the thing she waited for was already hers. But she is hardly a conscious thought in his mind, barely the echo of a ghost. The bones wizard is playing at his best tonight and nothing can stop him now.

When at last the final tune reels to an end, the audience, cheering, explodes. ("Well, we all finished at the same time, more or less," the fiddler will tell them later over beers, and they will take it as his highest praise.) The clapping quickly grows rhythmic, pounding.

The fiddler rises from his chair, laughing back at the audience, and waves. He bends forward to the mike and says something, laughing, that no one can hear. He waves again, stoops quickly and picks up the bodhran from beside the bones wizard, and starts to move away, upstage toward the black curtains, and the others move with him, the girl singer, the bouzouki player, the guitarist, the player of the button accordion.

The bones wizard remains sitting a moment longer as the others move out of the light. The bones are safely in his pocket. He stands, awkwardly, as the lights die out to darkness, and in the darkness, filled with pounding applause, he feels for the crutches on the floor behind his chair. He finds his balance on one foot—this is recent and he is still getting used to it—and settles the crutches beneath his arms. In the dimness, he sees the fiddler waiting by the black curtain to give him a hand if he needs it. There is a step back there, he remembers, just behind the curtain, and he still has trouble with steps. Steps are hard for a man with only one good leg and another that ends at the knee. He still has some pain there, and sometimes itching in the nonexistent foot, but the bones wizard doesn't care. The bones wizard is playing at his best these days and nothing can stop him now.

Steve Rasnic Tem's stories, like good friendships, never leave you. He is able to capture a part of the reader's mind that sucks up his creation, and like the last remnants of a tube of toothpaste, it cannot ever be squeezed out.

LEAKS

By Steve Rasnic Tem

"A family's got to do things together, each and every day," Owen's father always said. "And do things best as you can, like you mean them. That's what makes right living. Those little things you do every day. Like working in the garden, or working on the house, even going to a ball game together. You do them regular and it's just like praying. Even if you got nothing else but that, everything'll turn out okay."

His father's rituals. Owen used to think they'd drive him crazy. Maybe they had. Maybe he should have asked his wife if they had—Marie would know. But he hadn't even talked to her on the phone since she'd left him two years ago. He had no idea where she was. She hadn't even tried to contact their older son Wes, and that surprised him. Her leaving in the first place had surprised him. As had her taking Jimmy, the younger, and leaving ten-year-old Wes alone in the house that day. Owen couldn't imagine what she'd been thinking.

He hadn't really known Marie at all. And now, he had to admit, he knew his sons even less. His family must have been slipping through his fingers for years and he hadn't noticed a thing.

"I hate it here." That was Owen's mother. But it might have been Wes. He'd said that when they weren't more than three feet inside the doorway of the old house. Owen had felt like hitting him. "I hate it here," she always said. The regular, ritualistic complaints, day after day. "Everything's so *damp*. I can't leave any of my clothes in the trunks for fear they'll mildew on me. And it's so plain. It's like living in a box!" Then she'd drag Owen to her closet door and make him look in. The mildew spread over the old floorboards like pale green paint. It nauseated him. He'd look back over his shoulder at his father, who watched them from just outside the door but never came in. It embarrassed Owen, the way she'd show him things wrong with the house as if his father weren't standing right there.

"It's a great deal, hon." That was Owen's father. "County used to use it for storage, I think. Marine equipment, or something. That's why it's plain. But hell, doesn't have to be that way forever. We'll fix 'er up. Besides, it's the only way we're going to get a house right now."

"But it's so *wet* here. Makes my skin crawl. Like I'm always tasting bad water."

"It's close to the water, don't you know," he said, and laughed each time. Each time Owen's mother trembled, and after a few years in that house Owen understood why.

The voices were so clear, only slightly muted as he recalled them. As if they'd leaked from the walls that had stored them these many years.

His father's attempts to placate his mother were useless. Owen didn't think he'd really tried. Most of the time he ignored her complaints, as if he had other things on his mind and counted on the rituals to make things right in the family.

"Almost sunset. Let's get those chairs ready and head down to the creek bank." He never said it loudly, but the firmness of his expectation was clear. It was something the family did every night, even in the coldest weather. "Owen, you shut the door behind your mother." Always the same instruction.

The family trooped the hundred feet to the creek bank, a hundred muddy feet most of the time, the brownish-yellowish grass lying flat over the wet loam like a badly done toupee. Owen's father always in the lead. "In case of water snakes," he said and winked at Owen's mother. A little cruelly, Owen always thought. One evening she'd been terrified to distraction by one of the enormous earthworms that were always lying around, forced out of their holes by all the water that saturated the ground near the creek. Owen had to admit it was the biggest earthworm he'd ever seen. Freakishly big.

They each carried a lawn chair. "Okay, now you sit there, Mother. And you there, Owen." His father stared at them as they struggled to unfold the stiff old chairs. It always made Owen terribly self-conscious. And then inevitably his father would grab the chairs out of their hands and show them how to grip the aluminum tubing, how to snap the chair out just so. "Why can't you people ever learn the proper way to unfold a lawn chair?" Then they'd all sit facing the creek. "Good to do things together," his father would say several times during the next hour. "Family needs its routine." And that would begin the lecture for the evening.

They'd sit there, watching the sunset redden the greasy water below them, dark water that seemed too thick somehow, too substantial, that lapped at their feet so hungrily.

"Beautiful evening," his father would say. "And look at how pretty the water!" Owen could *taste* the creek—the air was full of it. It was like drowning.

That was a long time ago. Now he and Wes were back.

The first day back in the house Owen wandered aimlessly from room to room. Wes stayed in the backyard and complained. Sometimes Owen would catch a glimpse of him through a yellowed windowpane. At thirteen he was tall and lanky, a dishwater blond much like Owen himself, much like Owen's father. Owen felt a sudden pride in his son at that moment, but he doubted he ever would tell him. Something made it too hard.

Several times Owen had to stop Wes from throwing rocks at the house. He was rapidly losing his patience; he was sure if Wes didn't stop he'd take a backhand to the boy. He couldn't understand why his son would do that; he couldn't understand why he was so angry all the time. He'd talked to him, when he could, about Marie's abandoning the two of them, and Wes really seemed okay about all that.

But Owen knew he was overstating things—Wes certainly wasn't angry all the time. He just had a talent for picking the *wrong* times to be unruly.

Once during that first afternoon in the house Wes brought Owen flowers. "For the lady of the house," he said with a grin.

Owen was touched. "Lady?"

"Sure. You've been hanging closer to home than an old maid, Dad."

Owen sighed. "I am being a little silly, I guess." He laughed when Wes nodded in an exaggerated, comic fashion. Owen smelled the flowers. "Terrific. Where'd you find these?"

"Out by the back gate, near the woods. They're all over the place out there."

"Yeah. Seems like I remember my father having a bed of perennials out there." He looked up. "I'm sorry, Wes. How are you doing?"

Wes let loose a lopsided grin. "Hey, no sweat. I just feel a little strange out here, is all. What can *I* do for you?"

"You're already doing it, Wes. You're already doing it."

He left his own and Wes's meager pile of belongings in the front hallway, right where they dropped them. He traveled light, never thinking of any particular place as home, determined not to let his own possessions tie him down.

Very little had changed in the house in fifteen years. In his mother's sewing room a swatch of bright blue cloth still wedged under the needle. The dust had only now begun to accumulate; his father had been dead a week, the house untended for two.

He knew the house would dirty quickly. There seemed no end to the work required to maintain a house. Owen found himself listening to the walls.

"It doesn't stop! I've cleaned the floor twice today already!" His mother was on her hands and knees, her back hunched, scrubbing at the kitchen tiles. No matter how much she scrubbed, the seams still looked muddy. Her face was red. Her hands raw, nearly bleeding. She was sobbing.

In his father's den a newspaper from last month was neatly folded on his overstuffed chair, the same soft brown chair Owen remembered. The house had been a lifetime of work. His father's lifetime.

His father had seen Wes only once or twice; he'd never seen Jimmy at all. "Can't come out there now, Owen. The house needs too much work right now." The same excuse, again and again. "No time for visiting with all this work to be done."

"I can't do this anymore!" His mother said it almost daily, ritualistically, her hand clutching a filth-encrusted rag, her eyes red from the dust and crying. The mold came back no matter how thoroughly she scraped it away. The tiles peeled from the floor. The windowsills warped. The paint flaked away. "This house! This house!" She complained all day when his father wasn't home, complained just to Owen, and to those always damp, clammy walls. His father made her sound crazy.

"It's that fancy house your mother's folks own." His father spoke to him as if his mother weren't standing right there, slamming pans around as she fixed dinner. "It's got her spoiled, I think. Your mother doesn't seem to know about working to *make* something good. Like this house. It'll be a showplace someday. If we all aren't afraid of a little work."

A lifetime of work. Owen knew he should have sold the house, or denied the will, anything other than, in fact, to take possession of it. But his father had worked so hard. His father had told him again and again that children owed their parents, and Owen believed that. His father had manipulated him as skillfully and persistently as he had manipulated the rules by which houses fall into disrepair.

All the furniture and appliances looked new in that house. It was only by looking very closely that Owen could see the countless, minute indications of repair—the reweavings, the welds, the glue repairs, the parts replaced by parts of ever-so-slightly different color. Such fine repair work. So much effort spent to gain such small results.

He could smell the dampness in the house.

It was only after dark that Owen realized he and Wes really didn't have to stay in the house. Wes had known, had insisted they didn't have to stay, but Owen had other voices to listen to.

"We can leave all our stuff here, Dad. None of it really matters that much; isn't that what *you're* always saying?" Owen gazed at his son in surprise. Wes was almost in tears. Owen wondered how the boy could even know.

A battered suitcase and a few boxes of clothes and paperbacks. Owen could hire an agent to handle the sale of his father's house.

He gazed at the new woodwork around the doors and windows, the new paint that had replaced the old, the carefully wrought repairs in the furniture. It was insane, the amount of wasted labor, wasted life that had gone into keeping this house alive.

When next he looked out the window it was dark. Wes had fallen asleep on the couch. He could hear the creek lapping at the muddy bank only a short distance away. A damp sensation crept into his throat. Suddenly Owen was afraid to step out onto the soft, fog-shrouded ground that surrounded his father's showplace. Wes was asleep; it was best to spend the night. Owen covered him with a blanket—it had always been easy to catch colds in this house.

Owen left their things in the hallway and slept upstairs that night. First he tried his old bedroom, but after gazing at all its carefully repaired toys he discovered he could not sleep there. He used his father's old bedroom.

His mother left the house, and the creek, when Owen was thirteen. He never saw her again. He knew it was that nightly ritual that finally did it, for his mother had always hated that creek. She said she'd never seen water like that anywhere.

Owen woke up on his second day in the house with an enormous headache, his chest sore, and his body riddled with aches and pains. Opening his eyes seemed unusually difficult, as if the wet headache were pushing his eyelids down.

The wooden floorboards creaked—too loudly—as he padded his way toward the bathroom. He stopped at the bathroom door and looked down. He felt dizzy. The floor looked warped, buckled toward its center. He grew nauseous and fled into the bathroom.

He hovered over the sink, barely able to control his sickness, his arm supporting him against the wall. The wall tiles felt slick, slimy beneath his palm. He wanted to remove it from the tile, but he hadn't regained his balance yet. He stared down at the faucet. Water was flowing in a silver line into the drain, noiselessly, with almost no splash, like an unbroken tube. He suddenly couldn't bear the thought of touching it, of breaking its symmetry.

He dressed quickly and went downstairs. Wes's bags were gone. He started to call him when he heard the footsteps overhead, in his old room. He couldn't suppress a smile as he walked past his stuff and opened the front door.

With his first steps outside he noted how quiet it was. You couldn't even hear the creek.

He walked around to the patio facing the garden. The cement slab was cracked—you could see the traces of patching material. It had cracked every spring when the water pushed the ground up under it, and his father had repaired it every spring with the same patching compound, which made the slab good until the next spring. Owen looked out on the garden; it was badly in need of weeding. Several potted plants left out on the gravel pathways had tilted where the gravel had sunk beneath them. The little garden house his father had built when Owen was thirteen had lost some roof tiles. They protruded from the barren garden like praying hands. The bright yellow paint on the back fence had paled and was peeling away from the damp wood. The woods drooped over the fence, leaves dripping steadily.

The ground seemed to shift beneath his feet. Owen lifted one shoe and it came away muddy. As he stared into the early morning fog he imagined his father there, laboring furiously over first one area of the yard and then another. Only to repeat these small repairs a few days later.

It took a special person to take good care of a house. A talented and dedicated person. His father had said that many times. Owen wondered if he had it in him. There was so much work to be done here.

After Owen's mother left, his father began insisting that they "do more father-son things." And so he had instituted the ritual of the late-afternoon swim. His father expected him to be dressed in his swimming trunks by the time he got home from work each day.

It was cold in his bedroom, as it was always cold in his bedroom, which made Owen change quickly into his trunks. But he let his father believe it was an example of the eagerness he insisted on.

"Hurry up, boy! The creek don't like a reluctant swimmer, you know." His father said it each time, and Owen always wondered at his meaning. Maybe it was a joke, but it always made him even colder.

In any case Owen knew it was a mistake to keep his father waiting. As they walked toward the creek bank, his father led the way with a brisk, long-legged stride. When they reached the bank, Owen was to drop his towel immediately and jump into the shiny water. He learned to make the leap into the creek without thinking, resigned to it as one might become resigned to a repetitive bad dream.

Owen leapt, eyes closed, struggling to force his thoughts into a stillness, into the bad dream.

The water was cold. He got some in his mouth. Bitter, and thick. It made him spit and choke.

"That's just from the plants living on the bank . . . give it a bad taste." His father said that every time. And not once had Owen believed him.

It was hard to swim here—however calm the water appeared, it roughened when Owen tried to swim in any particular direction, the small waves pushing against him. The water was heavy on his back. As if someone were sitting on him, trying to push him into the scummy bottom. The surface was oily and burned his eyes. It had taken him a long time to find the right word for it and then he couldn't get it out of his mind: It was an *unfriendly* place to be.

A hundred times Owen thought of refusing the swim.

"It's important for us to do these things together, son."

"You never spend time with Wes. You should be doing things together!" That was Owen's wife. He agreed with her, and the desperation he heard in her voice pained him. It wasn't that he didn't *like* Wes. He loved him deeply. And he made attempts to plan activities they could do together—movies and ball games and museums and such. But it always felt so forced. So dangerous.

And now it was all his. The house. The grounds. The bank. The creek. Owen turned and stared at it. Now, the creek was making noise, splashing and sucking, as if it had awakened from a very long sleep. He tried in vain to remember its name, and wondered if it even had a name.

On the morning of the third day back, Owen quickly put away his own gear, then set about on the first repairs. He would wonder for some time why he felt compelled to do this—he wondered even at the time. There was no reason for him to follow in his father's footsteps. He could live a completely different life. And when he woke up that morning he had pretty much decided that was the way it was going to be—he was going to keep the repairs down to a necessary minimum. Shabbiness was one thing that could not get to him. It wouldn't define his life.

Wes, of course, wasn't happy about Owen's decision. "You promised we'd only be here a little while!" was all he would say. His son's petulance angered him.

"Just for a little while, Wes. If I do just a few, small repairs then we can get a better price for this place. And I can afford to buy *you* some of the things you've always wanted. Now doesn't that make sense?"

"I don't want you to buy me anything. I just want to get out of this place. It's cold and wet . . . I *hate* it!"

It hurt.

But then there were things to do. Several of the fake-marble tiles popped off the wall when he went into the bathroom. He examined the exposed surfaces, and discovered the old plaster beaded with water. No doubt the caulking had eroded, letting the water from the shower seep in. Then he noticed the small rust stain in the sink, a stain he could swear had not been there the day before. Then a section of wallpaper peeled loose in the living room. And a piece of brick fell down from the fireplace —he picked it up and it crumbled nearly to dust in his hand. He examined the rest of the brickwork and found it full of tiny holes, soft and brittle. As if alternating damp and dry had made it deteriorate.

The house was falling apart around him, and he couldn't bear the thought of that happening so soon after his father's death, while he was in charge. If nothing else he had to save the house for his own son's future. Maybe eventually he would put it on the market and sell the problem to someone else, but he couldn't let it all disintegrate while he was staying there.

On the living room shelves were countless books on home repair. Owen spread one across his lap. The pages smelled musty, and felt a bit like dough beneath his fingertips. He stared at a shiny splotch lying on the contents page. When it started to move he recognized it: a silverfish. He sucked in his revulsion and brushed the insect away.

The plastic wall tile in the bathroom was easy. He spent about an hour scraping the old adhesive off the backs of the tiles and the exposed wall. The wall had dried during the morning and seemed pretty solid. He found new plastic-tile adhesive in a storage room in the basement, as well as virtually every other home repair compound, chemical, tool, and material imaginable. He stood there, adhesive in hand, and tried to calculate the value of such a stock. Probably in the thousands. He spread the backs of the tiles with the adhesive and pressed them firmly into place. Then the joints had to be smoothed. Owen found himself using the flat end of a toothpick, as if he were sculpting a miniature. An old house like this never forgave shoddy work. Before you knew it, something adjacent would need repair—like a spreading infection. His father must have told him that a hundred times.

Wes spent a great deal of time wandering the grounds and reading. He didn't like sitting on the ground, so he always carried a folding chair with him. Sometimes Owen would discover him behind a bush or some other object, watching Owen make the repairs. Owen thought he seemed content enough.

Rubbing paraffin on all the edges of a sticking kitchen cabinet door seemed to solve that problem immediately. Replacing a door spring with a pneumatic closer from the basement storage room stopped the back screen door from banging. The wobbly legs on the dining room table were repaired by forcing new glue into the joints. A small hole in one of the walls was filled with gypsum-board joint compound and sanded smooth. Owen discovered a small hole in one of his mother's favorite pewter mugs; he cleaned the metal inside the mug with steel wool, then covered the hole with epoxy mender.

When he returned the epoxy to the basement he discovered that several of the water pipes were sweating, and a puddle had formed on the concrete floor. He stared at the pipes, fascinated by the way moisture just seemed to ooze out of solid metal, then wrapped them with fiberglass tape.

Over the next few days Owen discovered he had a knack for this sort of work, something he never would have imagined. Some repair solutions came to him naturally, unbidden. And for the knottier problems he discovered, by dipping into his father's library, that there were tricks he could use, that the mysteries had discoverable keys. By drilling holes almost through the wood slightly smaller than the nails he was going to use he could prevent the wood from splitting when he nailed two pieces together—especially useful when working with oak or yellow pine. Coarse sand was required for making good concrete. Cellulose cement made a neater joint than epoxy glue but it broke down under heat. Pyrethrin was a good spray for centipedes, but since they kill many other insects perhaps they'd best be left alone.

The air seemed drier in the house. It had been unexpectedly easy to conquer the dampness. Owen breathed more easily.

Wes spent a great deal of time in Owen's old bedroom, playing with his ship models, taking them apart, reassembling them. And some days he took long walks by himself. But never by the creek.

"Why don't you ever go down to the creek?" Owen had been repairing the porch swing, replacing some of the slats, when Wes walked up behind him. It startled Owen at first; his son had paid a noticeable amount of nonattention to the repair work up until this time. "There's a lot of interesting animals living by the creek, birds and reptiles and things," Owen continued, "and it's a lot cooler down there." To his dismay, Owen usually found himself taking up a semilecturing tone when speaking to Wes. The canned sentences almost led him to propose that Wes take a swim in the creek. But the suggestion died in a sour taste that filled his mouth.

"I don't like the creek," Wes said. Then, when Owen thought the boy wasn't going to say anymore, "There's something wrong with it."

Owen laid his tools down and turned from the job. "I don't understand what you mean."

"What are we *doing* here, Dad? You said just a couple of days!"

Owen closed his eyes. He was angry, but he also felt an unaccountable kind of grief. He reached out and touched Wes's tennis shoe. Maybe it was silly—he wanted to hold his son, grab his hand, but the shoe was all he could reach at that moment. "I'm sorry. I know. But I'm real close to settling something, Wes. I can't explain it, but we have to stay just a little while longer. I feel so close now."

He must be babbling like an idiot. He expected his son to look confused or appalled or miffed, but the boy looked almost kindly. "Okay, Dad. But let me help you fix some of this stuff. Maybe then we can get out of here."

Owen nodded.

Owen discovered it relaxed him to make the walk from the house to the creek after a long day repairing the house. He'd sit in an old chair on the bank and nearly fall asleep watching the slight, restless waves. He wanted badly for Wes to join him there, but wasn't about to force him. He could see now why such a ritual might have appealed to his father.

Owen had noticed a peculiar coincidence. The better the repairs proceeded, the nearer some intangible ideal of "finishedness" the old house approached, the lower the level of the creek against his bank. And the dryer and firmer the ground. If repairs were going exceedingly well, he could hardly see the surface of the water.

Owen spent several more weeks making repairs. He had little time to think about why he was doing them; they just seemed to need doing. But after a while, after long stretches of labor, usually on a weekend when he thought he could rest, things seemed to go all wrong somehow. Concrete and brick he'd repaired three days before crumbled. Chair legs warped, popping their joints. Wallpaper buckled.

The damp was back, undoing Owen's repairs one at a time.

He had grown more and more irritable—he couldn't help himself—but Wes seemed to know enough to stay out of his way. Occasionally he allowed the boy to help out with the small things—the unskilled labor tasks like carrying supplies or bracing beams—but most of the time he refused help. Wes spent more and more time inside Owen's old room, with the shades drawn. Some days they didn't see each other at all. He ate his meals, sandwiches usually, wherever he was working. Wes seemed good at fending for himself.

Once his father had spent most of a week carefully laying flagstones for a patio that was to abut one of numerous flower gardens he had established on the grounds behind the house. By that time his father's anxieties about the house and yard were obvious to Owen. The number of lines webbing his face had increased dramatically, and there was a barely perceptible tremor in his hands. More than once Owen had seen him drop a hammer or screwdriver, then rub his hands violently, as if to work the circulation back into them.

But on this particular day his father seemed worse than usual. He walked around as if on eggshells, as if a cake might fall, or a castle of playing cards topple if he did not move softly enough. He carried the flagstones out to the prepared ground carefully, looking at the ground in front of him before each step. Then he knelt slowly, positioned the stone, then tamped it gently into place with a rubber mallet.

Owen didn't exactly see what happened next, but he heard his father fall and felt the ground shake. And saw, although from a distance, the flagstones sinking into mud. Later he examined the ground there; it had been seriously undermined by the water.

He could have gone to his father that long-ago day. He could have comforted him. But could not. Just as Wes could not. They'd always been like that, the two of them. The three of them. They were past changing, past any piecemeal repair.

Owen dreamed about plans for the house—his father's plans, his own plans. If he could only solve the dampness problem, they could have a rec room in the basement. His father had talked about that for years. It would

give them more time for each other. Wes would like that. It was important for a father and son to do things together.

Each night Owen would awaken from the dream of a house that demanded no labor, to the sound of the dripping. He'd leap from the bed
and roam the house, checking the faucets, the windows, the roof, examining the ground outside. No moisture. And yet when he crawled back into
bed he could hear it louder than ever, impossibly loud.

He wondered how Wes could sleep through it all.

He'd remodel the house completely, he thought. He'd put in a den, a
children's room. Wes would have his own workshop, his own tools. He'd
really like that. Reshingle the roof, panel the living room, change the
ceiling fixtures, update the wiring. Once the house was unrecognizable
perhaps there'd be no more problems.

Owen would walk into the bathroom in the morning and find the
faucet running, a continuous silver line as if the metal were leaking into
the bottomless pit of the drain. He'd tighten the handle but the leak
couldn't be stopped, and he'd stand there watching the metal dissolving,
being stolen so quickly by something that lived at the bottom of the drain.

Some nights he'd awaken and wander sleeplessly from room to room.
Every faucet in the house would be running in that continuous, echoing,
dreamlike way. He'd go back to bed wondering when the porcelain sinks
themselves would begin their silent journey into the dimension at the
other end of the drain.

He'd build a children's room. A silly thought. But what was a house
without children? There was so much work to be done—who had time for
a family?

Drip . . . drip . . .

There were hidden leaks in the house. All the good air escaped through
the poorly insulated roof and walls. Some energy projects would be good
for next fall. Maybe an insulating blanket around the water heater would
help.

He'd wake up in the middle of the night because of the awful subtlety
of the noise it made. Drip. He'd pull up the bedclothes and check his toes
for cracks in the toenails leaking his life away. His father would be surprised to see how well he'd managed the repairs.

He'd wake up in a heavy sweat, the bedroom impossibly humid, the
walls warping inward from the damp. He'd check his damp head, fearing
his brain fluid was leaking away.

He had a plan for getting remarried if he ever got out of the house to
meet someone. She would be enormously impressed with the improve-

ments he had made. And once she saw his sensitivity demonstrated in his plans for the new children's playroom, she would fall in love with him. They would be married in the living room, if he could keep it dry long enough.

They would have children. He'd always wanted more children.

His bed rotted under his thrashing body. His sheets tore to damp rags in his fists. The wallboard began to decompose, releasing gases into the room that reminded him of swamps and old spring houses. *You can smell history in these rooms,* he thought, and wondered if he had stumbled across an important discovery.

He woke up with the water in his ears. He stumbled into the bathroom —the liquid oozed from the tap like clear molasses. He went to the kitchen and the water was full-force from that faucet. The "hot" and "cold" handles no longer controlled it. He wandered into the turgid air of the living room; the walls had begun to sweat.

Where was Wes? Owen scrambled up the stairs and into his old bedroom. The bed was soaked, the sheets falling apart, the models suspended from the ceiling so damp they periodically dropped pieces onto the floor. Like rotting carrion.

But he couldn't find Wes. He fell running back down the stairs. The steps were slick, insubstantial.

Someone was calling for help. A child was lost in the creek, drowning. The child's voice was badly garbled by the fog, each syllable filled with cold and damp. But Owen had momentarily forgotten where the creek was. If anything, the creek surrounded him.

It was quieter outside. The creek kept peace tonight. He could not decide what had made him so anxious.

When his father beckoned from the house for their evening swim, Owen did not hesitate.

EVERYTHING TO LIVE FOR

by Charles L. Grant

Hate is a word I only use about my father.

Not him personally, not exactly, but about the things he does that make me want to punch a hole in the wall, or a hole in his face. Like telling me that I can't get on my little sister for going into my room without me saying she can—because Peggy doesn't know any better, Craig, she's too young to understand about privacy; like yelling at me for not listening to my mother when she's talking to me, even though she's always saying the same stuff—that I don't respect her, that I don't care about all the things she's done for me, that I'd better watch my mouth because I'm not too old to be spanked; like wanting me to practically punch a stupid time clock every time I step out the door so, he says, he'll know where I am in case of an emergency, as if I could be back here like Superman if the house were burning down.

Like I have no business in the shed and I damned well better stay the hell away from his stuff or I'll be grounded for just about the rest of my life.

In fact, I've never been in there, not since we moved here almost ten years ago. It's a little thing made of wood he built himself, not more than ten feet on a side, with a flat roof and one window; it's stuck in the back corner of the yard under a weeping willow that almost buries it year-round. He doesn't use it much, and when he does go out it's like an army on secret maneuvers or something. He puts on a coat no matter what month it is, picks up his briefcase with his pens and pencils and things, and gives Mother a kiss like he's going to the office.

He likes to think in private, he says.

He comes up with his electronics designs better at night, like writers and artists, poets, and other nuts like that.

I thought maybe he kept some booze there and some porn, and used it to get away when my mother was in one of her moods.

I never figured the real reason at all, until last night.

Two weeks ago, after school, I was hanging around the practice field because I wanted to talk to Muldane. He was trying, for the third year in a row, to make first-string catcher, and it was really sad the way he worked so hard out there and failed so badly. I'd been telling him for days to loosen up, get stoned if he had to, but not think that the world would end if he didn't get the spot. But he wouldn't believe me. And he wouldn't believe Jeanne, who stayed away that day because she knew she'd only make him nervous.

So he fell right on his ass a couple of times, missed second base by three or four miles trying to cut down a steal, and generally acted like a goofed-up, hyper freshman. I couldn't watch, and I couldn't look away, so I spent most of the time staring at the grass and listening to the coach hollering and thinking maybe I should go home and apologize to my sister for tying her sheets into knots the night before.

I didn't know Muldane was done until he flopped down beside me and tried to bend the bars off his catcher's mask.

"Bad, huh?" I said.

"Craig," he said, "I am quitting baseball forever."

"No, you're not."

"I am. No shit, Denton, I really am. I am going to join the debate club and talk my way into college, the hell with scholarships and crap like that."

We sat for a few minutes, watching the coaches weed out the other goofs, watched the creeps from last year strutting around with their chests puffed out to here, and finally watched Tony Pelletti run on the cinder track that goes around the field. He was taller than either of us, and about a hundred pounds skinnier, and probably the fastest man in the world.

"God," Muldane said glumly. "He's going to catch his own shadow if he doesn't watch out."

"Yeah."

We were jealous. Pelletti would probably go to college for nothing and end up as a wide receiver for some pro football team, making a zillion bucks a season and doing commercials on TV. And the worst part about it was, he was our friend so we couldn't hate him and make up lies so we'd feel better.

Pelletti saw us then and waved, pointed at the coach's back and gave him an elaborate and elegant finger.

I laughed, and Tony bowed as he ran by.

Then Muldane slammed his mask against the ground a few times, and I checked the sky to see if it would rain.

This wasn't the way I'd planned things to happen. I was the one who needed someone to talk to; I was the one who had just been with the principal, getting suspended for a week because I cut a few lousy classes. Muldane was supposed to cheer me up, and this wasn't like him. He knew he was a rotten catcher; he knew he'd never play anything more than park baseball with the guys; he knew that, and now he was acting like he was going to bust out crying.

I was disgusted. The jerk was letting me down when I needed him the most.

I got up and nudged him with a toe. "C'mon, let's go find Jeanne and get a burger or something."

He shook his head, yanking at his cap, slapping that mask on the ground again and again.

"Mike, for crying out loud, it isn't the end of the world, you know. You can always—"

"Craig, shut up, will you?"

I stared at the top of his head. He'd never told me to shut up before, not that way, and I didn't know whether to feed him a knuckle sandwich or kick in his butt.

Then he looked up at me, fat cheeks shining and those pale eyes all watery, and he said, "My old man, the sonofabitch, will call my brother at college tonight. He's gonna tell him what happened, and my brother's gonna laugh." He looked away, at the ball field. "I could've done it, Denton. I was trying, you saw me trying out there. But he's like everybody else, y'know? Always pushing, never giving you a chance to think, and you gotta think once in a while, you gotta rest, right? I could've made it if he'd just given me the chance. I ain't great, but he just wouldn't let up, and he made me blow it. You know what I mean? He made me blow it."

There was nothing more then but the guys laughing, a plane overhead, the wind against the ground; and Mike just sitting there, pulling on his cap.

I should have talked to him then, I guess. I should have gotten back down beside him and made him laugh. But I was so mad, so damned mad because he didn't know the trouble I was in and didn't care because he hadn't made the stupid baseball team, that I shoved my hands in my pockets and said, "Christ, Mike, when the hell're you gonna grow up, huh?"

And I walked away, across the grass, across the cinder track, and around the side of the school to the front.

I thought about going home and telling the folks the truth right off and getting it over with. But that was a scene I wasn't about to rush, especially since it meant I would probably have to spend that whole week in my room, studying, and then doing everything around the house I hadn't done in the past sixteen years.

So I walked without knowing where I was going, just hoping that an angel would suddenly land beside me and get me out of this mess before I was skinned alive and hung out to dry.

I was scared.

I was never so scared in my whole life.

And I was mad because I was feeling like a little kid, flinching every time a grown-up looked cross-eyed at me, thinking that everyone in the whole world was pointing a finger at me because they knew what I had done.

And it really wasn't all that bad. Mr. Ranto, my chemistry teacher, kept telling me I should be working harder, that I was smarter than I let on, and he wasn't going to be the one to pass me on to the next level just on my good looks. So he made me miserable, giving me work and work and work until I couldn't take it anymore and just stopped going. Just like that. I either hid out down in the gym, or out behind the school, taking a smoke with the greasers who couldn't figure out what the hell I was doing there, but as long as I had the butts they weren't going to argue.

Ranto caught me that morning.

A few minutes later, wham!—suspension, no appeal.

I walked for over an hour, I think, through parts of town I never knew existed. Houses that looked like they were painted every month, with big cars in the driveway, green lawns a mile long, porches big enough to hold the whole junior class. And down below the shopping district, houses just the opposite—brown no matter what color they were, hardly any grass, hardly a window that didn't have a shade that wasn't crooked or a curtain that wasn't torn. They looked the way I felt.

And when I passed Muldane's place, I saw it in a way I never had before—a place to get away from for the rest of your life, not a place to go home to when you've had a rotten day.

Jesus, I thought, and remembered what I'd said—*when the hell're you*

gonna grow up? I hated myself because I sounded just like my father—
grow up, boy, but don't forget to act your age.

I turned around right away and ran back to the school, thinking maybe
Mike was still there so I could talk to him and make a joke about my
sudden vacation.

He was gone.

The field was deserted, and so was the school.

And there isn't anything quite so empty as a school that doesn't have
anyone in it. Then it looks just like a small factory. It doesn't make any
difference how new it is, how fancy—it's worse than a prison, it's a grave-
yard hidden by brick and tinted glass.

Thinking all that, and wondering where it was coming from, I was
beginning to spook myself, so I headed home and thanked all my good
luck charms that Dad was still at work and Mother and Peggy were at the
store. It gave me a chance to work on my story, to look for the right
buttons to push so I wouldn't get killed when they heard my big news.

And just as it was getting dark, I looked out the kitchen door, down to
the shed. It was a black hole in the twilight, the window not even reflect-
ing the lights from the house.

What the hell, I thought; I can't get into worse trouble than I am.
Besides, Dad had been going out there a lot lately, and I was getting
curious as to what he really did there at night.

I went outside, and suddenly felt as if a spotlight were going to pin me
to the ground the minute I took another step. It was stupid, but I couldn't
help it, and I almost turned around and went back. I didn't. I walked
across the wet grass, went to the door, and turned the knob; it was locked.
I cupped my hands around my eyes and peered through the window.

I knew my father had some kind of workbench in there, but whenever
I'd snuck looks before, it was always covered. There was also an armchair,
a side table, and shelves on the walls.

And something else.

Something I thought I saw in the far corner when, before I could move,
headlights slashed up the driveway and washed the lawn a dull white.

I wasn't sure, but I thought it looked like a crate.

I ran back before I was caught, went around the house to the front to
wait for dear old Dad to get out of his fancy car. But he didn't. He just sat
there, his head all dark like an executioner's mask, and I could only stare
back at him until he rolled down his window and told me to get in.

He didn't look happy.

Oh shit, I thought; and walked over. It wouldn't do me any good to make him madder than he was.

"A little trouble, huh?" he said as soon as I got in.

I shrugged.

"You don't like chemistry or something?"

"It's okay."

"You don't like Mr. Ranto, then? What?"

I tried to explain. How they kept pushing me, kept coming at me, kept giving me all this load of crap about how good I was and how clever I was and how I ought to make my family proud because I was the smartest person in it for a hundred generations. They wouldn't let me alone, so I left them alone instead.

He didn't interrupt me once.

And when I was done, feeling shivery and stiff and wishing he would at least look at me when I was talking, he tapped a finger on the steering wheel and stared at the silver ornament at the end of the hood.

It was darker now, the moon lifting over the house, and the headlights made the glass in the garage door grow glaring white eyes.

"You're a jackass, you know," he said very calmly.

"Wonderful," I muttered, and reached for the handle.

That's when he grabbed me.

That's when he took my arm and yanked me back so that I was lying half on my side and staring up into his face.

"Listen, you shit," he said, still calmly, "I will think of a way to explain this to your mother so you don't get killed and she doesn't get hysterical. But you'd damned well better swear to me right now—and I mean right now, boy—that you won't pull a stunt like this again for as long as you live or I'll swear to you that you won't live long enough to see it happen a third time."

"Let go of me," I said, but he only tightened his grip and I felt as if my arm were coming out at the shoulder.

"Swear," he said, sweat suddenly lining his forehead.

"All right, all right!"

He smiled.

He actually smiled at me when he let me up; and as he slid out, he said, "Hey, I heard on the radio some kid killed himself this afternoon. Hung himself in the backyard, I think. You know him? Name's Falkenberg, I think."

I did—not like a friend, just someone you saw around in the halls. But it chilled me just the same. A boy, my age, taking his own life. Something, it said on the news that night, about pressures, grades, maybe drugs and liquor. Mother said it was a shame; Dad only looked at me as if I should be grateful she had something else to think about instead of me, for a change.

I didn't say anything. I didn't even object when, the next morning, he took me to school and we had a long session with the principal. When it was over, I was reinstated, my name practically in blood that I would go to every class, do every bit of homework, and respect my teachers for the betters they were.

I almost threw up.

But it was too close to the end of the year for me to really screw up, so I smiled like a jerk, nodded, promised the moon, and spent the rest of the day explaining to the others how I'd beaten the rap.

To everyone, that is, except Mike, who didn't come to school.

Jeanne wouldn't talk to me, either, and I couldn't figure that out. She acted like she was really mad at me, but she wouldn't tell me why, and no one else could, either.

At the time, I didn't push it. Girls had never been my strongest subject. I knew, sort of, what I was supposed to do with them, but there was something that always held me back whenever I tried to talk to them. They seemed so much smarter than me, so much older, that they only made me confused, and that made me angry.

When I called Muldane that night, his father told me he didn't want to talk to anyone. He sounded drunk. I wasn't surprised.

Mike wasn't in school the next day, or the day after, he wouldn't answer my calls, and when I went over there once he wouldn't come to the door.

I didn't cut a single class.

That's important. I was trying. I was really trying. I smiled at the teachers, I didn't argue with my mother, I even helped my little sister with her homework one night.

I was trying. Honest to god, I was trying.

And I think it was because of Mike. We were a lot alike, and always had been. Our folks didn't understand us, not really, and they didn't seem to want to try. My father just disappeared into his workshop and shut me out with a key; Mike's old man shut him out with a slap to the jaw and a bottle. We were both counting on college to get us away, but the more we worked, the harder it was to please anyone, much less those we had to.

It was like Pelletti, in a way—running around and around on that stupid red-cinder track and not getting anywhere at all except back where you started, back in the kitchen where they told you you were no good.

On Wednesday night, late, Dad had a phone call, kissed my mother good-night, and told me to go to bed.

"Something wrong?" I asked.

"No," he said, pulling on a worn leather jacket. "I just have to do some work, that's all. You gotta do things yourself, you know, if you want to get them right. Go to bed."

I did.

And Thursday, at dinner, he finished the apple pie my mother had made especially for him, and said, "It's getting to be an epidemic, a real damned shame."

"What, dear?" Mother said.

"Another kid killed himself today."

Mother poured another cup of coffee.

Dad turned to me. "His name was Muldoon, or something like that. Did you know him, Craig?"

I went right to my room. I went right to my bed. I laid down and I stared at the ceiling until I couldn't see it anymore; then I stared at the dark until I fell asleep and dreamed about Mike Muldane hiding in the shed.

I went to school on Friday, but I didn't go to classes. I didn't give a damn. They could hang me for all I care; I just didn't go.

I found a place near the track to sit in the sun. It was cool, still April, and I was beginning to wish I'd worn something else besides my denim jacket. The gym classes were out, though, and those who saw me either nodded or looked away—the word was still around that I had copped a plea to stay in, and I had a feeling that maybe only Pelletti cared about my reasons.

At lunch, just when I was growing tired of sitting alone and trying to figure out what kind of idiot Muldane was to take himself like that, Jeanne walked up. She was dressed in black, her red hair pulled tight into a ponytail that made her face look a hundred years older. She had been crying. She still was, but there weren't any tears left.

I started to get up, feeling worse than I had when my father dropped the bomb, but she waved me down again. And stared. Tilting her head from one side to the other until I couldn't take it anymore.

"What's the matter? Did I grow another head or something?"

"What did you say to him, Craig?" she asked. "What did you say to him?"

"What?"

I did get up then, but she backed away quickly.

"He was fine until he talked to you. He was—"

"Jesus Christ, Jeanne!" I said, practically yelling. "Are you trying to tell me I made him kill himself?"

She didn't answer, not in words. She only stared a minute longer, turned, and ran away. I started after her, but she buried herself in a group of her girlfriends and, with looks back that would have fried me if wishes were real, they hustled her inside.

I got so excited, so upset, so angry, I could feel the blood in my face, bulging my eyeballs and making my temples pound. I took another step toward the school, then spun around and started running, found myself on the track going around and around and around until I was sweating so much I was freezing. My legs locked on me, the green started to blur, and I dropped and leaned against a bench where the team sat during breaks in practice.

By then I figured she was just crazy with grief. She'd been going with Mike since seventh grade just about, and she was just crazy, that's all.

The bench jumped, then, as someone sat hard on the other end. I looked up, and it was Tony. He was cleaning his glasses with a fold of his gray sweatshirt, and with his long nose and long chin, his straight-back hair, and squinty eyes, he looked like a heron surveying the swamp for a lost meal.

"Bad news, huh?" he said.

"Tell me about it."

"He . . . he ever say anything to you?"

I scrambled up from the ground to sit beside him. "Tony, I swear to God, he never said a word! The last time . . ." I cleared my throat. I cleared it again. "The last time I saw him was at tryouts on Tuesday."

"You talked to him, though."

"On Tuesday, sure. But he wouldn't talk to me after. He was pissed because—"

I stopped. Tony didn't believe me, I could see it when he put on his glasses and examined me, head to toe and back again. He didn't believe me.

"Tony, what's—"

"I gotta go, man," he said. "I can't afford to cut classes like you." He was a couple of steps away before he looked back at me and frowned. "And look," he warned, "stop calling the house, huh? I feel bad enough. You're just making it worse."

And he was gone before I could stop him. Just like Jeanne. An accusation, an exit, and I was alone on the track, staring at the school and wondering what was going on. Two people had practically accused me of murder to my face. Two friends. Two of the only friends I had left in the world.

I didn't care about the deal; I left the school grounds and went for a walk. A long walk. That took me in and out of places I had grown up in, played ball in, smoked secret cigarettes in all my life.

I didn't go home for supper, and I didn't call to tell them where I was.

At nine I found myself on Jeanne's porch, knocking on the door.

She almost slammed it in my face when she saw who it was, but there must have been something there that made her change her mind. She signaled me to wait, closed it partway, and returned a few minutes later with a sweater over her shoulders. Inside, I could hear the television blaring and her two sisters arguing about somebody's boyfriend.

"Walk?" I said, though my legs were starting to turn to rubber.

"Sure."

So we did. Our shoes loud on the sidewalk, our shadows vanishing under the trees that were just getting their new leaves. We didn't say anything for a long time, until we started our second turn around the block and I took her arm and stopped her.

"Jeanne, he was my best friend."

The fingers of one hand lay across her cheek, spread over to her mouth while she swallowed and looked away.

"He was. And I swear to God, the last thing I said to him was that we should find you and get some burgers. That's all." I was almost crying. I almost dropped to my knees. "Jesus, that's all, I swear."

She didn't look at me, but she took my arm and we started walking again. Around the corner. Up the street. Houses lighted and houses dark, and cats running in the alleys.

"He called me the night . . . before," she said, her voice high and hoarse. "He said . . . he told me—Denton says I should take the big one because it ain't worth it anymore." A shudder nearly took the sweater from her shoulders. "Those were his exact words, Craig. His very same words."

I looked at her, stunned, and shook my head. "Jeanne, it wasn't me. You think I'd tell him to do . . . to do what he did? You think I could do that to my best friend?" When she didn't answer right away, I almost hit her. "And even if I did, which I didn't, he wouldn't do it. You know him. You know him as long as I have. He wouldn't do it, Jeanne, he wouldn't!"

"He did," she whispered. "But he did, Craig."

The third time we got to her house I knew she believed me even though I hadn't said another word. She held my hands tight and she looked hard into my face, and suddenly she looked as frightened as I suddenly felt.

When she ran inside, I didn't try to stop her.

I only ran home, just in time to meet my father coming out the front door.

"I was going to look for you," he said.

"I was walking," I told him, pushing inside to hang up my coat. "I had to think, that's all. About Mike. Stuff."

"Your mother was worried. She wanted me to call the police. Thank God, Peggy doesn't pull stunts like this."

"I'm sorry."

"Tell her yourself. She's in the kitchen."

Which she was, and which I did; and though I told her I saw Jeanne, I didn't tell her what she said.

"Michael Muldane was a very sick boy," was all she said as she put cookies in the jar and plates in the dishwasher. "I think his little girlfriend isn't well, either. I accept your apology, and I don't want you to see her again."

"What?"

Father came to the doorway. "Don't argue, Craig. Just go to bed, please. You're upset, your mother's upset. We'll talk about it in the morning."

I didn't want to talk about it in the morning; I wanted to talk about it now. Right now. But there's no justice for a kid my age, no justice at all. You have to stand there, that's all, and take it like a man, and hope that tomorrow they'll forget all about it and leave you alone.

I was lucky that time. They did, until the next weekend, when Jeanne called me, in tears, nearly hysterical.

Dad, who had just come in from the shed, his briefcase under his arm, answered the phone, listened a minute, and handed me the receiver with a scowl. "Don't be long," he ordered. "She sounds drunk or something."

She wasn't drunk. She was terrified.

Tony was dead.

He had gone out for a drive in his father's new car and had plowed it head-on into a bus on the far side of town. The police weren't sure it was an accident at all.

Mike's funeral had been private, family only. Not Tony's. A bunch of us left school early on Tuesday and went to the cemetery to say good-bye. Jeanne was with me, holding on to my arm so tight it almost cramped. The girls were kind of crying, the guys trying to be like they were supposed to—brave and cool and only looking sad.

When a tear got away from me, Jeanne wiped it away and smiled.

While the priest was talking, I started thinking—not about that shiny coffin with all the flowers on it that was supposed to hold Tony but how could it because he was probably right now running around the track; not about that, about me. How all of a sudden it seemed that every time I picked up the phone it was bad news. Somebody dead. A kid. And I thought about Jeanne and how scared she was, scared like me because kids aren't supposed to die like this. I know it happens, sure. I read the papers, I see the news, but not in this town. Not here. Not to people we know.

An epidemic, my father said.

And suddenly I went cold. Colder than the breeze that came at us from the tombstones.

Muldoon or something, he had said.

But he knew Mike. He'd known him for years, Mother fed him dinners and lunches, and he once even went on a vacation to the seashore with us.

Muldoon or something.

That's when I thought I was starting to go crazy; that's when I put my arm around Jeanne and held her so tightly she looked up at me and frowned, felt me trembling and held me back. And when it was over and we were walking away, she asked me what was wrong, and I told her.

"So?" she said. "I don't understand."

Neither did I, but it wouldn't let go once it took hold. All day. All night. All the next day, even when Mother said a neighbor saw me walking Jeanne home after school and didn't she tell me not to see her again?

Last night . . . last night was only a few hours ago.

I was lying on my bed, not undressed, just lying there with my hands behind my head and thinking about Jeanne and how Mike wouldn't mind if we got together or something; we'd been best friends, and Jeanne was . . . she was special. Mike knew it. I knew it, and I didn't have to worry with her about what to say or how to act. When I got stupid, she told me; when I did something nice, she told me. Mike wouldn't care. Mike was dead, and God, I missed him.

Then I heard voices downstairs. Arguing. My mother and father in the kitchen, and Father suddenly telling her to quiet down or the boy would hear.

That was my signal. Whenever one of them said that, my ears got
sensitive and I turned into a ghost, sneaking out of the room and into the
hall, to the head of the stairs and down to the one I knew creaked when
you breathed on it. All the lights were out, except over the kitchen table,
and all I could see were moving shadows on the hall wall.

"I think," Father said, "it's much too soon. He isn't going to be able to
take much more."

Mother was doing something at the stove. Probably baking another pie.
"I don't like bad influences, dear."

"She's only a little girl."

"Big enough to cause trouble."

"I don't know. I—"

"Just get your coat, dear. And please watch the noise. I don't want to
wake Peggy."

Father's voice changed. "An angel, you know that? God, I almost cry
every time I look at her. She has so much to live for. Not like—"

"I know, dear, I know."

"And when I think about Craig, I could—"

"Your coat, dear. Please."

I backed away from the bannister and watched the dark figure that was
my father go to the closet and take out his leather jacket, walk back into
the kitchen, and say something I couldn't hear. The back door opened,
closed, and I sat there with my knees close to my chest, my head turning
side to side like something had broken in my neck and I couldn't work it
right anymore.

I couldn't really be sure what it was I heard, but it was the tone of their
voices that frightened me. So controlled, so sure, and at the same time so
threatening that I almost screamed.

Instead, and I don't know why because I was so scared, I crept down
the rest of the steps and out the front door, then ran around the side of
the house, back toward the shed.

A light was on.

I crouched beside the wall and hugged myself, my teeth chattering so
loud I had to put a fist against my jaw to keep from biting my tongue in
half.

Then I looked in the window.

Father had turned the chair around and was sitting in it, leaning forward a little and looking at the large wooden crate I had seen the week
before. But it was black. So black the light didn't touch it, and when I
stared at it long enough I could see right through it, into more blackness,

solid dark; and Father was rocking a little now, and I could hear him grunting every so often, rocking, and grunting, shaking his head once and rocking even faster. Grunting. Then, suddenly, he was humming in a high quiet voice, like a song without words, without notes, a child's chant against the dark, driving away the demons until mommy or daddy could come in and save them.

A car drove down our street, its radio loud with rock music.

Humming. Chanting. Parting the black for more black, this time freckled with points of white light.

A window was open in a neighbor's house, and a telephone rang for almost a full minute before someone answered.

Chanting. Rocking. The points beginning to swirl into a dense white cloud whose light was swallowed by the black.

And in the white I saw something that looked like a face.

I blinked quickly because I felt myself crying, felt the tears on my cheeks and I didn't know why. It was stupid. There was some kind of electronic thing in my father's stupid shed, and all that black and all that dead white were making me cry like a stupid little baby.

For a minute, just a minute, I wanted to die.

Father stopped.

The white vanished.

The black faded to normal black, and the wood crate was back.

It was a few seconds before I was able to shake myself into moving around the corner so that, when he came out, whistling to himself, he wouldn't see me. He strolled back to the house with his hands in his pockets, and Mother opened the door for him, nodded, and kissed his cheek.

Then I looked up to the moon, saw the face, and I knew. One thing, then another, and something jumped inside my head and I knew what was going on, and I fell to my knees and put my head in my hands.

Hate is a word I use only about my father, but I know now it's a word both my folks use about me.

It's almost dawn. I've been sitting here so long I'm touched with dew, and I can't move. Not an arm, not a leg, though my teeth stopped chattering a long time ago.

Mike said his big brother was the favorite; Jeanne said it was her two sisters; Tony didn't have anyone; and I have Peggy.

So what can you do about it if you're a parent? You give birth to the kid and you watch it grow up and into a person, and then you decide if you like it or not. Someone you meet that you don't like you don't have to see again, or you can be polite to, or you can ignore. A kid is there all the time —all day, all week, all year, all your life.

It's cold out here.

So what can you do about it if you're a parent and you don't like your kid? What can you do if you don't want him anymore?

It's very cold, and it's dark.

I think . . . I think some parents go from hate to not caring, and that's the worst of all. And if they look right, they can find someone who can see that, see the dark of it, and make it almost alive. Like a cloud, a black cloud that hangs over you in November, telling you it's going to rain but not telling you when. Those kinds of days are the most rotten, and they make you feel rotten, on the outside where it's raw, and on the inside where you wish you could just go away and find a place that has the sun.

If the cloud stays long enough, you don't wait for the next day, or the rain, or the snow—you go on your own, and you never come back.

I didn't call Mike. My father did.

I didn't talk to Tony. My father did.

I wonder if Mr. Falkenberg hated his son?

I keep trying to remember, but I can't. Jesus, I can't remember whose face I saw in that dying white light.

But there's no sense in running.

I won't go back in the house, but there's no sense in running.

I'm just going to wait here, and maybe think of a way to stop it.

But sooner or later, when the sun comes out and the birds start flying and the kids are off to school and Peggy is laughing with my mother and my father is off to work, a telephone is going to ring.

My father did the magic; my mother told him who to get.

When that telephone rings, somebody is going to tell someone else that another kid is dead.

Oh shit, Jeanne, don't hate me, but I hope that it's you.

Despite the fact I once disparaged, to put it mildly, his brother's artwork, I am still able to call Al Sarrantonio a friend. Although this is his first appearance in a Whispers *book, we go back to the first* Whispers *anthology when he was my Doubleday editorial assistant. We both love traditional horror fiction, as this neat scare will show you.*

BOGY

by Al Sarrantonio

It was Old October, but no one was scared.

Pumpkins sat rotting on doorsteps. The air was cold but not crisp: apples wouldn't bob in tubs, and the trees held their wet green leaves and wouldn't let them fall, brown and whipping, to the ground. The Moon rose each night, but pale and quiet: a sick Man. Children were bored and lazy, their Halloween costumes—white plastic bone suits, coal-black witch cones and flapping ghost sheets—neatly folded in boxes on the top shelves of hall closets.

It was Old October, but there were no *Boo*s in the air.

No silvery shudders at midnight.

No howling wolf-dogs, wax fangs, velvet capes.

No creaking doors, opening coffins, dropping spiders.

No Telltale hearts.

No clouds; no wind.

It was Old October and something was wrong:

Fear was fading from the world.

Here were four Bogy-boys, count 'em: Spook and Butch and Bill and Augie the new boy: four Bogy-boys more bored and tired and unghoulish than the rest. Here were four Bogy-boys in their Bogy Clubhouse, cheats to their name: surrounded by the implements of their fraternity collecting dust. Boxes of rubber things—worms and centipedes and snakes and green glowy doo-dads with eyes all over—went unused in one corner. Crepe paper, orange and black and orange again, dangled limply, half-hung from the dry rafters. Frankenstein boots went unshined; ghost tarps gray and unwashed; coffin nails rusted in their unopened boxes. Creature models sat half-finished on neglected workbenches, glue-smeared, forlorn; and, worst offense of all, a life-size mummy stood uncoiled, revealing a real, smiling human face, a plaster of Paris head of some long-forgotten celebrity revealed in all its obscene unfrightfulness.

"We've got to do something scary," Spook said to Butch, and Butch nodded lazily. Bill nodded too, his tall straight back against the cool but unclammy wall. He stretched and said, "Yes," but the word didn't quite make it to his lips and rolled back down his tongue to disappear somewhere in his throat.

Augie, the new boy, yawned.

Spook, lean and long with wild, uncombed hair, leader of the Club, began (though he wanted more than anything to just lie down, to nap, to yawn) to speak.

"We went down to the golf course and prayed for lightning to strike."

A slight, tiny, almost happy smile played around Butch's lips for a moment as he remembered two years before, when that Shriner almost got it. The smile went lax.

"But there wasn't any lightning," he said. "There weren't even any dark *clouds*."

"We went up to the Old home to scare be-Jesus out of Miss Hammer," Bill went on, his voice climbing up from the chasm of his chest, slowly, the words falling to the cement floor as they left him. He was big and wide and bound someday for the army like his three brothers before him.

"And found that Miss Hammer passed away in April," Spook finished sadly, and then he continued weakly, as a pall of exhaustion overcame his words, "I don't know what else there is . . ."

They tried to move but could not. Even the comic books at their feet, the *Creepies* and *Scaries* and vintage *Eeries*, along with the single thumbed *Popular Photography* with the two frayed pages where artfully naked ladies against sand dunes were printed, seemed to sink deeper into the dry floor at their feet. The day outside, like high summer, was clear and still, bright as a photograph, unghastly. There was a high slim sliver of afternoon Moon that lost mightily to the renewed October Sun.

The day, the season, the battle—all were lost.

"Maybe," Augie, the new boy, said, his mouth forming a presleeping "O" as he spoke, "there's something wrong with Bogy."

A spark—small, incandescent as a candle before a star—danced up into his companions' eyes. Butch said, "Ah." Suddenly, Spook felt almost renewed. Bill pushed himself back up straight against the wall and flicked away the *Eerie* lying like a sleeping dog against his leg.

"Maybe," Butch said, his small eyes glinting in his face, "there is."

Spook began to catch fire. Before the other three could move he was up on his feet, standing over them, his hands moving through his hair, pushing it up into straight static shock lengths, his eyes bug-bulbs, his legs twitching.

"*What's the motto of the Bogy Club?*" he said in a rallying cry.

Without pause, his companions shouted:

"*To fright and scare*

"*No matter where!*

"*To scare and fright*

"*Day or night!*"

Spook twirled away, throwing himself into the boxes around them: one from this, one from that: when he twirled back he was decked out head to toe in black and red—cape and hat, shoes and buttons, bushy eyebrows and white fang-teeth.

"*So?*" he shouted; and then he hissed, one word at a time, into their faces: "We'll-go-see-if-something's-wrong-with-Bogy!"

"*Yes!*" Butch and Bill cried.

"But—" Augie, the new boy, suddenly protested.

"What's the matter?" Spook said in his best Bela Lugosi voice, looming over Augie as the new boy tried to cover his face with a comic. "You believe all those stories we told you?" He pulled the comic away, and it fluttered like a bat into the far corner of the cellar. "You believe Bogy is the source of all fear? That his face is wild, and hairy, and wide-eyed; that his hands are long-nailed and dirty and creased deep with earth, with worms crawling over his knuckles and around his wrists—that his feet are covered with spiked boots and his mouth is cavernous and sharp-toothed? You believe that he howls at the Moon, swims in foul water? That he lives deep in the woods in a moldy hut? That he changes shape and throws his voice? That he can only eat what he kills, and that he only kills"—Spook lumbered around, brandishing an imaginary weapon, stopping abruptly before Augie to haul it high above his head and then bring it down *chop*— "with his long tall axe?" Spook brought his face so close to the new boy that his wax fangs filled the other boy's eyes. "You afraid that fear is fading because Bogy is dying, and that Bogy is dying because he hasn't eaten in so long—that he's so hungry he'd eat even *you?*"

"*No!*" Augie screamed.

"Maybe," Butch screamed, jumping up and moving his legs like a wild man, "you *should* be afraid!"

"Bogy!" Bill shouted, jumping up next to him and howling.

"But you said it was just a story!" Augie whined as they danced around him. "You told me he wasn't real!"

"Maybe we lied!" Spook whooped, and then they put masks and wild wigs and teeth and warts on Augie.

And then they sang their Bogy song:

"To fright and scare
"No matter where!
"To scare and fright
"Day or night!"

And then they dragged the new boy out, to find the inspiration for their Club.

Old October was tight as calcium in the bones of the town. They passed everyday things—soda fountains, the movie theatre with "Fright Movie This Friday!" on its marquee in tired red letters that either dangled or were missing. They passed the school, with dusty, peel-taped, faded orange neglected pumpkin cutouts in the windows. They passed the mask shop, the well-known-to-them shopkeeper leaning in the doorway, threatening to doze off. Even Mad Lady Pinkerton, the town prophet, lay asleep under the slowly rotating barber pole, propped up like a scarecrow made of wet oats. She cocked a heavy eye at them as they passed, tried to raise a finger to exclaim something but instead fell back to sleep.

Even the dogs eyed them indolently.

Strange October tried to get at them. Once more they felt weak, drooped, lazy and unscared. They wanted to crawl back to the Clubhouse and sleep the whole season off.

"Fright and scare, scare and fright," Spook mumbled at their lead, but even he didn't believe it now.

"Fright and—" Butch began, but the rest was stifled by a yawn.

They pressed on.

In back of the old ball field, brown with October grass that even now looked ready for summer baseball, they passed into the outer reaches of the town. Now, abruptly, something woke within them. They passed an abandoned horse stable that threw long shadows out at them and seemed to creak louder from its leaning joints, just for them.

"Fright and scare, scare and fright," Spook tried again, and this time they began to believe it.

There was something present now—not strong, but getting stronger. With each step they took, their skins began to tingle and tiny icicles crawled up their backs.

Fear was returning.

"It's getting stronger as we get close to Bogy," Butch said mischievously, turning his eyes on the new boy. A delighted grin spread over his wax teeth.

"Maybe—" Augie began, turning around to look back toward the town, the safe, unscary town, but Bill cut him off.

"Look."

They looked at the wide high wall of woods in front of them, felt a dark and cold and creeping feeling when they looked at it, and then Spook said, "Wow."

"Maybe—" Augie tried again, but they took him by the arms as he held back, and, above them, as they melted into the woods, the Moon brightened and the Sun was truly gone.

There were *real* bats in here, not comic book bats, and other ghastly things. There were real bats around them, big brown leathery hinged things with sharp teeth and red rats' eyes, and though they didn't see those wings or teeth or ruby eyes they knew they were there just the same. Then one of them *was* there, breaking out of the dark to slap at Bill's head and then wheel flapping away.

"Wow," Spook said.

They fell deeper into the woods. A heavier darkness came down upon them. Each stepped-on twig called out, "Here we come!" and they found themselves huddled together. Their knees began to knock; their teeth began, imperceptibly at first and then like wind-up novelties, to chatter. Butch laughed nervously. Spook said, again, "Wow," only some of the amusement had vanished from his voice.

There were other creatures around them now, just out of sight, lurking. The Bogy-boys knew they were there. There were big things—things with green seaweed or damp soil hanging off their limbs, things with big saucer eyes and big thick black boots and crimson-lined capes and pointed ears. *Things* that were too white or too black. *Things* that slithered along the ground and dove clacking from tree to tree—*things* with long snouts that liked to bore into soft flesh; *things* the Bogy Club had talked about, dreamed about, now saw in snatches.

Their footsteps, like cannon, boomed around them. Up ahead, the darkness shifted.

"I don't like this," Butch said, and this time Bill did not cut him off.

"You know, I wouldn't mind going back to town," Bill said, but as he turned Spook held him.

"Fright and scare, scare and fright," Spook pleaded.

For a long moment Bill hesitated, and then he nodded and they crept on.

The darkness was different now. It was velvet curtains enfolding them, not only making night but something deeper than night, more final. There was no Moon here; no promise of even a tired Sun rising the next morning. It was as if they had stepped into a rip in the fabric of night, behind which the real darkness crouched waiting.

Once again Bill turned to leave, and once again Spook had to restrain him.

"Fright and scare," he said.

The four boys stepped ahead.

"Forget fright and scare," Bill said suddenly, and then he was gone, running back to town.

The three remaining looked one to the other. Butch's feet began to shift of their own accord, back toward Bill. Spook held him fast. Augie, the new boy, merely trembled.

The darkness darkened even more, and then they burst into a shallow valley with stark, nude tree branches twined like bone-fingers above them. They stopped abruptly, as one, at the sight of a mad jumble of bark and tar shaped into a hut. It was a dark igloo with eyes—tilted to one side with two hollow ovals and a grinning mouth doorway. The ground around the hut was brushed clean of leaves, leaving the stark black forest floor gleaming like dried ebony mud.

"Bogy," Augie breathed.

In answer, something sounded within the hut, a low, crawling cough.

In a flash Butch was gone, moving as fast as his shaking legs could crash him through the woods, shedding his costume, cape and wax teeth on the way.

Spook looked at Butch's retreating frame, and then at the new boy, who was shaking from head to sneakers.

Again a cough came from within, lingering and low, gravelly as the packed earth around them.

"I thought we made him up but he's *real,*" Spook said. His eyes behind his mask were wide and white and he began to turn away.

Just then there came a strangled weak sound from within the hut, and Augie's chattering voice said, "It sounds like he's dying."

Spook looked at the new boy, saw his own wild fright mirrored there and was ashamed. "Fright and scare," he said and he grabbed Augie's arm, high above the elbow and tight, and they stepped toward the doorway.

It was darker inside than out. Maybe it was a trick of the darkness: but one moment they were standing at the threshold of the door and the next they had been swallowed by that mouth and were inside.

Spook put his hand on the wall and there, leaning like a man with a pipe in his mouth and arms folded, was an axe handle a good four feet long and a blade sharp as the Sun's edge.

The cough came once more, off in a far corner, and when Spook looked in that corner something was there.

It was a bundle of rags. No, it wasn't that—it was a pile of clothing with something underneath. No, it wasn't that, either—it was a man, or something manlike, huddled or bent or collapsed, with arms and legs and trousers and coat attached here and there in the reasonably correct positions. Spook's eyes became used to this deep darkness, and now the man became more of a man: sitting with his back in the *V* of the corner, his legs pulled up to his chin and his arms, too long, they seemed, wrapped around his knees. His head was lowered.

The figure coughed once and then again—low, rattling sounds now, more far away than near.

"So hungry," the figure said, in a voice so weak and hoarse and artificial it sounded like something from a ventriloquist's dummy.

Spook edged closer.

"So," the figure said, "hungry."

"Fright and scare," Spook began, but even as he said this he knew the thing before him was dying. Around Spook, in the air and trees and soil, fear was truly fading away. He took another step forward and said, his voice filled almost with pity, "Bogy."

"All true," the thing before him said; its voice sounded even more hollow and false. "All the stories true. I'm the source of all fear. I howl at the Moon"—he made a sickly, sad try at a wail—"and swim in foul water. I live deep in the woods in a moldy hut. I . . . ." The voice trailed off into a reedy gasp and then there was dry silence.

Around Spook, the fear was just about gone.

He reached out slowly, carefully, inch by inch, and put his hand on Bogy's shoulder. The thing before him crumbled into a pile of rags and empty spiked black boots.

"Fright and scare—" Spook began, but then he called, "Augie?"

There was only silence behind him.

"All true," Bogy's voice came, but not from the rags and empty boots. It came from where Augie should be.

Like a stretching, waking cat, fear began to return. Shadows pushed out from the wall, making the room long and sinister; things dropped down from the ceiling and the corners became places you wouldn't want to back into. Spook got the shivers, and now when he got them they only got stronger and wouldn't go away. Fear was growing, and very fast. He looked at the pile of Bogy's clothing and a cold hand clamped over his heart and he was more frightened and scared than he had ever been.

"Augie?" he called once more, not wanting to turn around.

"I change shape and throw my voice," the new boy's voice said, not hollow anymore, "and I kill with my axe and eat what I kill—*so hungry.*"

Spook knew that fear would return to the town. He felt it radiating out from the hut, pushing out into the woods and beyond. Butch and Bill, wherever they were, would tremble in their boots. All the Halloween costumes would be yanked down from closet shelves; dogs would bay at the Moon, become mock wolves; and Mad Lady Pinkerton would rise from her sleep in front of the barber shop to cry doom upon all who passed.

Fear was back.

"Augie?" Spook called one final, desperate time, but he didn't turn around. He knew Augie was there. As he ran for the door he saw the monstrous shadow rising against the wall; saw the outline of huge clawed hands and heard the tread of monstrous feet. He heard the cavernous, sharp-toothed jaws behind him.

When he thought he was far enough away for his heart to beat slow and let him hesitate and turn, he saw the glint of the huge axe against the bursting bright October Moon.

People often talk of the Three Musketeers of Weird Tales *(Howard Phillips Lovecraft, Robert Ervin Howard, and Clark Ashton Smith). I hope that the future will find people talking about the Three Musketeers of* Whispers, *Manly Wade Wellman, Karl Edward Wagner, and David Drake. Although it was not until the third issue of* Whispers *magazine that I was able to announce my luck at obtaining Dave's expertise as my assistant editor, his influence was felt from the first issue, as it was David who convinced me that paying for original fiction (rather than hoping for free contributions from friends) would make* Whispers *go. I treasure his friendship as much as anyone's in the field. The following fantasy is part of a projected series, the first tale of which, hopefully, has been published in my* Whispers *magazine #23-24. "The Fool" is a David Drake tale told in the Manly Wade Wellman tradition.*

THE FOOL

by David Drake

"Now jest ignore him," said the buck to the doe as Old Nathan turned in the furrow he was hoeing twenty yards ahead of them.

"But he's *looking* at us," whispered the doe from the side of her mouth. She stood frozen, but a rapidly pulsing artery made shadows quiver across her throat in the evening sun.

"G'wan away!" called Old Nathan, but his voice sounded halfhearted even in his own ears. He lifted the hoe and shook it. A hot afternoon cultivating was the best medicine the cunning man knew for his aches . . . but the work did not become less tiring because it did him good. "Git, deer!"

"See, it's all right," said the buck as he lowered his head for another mouthful of turnip greens.

Old Nathan stooped for a clod to hurl at them. As he straightened with it the deer turned in unison and fled in great floating bounds, their heads thrust forward.

"Consarn it," muttered the cunning man, crumbling the clod between his long, knobby fingers as he watched the animals disappear into the woods beyond his plowland.

"Hi there," called a voice from behind him, beside his cabin back across the creek.

Old Nathan turned, brushing his hand against his pants leg of coarse homespun. His distance sight was as good as it ever had been, so even at the length of a decent rifleshot he had no trouble in identifying his visitor as Eldon Bowsmith. Simp Bowsmith, they called the boy down to the settlement . . . and they had reason, though the boy was more an innocent than a natural in the usual sense.

"Hi!" Bowsmith repeated, waving with one hand while the other shaded his eyes from the low sun. "There wuz two *deer* in the field jist now!"

They had reason, that was sure as the sunrise.

"Hold there," Old Nathan called as the boy started down the path to the creek and the field beyond. "I'm headed back myself." Shouldering his hoe, he suited his action to his words.

Bowsmith nodded and plucked a long grass stem. He began to chew on the soft white base of it while he leaned on the fence of the pasture which had once held a bull and two milk cows . . . and now held the cows alone. The animals, startled at first into watchfulness, returned to chewing their cud when they realized that the stranger's personality was at least as placid as their own.

Old Nathan crossed the creek on the puncheon that served as a bridge —a log of red oak, adzed flat on the top side. A fancier structure would have been pointless, because spring freshets were sure to carry *any* practicable bridge downstream once or twice a year. The simplest form of crossing was both easily replaced and adequate to the cunning man's needs.

As he climbed the sloping path to his cabin with long, slow strides, Old Nathan studied his visitor. Bowsmith was tall, as tall as the cunning man himself, and perhaps as gangling. Age had shrunk Old Nathan's flesh over its framework of bone and sinew to accentuate angles, but there was little real difference in build between the two men save for the visitor's greater juiciness.

Bowsmith's most distinguishing characteristic—the factor that permitted Old Nathan to recognize him from two hundred yards away—was his hair. It was a nondescript brown in color, but the way it stood out in patches of varying length was unmistakable. It looked as if the boy had cut it himself, using a knife.

The cunning man realized he must have been staring when Bowsmith said with an apologetic grin, "There hain't a mirror et my place, ye see. I do what I kin with a bucket uv water."

"Makes no matter with me," Old Nathan muttered. Nor should it have, and he was embarrassed that his thoughts were so transparent. He'd been late to the line hisself when they give out good looks. "Come in 'n set, and you kin tell me what brought ye here."

Bowsmith tossed to the ground his grass stem—chewed all the way to the harsh green blades—and hesitated as if to pluck another before entering the cabin. " 'Bliged t'ye," he said and, in the event, followed Old Nathan without anything to occupy his hands.

The doors, front and back, of the foursquare cabin were open when the visitor arrived, but he had walked around instead of through the structure on his way to find the cunning man. Now he stared at the interior, his look of anticipation giving way to disappointment at the lack of exotic trappings.

There were two chairs, a stool, and a table, all solidly fitted but shaped by a broadaxe and spokeshave rather than a lathe. The bed was of similar workmanship, with a rope frame and corn-shuck mattress. The quilted coverlet was decorated with a Tree-of-Life appliqué of exceptional quality, but there were women in the county who could at least brag that they could stitch its equal.

A shelf set into the wall above the bed held six books, and two chests flanked the fireplace. The chests, covered in age-blackened leather and iron-bound, could bear dark imaginings—but they surely did not require such. Five china cups and a plate stood on the fireboard where every cabin but the poorest displayed similar knickknacks; and the rifle pegged to the wall above them would have been unusual only by its absence.

"Well . . . ," Bowsmith murmured, turning his head slowly in his survey. He had expected to feel awe, and lacking that, he did not, his tongue did not know quite how to proceed. Then, on the wall facing the fireplace, he finally found something worthy of amazed comment. "Well . . . ," he said, pointing to the strop of black bullhide. The bull's tail touched the floor, while the nose lifted far past the rafters to brush the roof peak. "What en tarnation's *thet?*"

"Bull I onct hed," Old Nathan said gruffly, answering the boy as he might not have done with anyone who was less obviously an open-eyed innocent.

"Well," the boy repeated, this time in a tone of agreement. But his brow furrowed again and he asked, "But how come ye *keep* hit?"

Old Nathan grimaced and, seating himself in the rocker, pointed Bowsmith to the upright chair. "Set," he ordered.

But there was no harm in the lad, so the older man explained, "I could bring him back, I could. Don't choose to, is all, cuz hit'd cost too much. There's a price for ever'thing, and I reckon that 'un's more thin the gain."

"Well," said the boy, beaming now that he was sure Old Nathan wasn't angry with him after all.

He sat down on the chair as directed and ran a hand through his hair while he paused to collect his thoughts. Bowsmith must be twenty-five or near it, but the cunning man was sure that he would halve his visitor's age if he had nothing to go by except voice and diction.

"Ma used t' barber me 'fore she passed on last year," the boy said in embarrassment renewed by the touch of his ragged scalp. "Mar' Beth Neill, she tried the onct, but hit wuz worser'n what I done."

He smiled wanly at the memory, tracing his fingers down the center of his scalp. "Cut me bare, right along here," he said. *"Land* but people laughed. She hed t' laugh herself."

"Yer land lies hard by the Neill clan's, I b'lieve?" the cunning man said with his eyes narrowing.

"Thet's so," agreed Bowsmith, bobbing his head happily. "We're great friends, thim en me, since Ma passed on." He looked down at the floor, grinning fiercely, and combed the fingers of both hands through his hair as if to shield the memories that were dancing through his skull. "Specially Mar' Beth, I reckon."

"First I heard," said Old Nathan, "thet any uv Baron Neill's clan wuz a friend to ary soul but kin by blood er by marriage . . . and I'd heard they kept marriage pretty much in the clan besides."

Bowsmith looked up expectantly, though he said nothing. Perhaps he hadn't understood the cunning man's words, though they'd been blunt enough in all truth.

Old Nathan sighed and leaned back in his rocker. "No matter, boy, no matter," he said. "Tell me what it is ez brings ye here."

The younger man grimaced and blinked as he considered the request, which he apparently expected to be confusing. His brow cleared again in beaming delight and he said, "Why, I'm missin' my plowhorse, and I heard ye could find sich things. Horses what strayed."

Lives next to the Neill clan and thinks his horse strayed, the cunning man thought. Strayed right through the wall of a locked barn, no doubt. He frowned like thunder as he considered the ramifications, for the boy and for himself, if he provided the help requested.

"The Bar'n tried t' hep me find Jen," volunteered Bowsmith. "Thet's my horse. He knows about findin' and sichlike, too, from old books. . . ." He turned, uncomfortably, to glance at the volumes on the shelf here.

"I'd heard thet about the Baron," said Old Nathan grimly.

"But it wuzn't no good," the boy continued. "He says, the Bar'n does, must hev been a painter et Jen." He shrugged and scrunched his face up under pressure of an emotion the cunning man could not identify from the expression alone. "So I reckon thet's so . . . but she wuz a good ol' horse, Jen wuz, and it don't seem right somehows t' leave her bones out in the woods thet way. I thought maybe . . . ?"

Well, by God if there was one, and by Satan who was as surely loose in the world as the Neill clan—and the Neills' good evidence for the Devil— Old Nathan wasn't going to pass this by. Though *finding* the horse would be dangerous, and there was no need for that. . . .

"All right, boy," said the cunning man as he stood up. The motion of his muscles helped him find the right words, sometimes, so he walked toward the fireplace alcove. "Don't ye be buryin' yer Jen till she's dead, now. I reckon I kin bring her home fer ye."

A pot of vegetables had been stewing all afternoon on the banked fire. Old Nathan pivoted to the side the prong holding the pot and set a knot of pitchy lightwood on the coals. "Now," he continued, stepping away from the fire so that when the pine knot flared up its sparks would not spatter him, "you fetch me hair from Jen, her mane and her tail partikalarly. Ye kin find thet, cain't ye, clingin' in yer barn and yer fences?"

Bowsmith leaped up happily, "Why, sure I kin," he said. "Thet's all ye need?" Then his face darkened. "There's one thing, though," he said, then swallowed to prime his voice for what he had to admit next. "I've a right strong back, and I reckon there hain't much ye kin put me to around yer fields here ez I cain't do fer ye. But I hain't got money t' pay ye, and since Ma passed on"—he swallowed again—"seems like ever' durn thing we owned, I cain't find whur I put it. So effen my labor's not enough fer ye, I don't know what I could give."

The boy met Old Nathan's eyes squarely and there weren't many folk who would do that, for fear that the cunning man would draw out the very secrets of their hearts. Well, Simp Bowsmith didn't seem to have any secrets; and perhaps there were worse ways to be.

"Don't trouble yerself with thet," said Old Nathan aloud, "until we fetch yer horse back."

The cunning man watched the boy tramping cheerfully back up the trail, unconcerned by the darkness and without even a stick against the threat of bears and cougars which would keep his neighbors from traveling at night. Hard to believe, sometimes, that the same world held that boy and the Neill clan besides.

A thought struck him. "Hoy!" he called, striding to the edge of his porch to shout up the trail. "Eldon Bowsmith!"

"Sir?" wound the boy's reply from the dark. He must already be to the top of the knob, among the old beeches that were its crown.

"Ye bring me a nail from a shoe Jen's cast besides," Old Nathan called back. "D'ye hear me?"

"Yessir."

"Still, we'll make a fetch from the hair first, and thet hed ought t'do the job," the cunning man muttered; but his brow was furrowing as he considered consequences, things that would happen despite him and things that he—needs must—would initiate.

"I brung ye what ye called fer," said Bowsmith, sweating and cheerful from his midday hike. His whistling had announced him as soon as he topped the knob, the happiest rendition of "Bonny Barbry Allen" Old Nathan had heard in all his born days.

The boy held out a gob of gray-white horsehair in one hand and a tapered horseshoe nail in the other. Then his eyes lighted on movement in a corner of the room, the cat slinking under the bedstead.

"Oh!" said Bowsmith, kneeling and setting the nail on the floor to be able to extend his right hand toward the animal. "Ye've a cat. Here, pretty boy. Here, handsome." He clucked his tongue.

"Hain't much fer strangers, that 'un," said Old Nathan, and the cat promptly made a liar of him by flowing back from cover and flopping down in front of Bowsmith to have his belly rubbed.

"Oh," said the cat, "he's all right, ain't he," as he gripped the boy's wrist with his forepaws and tugged it down to his jaws.

"Watch—" the cunning man said in irritation to one or the other, he wasn't sure which. The pair of them ignored him, the cat purring in delight and closing his jaws so that the four long canines dimpled the boy's skin but did not threaten to puncture it.

Bowsmith looked up in sudden horror.

"Don't stop, damn ye!" growled the cat and kicked a knuckle with a hind paw.

"Is he . . . ?" the boy asked. "I mean, I thought he wuz a cat, but . . . ?"

"He's a cat, sure ez I'm a man"—Old Nathan snapped. He had started to add—"and you're a durn fool," but that was too close to the truth, and there was no reason to throw it in Bowsmith's face because he made up to Old Nathan's cat better than the cunning man himself generally did.

"Spilesport," grumbled the cat as he rolled to his feet and stalked out the door.

"Oh well," said the boy, rising and then remembering to pick up the horseshoe nail. "I wouldn't want, you know, t' trifle with yer familiars, coo."

"Don't hold with sich," the cunning man retorted. Then a thought occurred to him and he added, "Who is it been tellin' ye about familiar spirits and sechlike things?"

"Well," admitted the boy, and "admit" was the right word for there was embarrassment in his voice, "I reckon the Bar'n might could hev said somethin'. He knows about thet sort uv thing."

"Well, ye brung the horsehair," said Old Nathan softly, his green eyes slitted over the thoughts behind them. He took the material from the boy's hand and carried it with him to the table.

The first task was to sort the horsehair—long white strands from the tail; shorter but equally coarse bits of mane; and combings from the hide itself, matted together and gray-hued. The wad was more of a blur to his eyes than it was even in kinky reality. Sighing, the old man started up to get his spectacles from one of the chests.

Then, pausing, he had a better idea. He turned and gestured Bowsmith to the straight chair at the table. "Set there and sort the pieces fer length," he said gruffly.

The cunning man was harsh because he was angry at the signs that he was aging; angry that the boy was too great a fool to see how he was being preyed upon; and angry that he, Old Nathan the Devil's Master, should care about the fate of one fool more in a world that already had a right plenty of such.

"Yessir," said the boy, jumping to obey with such clumsy alacrity that his thigh bumped the table and slid the solid piece several inches along the floor. "And thin what do we do?"

Bowsmith's fingers were deft enough, thought Old Nathan as he stepped back a pace to watch. "No *we* about it, boy," said the cunning man. "You spin it to a bridle whilst I mebbe say some words t' help."

Long hairs from the tail to form the reins; wispy headbands and throat latch bent from the mane, and the whole felted together at each junction by tufts of gray hair from the hide.

"And I want ye t' think uv yer Jen as ye do thet, boy," Old Nathan said aloud while visions of the coming operation drifted through his mind. "Jest ez t'night ye'll think uv her as ye set in her stall, down on four legs like a beast yerself, and ye wear this bridle you're makin'. And ye'll call her home, so ye will, and thet'll end the matter, I reckon."

" 'Bliged t' ye, sir," said Eldon Bowsmith, glancing up as he neared the end of the sorting. There was no more doubt in his eyes than a more sophisticated visitor would have expressed at the promise the sun would rise.

Old Nathan wished he were as confident. He especially wished that he were confident the Neill clan would let matters rest when their neighbor had his horse back.

Old Nathan was tossing the dirt with which he had just scoured his cookware off the side of the porch the next evening when he saw Bowsmith trudging back down the trail. The boy was not whistling, and his head was bent despondently.

His right hand was clenched. Old Nathan knew, as surely as if he could see it, that Bowsmith was bringing back the fetch bridle.

"Come and set," the cunning man called, rising and flexing the muscles of his back as if in preparation to shoulder a burden.

"Well," the boy said, glumly but without the reproach Old Nathan had expected, "I reckon I'm in a right pickle now," as he mounted the pair of steps to the porch.

The two men entered the cabin; Old Nathan laid another stick of lightwood on the fire. It was late afternoon in the flatlands, but here in the forested hills the sun had set and the glow of the sky was dim even outdoors.

"I *tried* t' do what ye said," Bowsmith said, fingering his scalp with his free hand, "but someways I must hev gone wrong like usual."

The cat, alerted by voices, dropped from the rafters to the floor with a loud thump. "Good t' see ye agin," the animal said as he curled, tail high, around the boots of the younger man. Even though Bowsmith could not understand the words as such, he knelt and began kneading the cat's fur while much of the frustrated distress left his face.

"Jen didn't fetch t' yer summons, thin?" the cunning man prodded. Durn fool, durn cat, durn *nonsense*. He set down the pot he carried with a clank, not bothering at present to rinse it with a gourdful of water.

"Worsen thet," the boy explained. "I brung the ol' mule from Neills', and wuzn't they mad ez *hops.*" He looked up at the cunning man. "The Bar'n wuz right ready t' hev the sheriff on me fer horse stealin', even thoughs he's a great good friend t' me."

The boy's brow clouded with misery, then cleared into the same beatific, full-face smile Old Nathan had seen cross it before. "Mar' Beth, though, she quietened him. She told him I hadn't meant t' take their mule, and thet I'd clear off the track uv newground they been meanin' t' plant down on Cane Creek."

"You figger t' do thet?" the cunning man asked sharply. "Clear cane-brake fer the Neill clan, whin there's ten uv thim and none willin' t' break his back with sich a chore?"

"Why I reckon hit's the least I could do," Bowsmith answered in surprise. "Why, I took their mule, didn't I?"

Old Nathan swallowed his retort, but the taste of the words soured his mouth. "Let's see the fetch bridle," he said instead, reaching out his hand.

The cunning man knelt close by the spluttering fire to examine the bridle while his visitor continued to play with the cat in mutual delight. The bridle was well made, as good a job as Old Nathan himself could have done with his spectacles on.

It was a far more polished piece than the bridle Eldon Bowsmith had carried off the day before, and the hairs from which it was hand-spun were brown and black.

"Where'd ye stop yestiddy, on yer way t' home?" Old Nathan demanded.

Bowsmith popped upright, startling the cat out the door with an angry curse. "Now, how did *you* know thet?" he said—in amazement, and in delight at being amazed.

"Boy, boy," the cunning man said, shaking his head. He was too astounded at such innocence even to snarl in frustration. "Where'd ye stop?"

"Well, I reckon I might uv met Mary Beth Neill," Bowsmith said, tousling his hair like a dog scratching his head with a forepaw. "They're right friendly folk, the Neills, so's they hed me stay t' supper."

"Where you told thim all about the fetch bridle, didn't ye?" Old Nathan snapped, angry at last.

"Did I?" said the boy in open-eyed wonder. "Why, not so's I kin recolleck, sir . . . but I reckon ef you say I did, thin—"

Old Nathan waved the younger man to silence. Bowsmith might have blurted the plan to the Neills and not remember doing so. Equally, a mind less subtle than Baron Neill's might have drawn the whole story from a mere glimpse of the bridle woven of Jen's hair. That the Neill patriarch had been able to counter in the way he had done suggested he was deeper into the lore than Old Nathan would otherwise have believed.

"Well, what's done is done," said the cunning man as he stepped to the fireboard. "Means we need go a way I'd not hev gone fer choice."

He took the horseshoe nail from where he had lodged it, beside the last in line of his five china cups. He wouldn't have asked the boy to bring the nail if he hadn't expected—or at least feared—such a pass. If Baron Neill chose to raise the stakes, then that's what the stakes would be.

Old Nathan set the nail back, for the nonce. There was a proper bed of coals banked against the wall of the fireplace now during the day. The cunning man chose two splits of hickory and set them sharp-edge down on the ashes and bark-sides close together. When the clinging wood fibers ignited, the flames and the blazing gases they drove out would be channeled up between the flats to lick the air above the log in blue lambency. For present purposes, that would be sufficient.

"Well, come on, thin, boy," the cunning man said to his visitor. "We'll git a rock fer en anvil from the crik and some other truck, and thin we'll forge ye a pinter t' pint out yer horse. Wheriver she be."

Old Nathan had chosen for the anvil an egg of sandstone almost the size of a man's chest. It was at a good location for easy lifting, standing clear of the streambed on a pedestal of limestone blocks from which all the sand and lesser gravel had been sluiced away since the water was speeded by constriction.

For all that the rock's placement was a good one, Old Nathan had thought that its weight might be too much for Bowsmith to carry up to the cabin. The boy had not hesitated, however, to wade into the stream running to mid-thigh and raise the egg with the strength of his arms and shoulders alone.

Bowsmith walked back out of the stream, feeling cautiously for his footing but with no other sign of the considerable weight he balanced over his head. He paused a moment on the low bank, where mud squelched from between his bare toes. Then he resumed his steady stride, pacing up the path.

Old Nathan had watched to make sure the boy could handle the task set him. As a result, he had to rush to complete his own part of the business in time to reach the cabin when Bowsmith did.

A flattened pebble, fist-sized and handfilling, would do nicely for the hammer. It was a smaller bit of the same dense sandstone that the cunning man had chosen for the anvil. He tossed it down beside a clump of alders and paused with his eyes closed. His fingers crooked, groping for the knife he kept in a place he could "see" only within his skull.

It was there where it should be, a jackknife with two blades of steel good enough to accept a razor edge—which was how Old Nathan kept the shorter one. His fingers closed on the yellow bone handle and drew the knife out into the world that he and others watched with their eyes.

The cunning man had never been sure where it was that he put his knife. Nor, for that matter, would he have bet more than he could afford to lose that the little tool would be there the next time he sought it. Thus far, it always had been. That was all he knew.

He opened the longer blade, the one sharpened to a 30° angle, and held the edge against a smooth-barked alder stem that was of about the same diameter as his thumb. Old Nathan's free hand gripped the alder above the intended cut, and a single firm stroke of the knife severed the stem at a slant across the tough fibers.

Whistling himself—"The Twa Corbies," in contrast to Bowsmith's rendition of "Bonny Barbry Allen" on the path ahead—Old Nathan strode back to the cabin. The split hickory should be burning to just the right extent by now.

"And I'll set down on his white neck bone," the cunning man sang aloud as he trimmed the alder's branches away, "T' pluck his eyes out one and one."

The Neill clan had made their bed. Now they could sleep in it with the sheriff.

"Gittin' right hot," said Bowsmith as he squatted and squinted at the nail he had placed on the splits according to the cunning man's direction. "Reckon the little teensie end's so hot hit's nigh yaller t' look et."

Old Nathan gripped the trimmed stem with both hands and twisted as he folded it, so that the alder doubled at the notch he had cut in the middle. What had been a yard-long wand was now a pair of tongs with which the cunning man bent to grip the heated nail by its square head.

"Ready now," he directed. "Remember thet you're drawin' out the iron druther thin bangin' hit flat."

"Wisht we hed a proper sledge," the boy said. He slammed the smaller stone accurately onto the glowing nail the instant Old Nathan's tongs laid it on the anvil stone.

Sparks hissed from the nail in red anger, though the sound of the blow was a *clock!* rather than a ringing crash. A dimple near the tip of the nail brightened to orange. Before it had faded, the boy struck again. Old Nathan turned the workpiece 90° on its axis, and the hand-stone hit it a third time.

While the makeshift hammer was striking, the iron did not appear to change. When the cunning man's tongs laid it back in the blue sheet of hickory flame, however, the workpiece was noticeably longer than the smith had forged it originally.

Old Nathan had been muttering under his breath as the boy hammered. They were forging the scale on the face of the nail into the fabric of the pointer, amalgamating the proteins of Jen's hoof with the hot iron. Old Nathan murmured, "As least is to great," each time the hammer struck. Now, as the nail heated again, the gases seemed to flow by it in the pattern of a horse's mane.

"Cain't use an iron sledge, boy," the cunning man said aloud. "Not fer this, not though the nail be iron hitself."

He lifted out the workpiece again. "Strike on," he said. "And the tip this time, so's hit's pinted like an awl."

The stone clopped like a horse's hoof and clicked like horses' teeth, while beside them in the chimney corner the fire settled itself with a burbling whicker.

"As least is to great. . . ."

Eldon Bowsmith's face was sooty from the fire and flushed where runnels of sweat had washed the soot away, but there was a triumphant gleam in his eyes as he prepared to leave Old Nathan's cabin that evening. He held the iron pointer upright in one hand and his opposite index finger raised in balance. The tip of his left ring finger was bandaged with a bit of tow and spiderweb to cover a puncture. The cunning man had drawn three drops of the boy's blood to color the water in which they quenched the iron after its last heating.

"I cain't say how much I figger I'm 'bliged t' ye fer this," said Bowsmith, gazing at the pointer with a fondness inexplicable to anyone who did not know what had gone into creating the instrument.

The bit of iron had been hammered out to the length of a man's third finger. It looked like a scrap of bent wire, curved and recurved by blows from stone onto stone, each surface having a rounded face. The final point had been rolled onto it between the stones, with the boy showing a remarkable delicacy and ability to coordinate his motions with those of the cunning man who held the tongs.

"Don't thank me till ye've got yer Jen back in her stall," said Old Nathan. His mind added, "And not thin, effen the Neills burn ye out and string ye to en oak limb." Aloud he said, "Anyways, ye did the heavy part yerself."

That was true only when limited to the physical portion of what had gone on that afternoon. Were the hammering of primary importance, then every blacksmith would have been a wizard. Old Nathan, too, was panting and worn from exertion; but like Bowsmith, the success he felt at what had been accomplished made the effort worthwhile. He had seen the plowhorse pacing in her narrow stall when steam rose as the iron was quenched.

The boy cocked his head aside and started to comb his fingers through his hair in what Old Nathan had learned was a gesture of embarrassment. He looked from the pointer to his bandaged finger, then began to rub his scalp with the heel of his right hand. "Well . . . ," he said. "I want ye t' know thet I . . ."

Bowsmith grimaced and looked up to meet the eyes of the cunning man squarely. "Lot uv folk," he said, "they wouldn't hev let me hep. They call me Simp, right t' my face they do thet. . . . En, en I reckon there's no harm t' thet, but . . . sir, ye treated me like Ma used to. You air ez good a friend ez I've got in the world, 'ceptin' the Neills."

"So good a friend ez thet?" said the cunning man drily. He had an uncomfortable urge to turn his own face away and comb fingers through his hair.

"Well," he said instead and cleared his throat in order to go on. "Well. Ye remember what I told ye. Ye don't speak uv this t' ary soul. En by the grace uv yer Ma in heaven whur she watches ye—"

Old Nathan gripped the boy by both shoulders, and the importance of what he had to get across made emotionally believable words that were not part of the world's truth as the cunning man knew it "—*don't* call t' Jen and foller the pinter to her without ye've the sheriff et yer side. Aye, en ef he wants t' bring half the settlement along t' boot, thin I reckon thet might be a wise notion."

"Ain't goin' t' fail ye this time, sir," promised the boy brightly. "Hit'll all be jist like you say."

He was whistling again as he strode up the hill into the dusk. Old Nathan imagined a cabin burning and a lanky form dangling from a tree beside it.

He spat to avoid the omen.

Old Nathan sat morosely in the chimney corner, reading with his back to the fire, when his cat came in the next night.

"Caught a rabbit nigh on up t' the road," the cat volunteered cheerfully. "Land *sakes* didn't it squeal and thrash."

He threw himself down on the puncheon floor, using Old Nathan's booted foot as a brace while he licked his belly and genitals. "Let it go more times thin I kin count," the cat went on. "When it wouldn't run no more, thin I killed it en et it down t' the head en hide."

"I reckon ye did," said the cunning man. To say otherwise to the cat would be as empty as railing against the sky for what it struck with its thunderbolts. He carefully folded his reading glasses and set them in the crease of his book so that he could stroke the animal's fur.

"Hev ye seen thet young feller what wuz here t'other day?" the cat asked, pawing his master's hand but not—for a wonder—hooking in his claws.

"I hev not," Old Nathan replied flatly. He had ways by which he could have followed Bowsmith's situation or even anticipated it. Such sources of information came with a price, however, and they graved an otherwise fluid future on the stone of reality. He would enter that world of knowledge for others whose perceived need was great enough, but he would not enter it for himself. Old Nathan had experienced no greater horror in his seventy years of life than the certain knowledge of a disaster which he could not change.

"Well," said the cat, "reckon ye'll hev a chanct to purty quick, now. Turned down yer trail, he did, 'bout time I licked off them rabbit guts en come home myself."

"Halloo the house!" called Eldon Bowsmith from beyond the front door, and the cat bit Old Nathan's forearm solidly as the cunning man tried to rise from the rocking chair.

"Bless en *save* ye, cat!" roared the old man, gripping the animal before the hind legs, feeling the warm distended belly squishing with rabbit meat. "Come in, boy," he cried, "come in en set," and he surged upright with the open book in one hand and the cat cursing in the other.

Bowsmith wore a look of such dejection that he scarcely brightened with surprise at the cunning man's incongruous appearance. A black iron pointer dangled from the boy's right hand, and the scrap of bandage had fallen from his left ring finger without being replaced.

"Ev'nin' t' ye, sir," he said to Old Nathan. "Wisht I could say I'd done ez ye told me, but I don't reckon I kin."

When the cat released Old Nathan's forearm, the cunning man let him jump to the floor. The animal promptly began to insinuate himself between Bowsmith's feet and rub the boy's knees with his tailtip, muttering, "Good t' see ye, good thet ye've come."

"Well, you're alive," said Old Nathan, "en you're here, which ain't a bad start fer fixin' sich ez needs t' be fixed. Set yerself en we'll talk about it."

Bowsmith obeyed his host's gesture and seated himself in the rocker, still warm and clicking with the motion of the cunning man rising from it. He held out the pointer but did not look at his host as he explained, "I wint to the settlemint, and I told the sheriff what ye said. He gathered up mebbe half a dozen uv the men thereabouts, all totin' their guns like they wuz en army. En I named Jen, like you said, and this nail, hit like t' pull outen my *hand* it wuz so fierce t' find her."

Old Nathan examined by firelight the pointer he had taken from the boy. He was frowning, and when he measured the iron against his finger the frown became a thundercloud in which the cunning man's eyes were flashes of green lightning. The pointer was a quarter inch longer than the one that had left his cabin the morning before.

"En would ye b'lieve it, but hit took us straight ez straight t' the Neill place?" continued the boy with genuine wonderment in his voice. He shook his head. "I told the sheriff I reckoned there wuz a mistake, but mebbe the Bar'n had found Jen en he wuz keepin' her t' give me whin I next come by."

Bowsmith shook his head again. He laced his fingers together on his lap and stared glumly at them as he concluded, "But I be hanged ef thet same ol' spavined mule warn't tied t' the door uv the barn, and the pinter wouldn't leave afore it touched hit's hoof." He sucked in his lips in frustration.

"Here, I'd admire ef you sleeked my fur," purred the cat, and he leaped into the boy's lap. Bowsmith's hands obeyed as aptly as if he could have understood the words of the request.

"What is it happened thin, boy?" Old Nathan asked in a voice as soft as the whisper of powder being poured down the barrel of a musket.

"Well, I'm feared to guess what might hev happened," explained Bowsmith, "effen the Baron hisself hedn't come out the cabin and say hit made no matter."

He began to nod in agreement with the words in his memory, saying, "The Bar'n, he told the sheriff I wuzn't right in the head sometimes, en he give thim all a swig outen his jug uv wildcat so's they wouldn't hammer me fer runnin' thim off through the woods like a durned fool. They wuz laughin' like fiends whin they left, the sheriff and the folk from the settlement."

Bowsmith's hands paused. The cat waited a moment, then rose and battered his chin against the boy's chest until the stroking resumed.

"Reckon I am a durn fool," the boy said morosely. "Thet en worse."

"How long did ye stop over t' the Neills after ye left here yestiddy?" Old Nathan asked in the same soft voice.

"Coo," said Bowsmith, meeting the cunning man's eyes as wonder drove the gloom from his face. "Well, I *niver*. . . . Wuzn't goin' t' tell ye thet, seein's ez ye'd said I oughtn't t' stop. But Mar' Beth, she seed me on the road en hollered me up t' the cabin t' set fer a spell. Don't guess I was there too long, though. The Baron asked me whin I was going t' clear his newground. And then whin he went out, me en the boys, we passed the jug a time er two."

He frowned. "Reckon hit might uv been longer thin I'd recollected."

"Hit wuz dark by the time ye passed the Neills', warn't it?" Old Nathan said. "How'd Mary Beth see down t' the road?"

"Why, I be," replied the boy. "Why—" His face brightened. "D'ye reckon she wuz waiting on me t' come back by? She's powerful sweet on me, ye know, though I say thet who oughtn't't."

"Reckon hit might be she wuz waitin'," said the cunning man, his voice leaden and implacable. He lifted his eyes from Bowsmith to the end wall opposite the fireplace. The strop that was all the material remains of Spanish King shivered in a breeze that neither man could feel.

"Pinter must hev lost all hit's virtue whin I went back on what ye told me," the boy said miserably. "You bin so good t' me, en I step on my dick ever' time I turn around. Reckon I'll git back t' my place afore I cause more trouble."

"Set, boy," said Old Nathan. "Ye'll go whin I say go . . . and ye'll do this time what I say ye'll do."

"Yessir," replied Bowsmith, taken aback. When he tried instinctively to straighten his shoulders, the chair rocked beneath him. He lurched to his feet in response. Instead of spilling the cat, he used the animal as a balancer and then clutched him back to his chest.

"Yessir," he repeated, standing upright and looking confused but not frightened. And not, somehow, ridiculous, for all his ragged spray of hair and the grumbling tomcat in his arms.

Old Nathan set the book he held down on the table, his spectacles still marking his place against the stiff binding which struggled to close the volume. With both hands free, he gripped the table itself and walked over to the fireplace alcove.

Bowsmith poured the cat back onto the floor as soon as he understood what his host was about, but he paused on realizing that his help was not needed. The table top was forty inches to a side, sawn from thick planks and set on an equally solid framework—all of oak. The cunning man shifted the table without concern for its weight and awkwardness. He had never been a giant for strength, but even now he was no one to trifle with either.

"Ye kin fetch the straight chair to it," he said over his shoulder while he fumbled with the lock of one of the chests flanking the fireplace. "I'll need the light t' copy out the words ye'll need."

"Sir, I cain't read," the boy said in a voice of pale, peeping despair.

"Hit don't signify," replied the cunning man. The lid of the chest creaked open. "Fetch the chair."

Old Nathan set a bundle of turkey quills onto the table, then a pot of ink stoppered with a cork. The ink moved sluggishly and could have used a dram of water to thin it, but it was fluid enough for writing as is.

Still kneeling before the chest, the cunning man raised a document case and untied the ribbon which closed it. Bowsmith placed the straight chair by the table, moving the rocker aside to make room. Then he watched over the cunning man's shoulder, finding in the written word a magic as real as anything Old Nathan had woven or forged on previous visits.

"Not this one," the older man said, laying aside the first of the letters he took from the case. It was in a woman's hand, the paper fine but age-spotted. He could not read the words without his glasses, but he did not need to reread what he had not been able to forget even at this distance in time. "Nor this."

"Coo . . . ," Bowsmith murmured as the first document was covered by the second, this one written on parchment with a wax seal and ribbons which the case had kept a red as bright as that of the day they were impressed onto the document.

Old Nathan smiled despite his mood. "A commendation from General Sevier," he said in quiet pride as he took another letter from the case.

"You fit the Redcoats et New Or-leens like they say, thin?" the younger man asked.

Old Nathan looked back at him with an expression suddenly as blank as a board. "No, boy," he said, "hit was et Kings Mountain, en they didn't wear red coats, the most uv them."

He paused and then added in a kindlier tone, "En I reckon thet when I was yer age en ol' fools wuz jawin' about Quebec and Cartagena and all thet like, hit didn't matter a bean betwixt them t' me neither. And mebbe there wuz more truth t' thet thin I've thought since."

"I don't rightly foller," said Bowsmith.

"Don't reckon ye need to," the older man replied. "Throw a stick uv lightwood on the fire."

Holding the sheet he had just removed from the case, Old Nathan stood upright and squinted to be sure of what he had. It seemed to be one of his brother's last letters to him, a decade old but no more important for that. It was written on both sides of the sheet, but the cuttlefish ink had faded to its permanent state of rich brown. The paper would serve as well for the cunning man's present need as a clean sheet which could not have been found closer than Hewitt's store in the settlement—and that dearly.

He sat down on the chair and donned his spectacles, using the letter as a placeholder in the book in their stead. The turkey quills were held together by a wisp of twine which, with his glasses on, he could see to untie.

After choosing a likely quill, Old Nathan scowled and said, "Turn yer head, boy." When he felt the movement of Bowsmith behind him, obedient if uncertain, the cunning man reached out with his eyes closed and brought his hand back holding the jackknife.

Some of Old Nathan's magic was done in public to impress visitors and those to whom they might babble in awe. Some things that he might have hidden from others he did before Bowsmith, because he knew that the boy would never attempt to duplicate the acts on his own. But this one trick was the cunning man's secret of secrets.

The knife is the most useful of Mankind's tools, dating from ages before he was even human. But a knife is also a weapon, and the sole reason for storing it—somewhere else—rather than in a pants pocket was that on some future date an enemy might remove a weapon from your pants. Better to plan for a need which never eventuated than to be caught by unexpected disaster.

"Ye kin turn and help me now, Eldon Bowsmith," the cunning man said as he trimmed his pen with the wire edge of the smaller blade. "Ye kin hold open the book fer me."

"Yessir," said the boy and obeyed with the clumsy nervousness of a bachelor asked to hold an infant for the first time. He gripped the volume with an effort which an axehelve would have better justified. The shaking of his limbs would make the print even harder to read.

Old Nathan sighed. "Gently, boy," he said. "Hit won't bite ye."

Though there was reason to fear this book. It named itself *Testamentum Athanasii* on a title page which gave no other information regarding its provenance. The volume was old, but it had been printed with movable type and bound or rebound recently enough that the leather hinges showed no sign of cracking.

The receipt to which the book now opened was one Old Nathan had read frequently in the months since Spanish King had won his last battle and, winning, had died. Not till now had he really considered employing the formula. Not really.

"Boy," lied the cunning man, "we cain't git yer horse back, so I'll give ye the strength uv a bull thet ye kin plow."

Bowsmith's face found a neutral pattern and held it while his mind worked on the sentence he had just been offered. Usually conversations took standard patterns. "G'day t' ye, Simp." "G'day t' ye, Mister/Miz . . ." "Ev'nin', Eldon. Come en set." "Ev'nin', Mar' Beth. Don' mind effen I do." Patterns like that made a conversation easier, without the confusing precipices which talking to Old Nathan entailed.

"Druther hev Jen back, sir," said the boy at last. "Effen *you* don't mind."

The cunning man raised his left hand. The gesture was not quite a physical threat because the hand held his spectacles, and their lenses refracted spitting orange firelight across the book and the face of the younger man. "Mind, boy?" said Old Nathan. "Mind? You mind *me,* thet's the long and the short uv it now, d'ye hear?"

"Yessir."

The cunning man dipped his pen in the ink and wiped it on the bottle's rim, cursing the fluid's consistency. "Give ye the strength uv a bull," he lied again, "en a strong bull et thet." He began to write, his present strokes crossing those of his brother in the original letter. He held the spectacles a few inches in front of his eyes, squinting and adjusting them as he copied from the page of the book.

"Ever ketch rabbits, feller?" asked the cat as he leaped to the tabletop and landed without a stir because all four paws touched down together.

"Good feller," muttered Bowsmith, holding the book with the thumb and spread fingers of one hand so that the other could stroke the cat. The trembling which had disturbed the pages until then ceased, though the cat occasionally bumped a corner of the volume. "Good feller. . . ."

The click of clawtips against oak, the scritch of the pen nib leaving crisp black lines across the sepia complaints beneath, and the sputtering pine knot that lighted the cabin wove themselves into a sinister unity that was darker than the nighted forest outside.

Yet not so dark as the cunning man's intent.

When he finished, the boy and the cat were both staring at him, and it was the cat who rumbled, "Bad ez all thet?" smelling the emotions in the old man's sweat.

"What'll be," Old Nathan rasped through a throat drier than he had realized till he spoke, "will be." He looked down at the document he had just indited, folded his spectacles one-handed, and then turned to hurl the quill pen into the fire with a violence that only hinted his fury at what he was about to do.

"Sir?" said Bowsmith.

"Shut the book, boy," said Old Nathan wearily. His fingers made a tentative pass toward the paper, to send it the way the quill had gone. A casuist would have said that he was not acting and therefore bore no guilt . . . but a man who sets a snare for a rabbit cannot claim the throttled rabbit caused its own death by stepping into the noose.

The cunning man stood and handed the receipt to his visitor, folding it along the creases of the original letter. "Put it in yer pocket fer now, lad," he said. He took the book, closed now as he had directed, and scooped up the cat gently with a hand beneath the rib cage and the beast's haunches in the crook of his elbow.

"Now, carry the table acrosst t' the other side," the cunning man continued, motioning Bowsmith with a thrust of his beard because he did not care to point with the leather-covered book. "Fetch me down the strop uv bullhide there. Hit's got a peg drove through each earhole t' hold it."

"That ol' bull," said the cat, turning his head to watch Bowsmith walk across the room balancing the heavy table on one hand. "Ye know, I git t' missin' him sometimes?"

"As do I," Old Nathan agreed grimly. "But I don't choose t' live in a world where I don't see the prices till the final day."

"Sir?" queried the boy, looking down from the table which he had mounted in a flat-footed jump that crashed its legs down on the puncheons.

"Don't let it trouble ye, boy," the cunning man replied. "I talk t' my cat, sometimes. Fetch me down Spanish King, en I'll deal with yer problem the way I've set myself t' do."

The cat sprang free of the encircling arm, startled by what he heard in his master's voice.

It was an hour past sunset, and Baron Neill held court on the porch over an entourage of two of his three sons and four of the six grandsons. Inside the cabin, built English-fashion of sawn timber but double-sized, the women of the clan cleared off the truck from supper and talked in low voices among themselves. The false crow calls from the lookout tree raucously penetrated the background of cicadas and tree frogs.

" 'Bout time," said the youngest son, taking a swig from the jug. He was in his early forties, balding and feral.

"Mar' Beth," called Baron Neill without turning his head or taking from his mouth the long stem of his meerschaum pipe.

There was silence from within the cabin but no immediate response.

The Baron dropped his feet from the porch rail with a crash and stood up. The Neill patriarch looked more like a rat than anything on two legs had a right to do. His nose was prominent, and the remainder of his body seemed to spread outward from it down to the fleshy buttocks supported by a pair of spindly shanks. "Mar' *Beth!*" he shouted, hunched forward as he faced the cabin door.

"Well, I'm comin', ain't I?" said a woman who was by convention the Baron's youngest daughter and was in any case close kin to him. She stepped out of the lamplit cabin, hitching the checked apron a little straighter on her homespun dress. The oil light behind her colored her hair more of a yellow than the sun would have brought out, emphasizing the translucent gradations of her single tortoiseshell comb.

"Simp's comin' back," said the Baron, relaxing enough to clamp the pipe again between his teeth. "Tyse jist called. Git down t' the trail en bring him back."

The woman stood hipshot, the desire to scowl tempered by the knowledge that the patriarch would strike her if the expression were not hidden by the angle of the light. "I'm *poorly,*" she said.

One of the boys snickered, and Baron Neill roared, "Don't I *know* thet? You do ez I tell ye, girl."

Mary Beth stepped off the porch with an exaggerated sway to her hips. The pair of hogs sprawled beneath the boards awakened but snorted and flopped back down after questing with their long flexible snouts.

"Could be I don't mind," the woman threw back over her shoulder from a safe distance. "Could be Simp looks right good stacked up agin some I've seed."

One of her brothers sent after her a curse and the block of poplar he was whittling, neither with serious intent.

"Jeth," said the Baron, "go fetch Dave and Sim from the still. Never know when two more guns might be the difference betwixt somethin' er somethin' else. En bring another jug back with ye."

"Lotta durn work for a durned old plowhorse," grumbled one of the younger Neills.

The Baron sat down again on his chair and lifted his boots to the porch rail. "Ain't about a horse," he said, holding out his hand and having it filled by the stoneware whiskey jug without him needing to ask. "Hain't been about a horse since he brung Old Nathan into hit. Fancies himself, that 'un does."

The rat-faced old man took a deep draw on his pipe and mingled in his mouth the harsh flavors of burley tobacco and raw whiskey. "Well, I fancy myself, too. We'll jist see who's got the rights uv it."

Eldon Bowsmith tried to step apart from the woman when the path curved back in sight of the cabin. Mary Beth giggled throatily and pulled herself close again, causing the youth to sway like a sapling in the wind. He stretched out the heavy bundle in his opposite hand in order to recover his balance.

"What in *tarnation* is that ye got, boy?" demanded Baron Neill from the porch. The air above his pipe bowl glowed orange as he drew on the mouthpiece.

"Got a strop uv bullhide, Bar'n," Bowsmith called back. "Got the horns, tail, and the strip offen the backbone besides."

He swayed again, then said in a voice that carried better than he would have intended, "Mar' *Beth*, ye mustn't touch me like thet here." But the words were not a serious reproach, and his laughter joined the woman's renewed giggle.

There was snorting laughter from the porch as well. One of the men there might have spoken had not Baron Neill snarled his offspring to silence.

The couple separated when they reached the steps, Mary Beth leading the visitor with her hips swaying in even greater emphasis than when she had left the cabin.

"Tarnation," the Baron repeated as he stood and took the rolled strip of hide from Bowsmith. The boy's hand started to resist, but he quickly released the bundle when he remembered where he was.

"Set a spell, boy," said the patriarch. "Zeph, hand him the jug."

"I reckon I need yer help, Bar'n," Bowsmith said, rubbing his right sole against his left calf. The stoneware jug—a full one just brought from the still by the Baron's other two grandsons—was pressed into his hands and he took a brief sip.

"Now, don't ye insult my squeezin's, boy," said one of the younger men. "Drink hit down like a man er ye'll answer t' me." In this, as in most things, the clan worked as a unit to achieve its ends. Simp Bowsmith was little enough of a problem sober; but with a few swallows of wildcat in him, the boy ran like butter.

"Why, you know we'd do the world for ye, lad," said the rat-faced elder as he shifted to bring the bundle into the lamplight spilling from the open door. It was just what the boy had claimed, a strop of heavy leather, tanned with the hair still on, and including the stiff-boned tail as well as the long, translucent horns.

Bowsmith handed the jug to one of the men around him, then spluttered and coughed as he swallowed the last of the mouthful he had taken. "Ye see, sir," he said quickly in an attempt to cover the tears which the liquor had brought to his eyes, "I've a spell t' say, but I need some'un t' speak the words over whilst I git thim right. He writ thim down fer me, Mister Nathan did. But I cain't read, so's he told me go down t' the settlemint en hev Mister Hewitt er the sheriff say thim with me."

He carefully unbuttoned the pocket of his shirt, out at the elbows now that his mother was not alive to patch it. With the reverence for writing that other men might have reserved for gold, he handed the rewritten document to Baron Neill.

The patriarch thrust the rolled bullhide to the nearest of his offspring and took the receipt. Turning, he saw Mary Beth and said, "You—girl. Fetch the lamp out here, and thin you git back whar ye belong. Ye know better thin t' nose around whin thar's men talkin'."

"But I mustn't speak the spell out whole till ever'thing's perpared," Bowsmith went on, gouging his calf again with the nail of his big toe. "Thet's cuz hit'll work only the onct, Mister Nathan sez. En effen I'm not wearin' the strop over me when I says it, thin I'll gain some strength but not the whole strength uv the bull."

There was a sharp altercation within the cabin, one female voice shrieking, "En what're *we* s'posed t' do with no more light thin inside the Devil's butthole? You put that lamp down, Mar' Beth Neill!"

"Zeph," said the Baron in a low voice, but two of his sons were already moving toward the doorway, shifting their rifles to free their right hands.

"Anyhows, I thought ye might read the spell out with me, sir," Bowsmith said. "Thim folk down t' the settlemint, I reckon they don't hev much use fer me."

"I wuz jist—" a woman cried on a rising inflection that ended with the thud of knuckles instead of a slap. The light through the doorway shifted, then brightened. The men came out, one of them carrying a copper lamp with a glass chimney.

The circle of lamplight lay like the finger of God on the group of men.

That the Neills were all one family was obvious; that they were a species
removed from humanity was possible. They were short men; in their
midst, Eldon Bowsmith looked like a scrawny chicken surrounded by rats
standing upright. The hair on their scalps was black and straight, thinning
even on the youngest, and their foreheads sloped sharply.

Several of the clan were chewing tobacco, but the Baron alone smoked
a pipe. The stem of that yellow-bowled meerschaum served him as an
officer's swagger stick or a conductor's baton.

"Hold the durn lamp," the patriarch snapped to the son who tried to
hand him the instrument. While Bowsmith clasped his hands and
watched the Baron in nervous hopefulness, the remainder of the Neill clan
eyed the boy sidelong and whispered at the edge of the lighted circle.

Baron Neill unfolded the document carefully and held it high so that
the lamp illuminated the writing from behind his shoulder. Smoke drib-
bled from his nostrils in short puffs as his teeth clenched on the stem of
his pipe.

When the Baron lowered the receipt, he removed the pipe from his
mouth. His eyes were glaring blank fury, but his tongue said only, "I
wonder, boy, effen yer Mister Nathan warn't funnin' ye along. This paper
he give ye, hit don't hev word one on it. Hit's jist Babel."

One of the younger Neills took the document which the Baron held
spurned at his side. Three of the others crowded closer and began to argue
in whispers, one of them tracing with his finger the words written in sepia
ink beneath the receipt.

"Well, they hain't words, Bar'n," said the boy, surprised that he knew
something which the other man—any other man, he might have said—
did not. "I mean, not like we'd speak. Mister Nathan, he said what he writ
out wuz the sounds, so's I didn't hev occasion t' be consarned they wuz
furrin words."

Baron Neill blinked, as shocked to hear a reasoned exposition from
Simp Bowsmith as the boy was to have offered it. After momentary con-
sideration, he decided to treat the information as something he had
known all the time. "*Leave* thet be!" he roared, whirling on the cluster of
his offspring poring over the receipt.

Two of the men were gripping the document at the same time. Both of
them released it and jumped back, bumping their fellows and joggling the
lantern dangerously. They collided again as they tried unsuccessfully to
catch the paper before it fluttered to the board floor.

The Baron cuffed the nearer and swatted at the other as well, missing
when the younger man dodged back behind the shelter of his kin. Deliber-

ately, his agitation suggested only by the vehemence of the pull he took on his pipe, the old man bent and retrieved the document. He peered at it again, then fixed his eyes on Bowsmith. "You say you're t' speak the words on this. Would thet be et some particular time?"

"No sir," said the boy, bobbing his head as if in an effort to roll ideas to the surface of his mind. "Not thet Mister Nathan told me."

As Baron Neill squinted at the receipt again, silently mouthing the syllables which formed no language of which he was cognizant, Bowsmith added, "Jist t' set down with the bullhide over my back, en t' speak out the words. En I'm ez strong ez a bull."

"Give him another pull on the jug," the Baron ordered abruptly.

"I don't—" Bowsmith began as three Neills closed on him, one offering the jug with a gesture as imperious as that of a highwayman presenting his pistol.

"Boy," the Baron continued, "I'm goin' t' help ye, jist like you said. But hit's a hard task, en ye'll hev t' bear with me till I'm ready. Ain't like reg'lar readin', this parsin' out things ez ain't words."

He fixed the boy with a fierce glare which was robbed of much of its effect because the lamp behind him threw his head into bald silhouette. "Understand?"

"Yessir."

"Drink my liquor, boy," suggested the man with the jug. "Hit'll straighten yer quill for sure."

"Yessir."

"Now," Baron Neill went on, refolding the receipt and sliding it into the pocket of his own blue frock coat, "you set up with the young folks, hev a good time, en we'll make ye up a bed with us fer the night. Meanwhiles, I'm goin' down t' the barn t' study this over so's I kin help ye in the mornin'."

"Oh," said Bowsmith in relief, then coughed as fumes of the whiskey he had just drunk shocked the back of his nostrils. "Lordy," he muttered, wheezing to get his breath. "Lordy!"

One of the Neills thumped him hard on the back and said, "Chase thet down with another, so's they fight each other en leave you alone."

"Thet bullhide," said the Baron, calculation underlying the appearance of mild curiosity, "hit's somethin' special, now, ain't it?"

"Reckon it might be," the boy agreed, glad to talk because it delayed by that much the next swig of the liquor that already spun his head and his stomach. "Hit was pegged up t' Mister Nathan's wall like hit hed been thar a right long time."

"Figgered thet," Baron Neill said in satisfaction. "Hed t' be somethin' more thin ye'd said."

Bowsmith sighed and took another drink. For a moment there was no sound but the hiss of the lamp and a whippoorwill calling from the middle distance.

"Reckon I'll take the hide with me t' the barn," said the Baron, reaching for the rolled strop, "so's hit won't git trod upon."

The grandson holding the strip of hide turned so that his body blocked the Baron's intent. "Reckon we kin keep it here en save ye the burden, ol' man," he said in a sullen tone raised an octave by fear of the consequences.

"What's *this*, now?" the patriarch said, backing a half step and placing his hands on his hips.

"Like Len sez," interjected the man with the lamp, stepping between his father and his son, "we'll keep the hide safe back here."

"Tar*nation*," Baron Neill said, throwing up his hands and feigning good-natured exasperation. "Ye didn't think yer own pa 'ud shut ye out wholesale, did ye?"

"Bar'n," said Eldon Bowsmith, emboldened by the liquor, "I don't foller ye."

"Shet yer mouth whin others er talkin' family matters, boy," snapped one of the clan from the fringes. None of the women could be seen through the open door of the cabin, but their hush was like the breathing of a restive cow.

"You youngins hev fun," said the Baron, turning abruptly. "I've got some candles down t' the barn. I'll jist study this"—he tapped with the pipestem on the pocket in which paper rustled—"en we'll talk agin, mebbe 'long about moonrise."

Midnight.

"Y'all hev fun," repeated the old man as he began to walk down the slippery path to the barn.

The Neill women, led by Mary Beth with her comb readjusted to let her hair fall to her shoulders, softly joined the men on the porch.

In such numbers, even the bare feet of his offspring were ample warning to Baron Neill before Zephaniah opened the barn door. The candle of molded tallow guttered and threatened to go out.

"Simp?" the old man asked. He sat on the bar of an empty stall with the candle set in the slot cut higher in the endpost for another bar.

It had been years since the clan kept cows. The only animal now sharing the barn with the patriarch and the smell of sour hay was Bowsmith's horse, her jaws knotted closed with a rag to keep her from neighing. Her stall was curtained with blankets against the vague possibility that the boy would glance into the building.

"Like we'd knocked him on the head," said the third man in the procession entering the barn. The horse wheezed through her nostrils and pawed the bars of her stall.

"Why ain't we done jist thet?" demanded Mary Beth. "Nobody round here's got a scrap uv use fer him, 'ceptin' mebbe thet ol' bastard cunning man. En *he's* not right in the head neither."

The whole clan was padding into the barn, but the building's volume was a good match for their number. There were several infants, one of them continuing to squall against its mother's breast until a male took it from her. The mother cringed, but she relaxed when the man only pinched the baby's lips shut with a thumb and forefinger. He increased the pressure every time the infant swelled itself for another squawl.

"Did I raise ye up t' be a fool, girl?" Baron Neill demanded angrily, jabbing with his pipestem. "Sure, they've a use fer him—t' laugh et. Effen we slit his throat en weight his belly with stones, the county'll be here with rope and torches fer the whole lot uv us."

He took a breath and calmed as the last of the clan trooped in. "Besides, hain't needful. Never do what hain't needful."

One of the men swung the door to and rotated a peg to hold it closed. The candleflame thrashed in the breeze, then steadied to a dull, smoky light as before.

"Now . . . ," said the Baron slowly, "I'll tell ye what we're goin' t' do."

Alone of the Neill clan, he was seated. Some of those spread into the farther corners could see nothing of the patriarch save his legs crossed as he sat on the stall bar. There were over twenty people in the barn, including the infants, and the faint illumination accentuated the similiarity of their features.

Len, the grandson who held the bullhide, crossed his arms to squeeze the bundle closer to his chest. He spread his legs slightly, and two of his bearded, rat-faced kin stepped closer as if to defend him from the Baron's glare.

The patriarch smiled. "We're all goin' t' be stronger thin strong," he said in a sinuous, enticing whisper. "Ye heard Simp—he'd gain strength whether er no the strop wuz over his back. So . . . I'll deacon the spell off, en you all speak the lines out after me, standin' about in the middle."

He paused in order to stand up and search the faces from one side of the room to the other. "Hev I ever played my kinfolk false?" he demanded. The receipt in his left hand rustled, and the stem of his pipe rotated with his gaze. Each of his offspring lowered his or her eyes as the pointer swept the clan.

Even Len scowled at the rolled strop instead of meeting the Baron's eyes, but the young man said harshly, "Who's t' hold the hide, thin? You?"

"The hide'll lay over my back," Baron Neill agreed easily, "en the lot uv you'll stand about close ez ye kin git and nobody closer thin the next. I reckon we all gain, en I gain the most."

The sound of breathing made the barn itself seem a living thing, but no one spoke and even the sputter of the candle was audible. At last Mary Beth, standing hipshot and only three-quarters facing the patriarch, broke the silence with, "You're not ez young ez ye onct were, Pa. Seems ez if the one t' git the most hed ought t' be one t' be around t' use hit most."

Instead of retorting angrily, Baron Neill smiled and said, "Which one, girl? Who do *you* pick in my place?"

The woman glanced about her. Disconcerted, she squirmed backward, out of the focus into which she had thrown herself.

"He's treated us right," murmured another woman, half-hidden in the shadow of the post which held the candle. "Hit's best we git on with the business."

"All right, ol' man," said Len, stepping forward to hold out the strop. "What er ye waitin' on?"

"Mebbe fer my kin t' come t' their senses," retorted the patriarch with a smile of triumph.

Instead of snatching the bullhide at once, Baron Neill slid his cold pipe into the breast pocket of his coat, then folded the receipt he had taken from Bowsmith and set it carefully on the endpost of the stall.

Len pursed his lips in anger, demoted from central figure in the clan's resistance to the Baron back to the boy who had been ordered to hold the bullhide. The horns, hanging from the section of the bull's coarse poll which had been lifted, rattled together as the young man's hands began to tremble with emotion.

Baron Neill took off his frock coat and hung it from the other post supporting the bar on which he had waited. Working deliberately, the Baron shrugged the straps of his galluses off his shoulders and lowered his trousers until he could step out of them. His boots already stood toes-out beside the stall partition. None of the others of the clan were wearing footgear.

"Should we . . . ?" asked one of the men, pinching a pleat of his shirt to finish the question.

"No need," the Baron said, unbuttoning the front of his own store-bought shirt. "Mebbe not fer me, even. But best t' be sure."

One of the children started to whine a question. His mother hushed him almost instantly by clasping one hand over his mouth and the other behind the child's head to hold him firmly.

The shirt was the last of Baron Neill's clothing. When he had draped it over his trousers and coat, he looked even more like the white-furred rodent he resembled clothed. His body was pasty, its surface colored more by grime and the yellow candlelight than by blood vessels beneath it. The epaulettes on the Baron's coat had camouflaged the extreme narrowness of his shoulders and chest, and the only place his skin was taut was where the potbelly sagged against it.

His eyes had a terrible power, and they seemed to glint even before he took the candle to set it before him on the floor compacted of earth, dung, and ancient straw.

The Baron removed the receipt from the post on which it waited, opened it and smoothed the folds, and placed it beside the candle. Only then did he say to Len, *"Now* I'll take the strop, boy."

His grandson nodded sharply and passed the bundle over. The mood of the room was taut, like that of a stormy sky in the moments before the release of lightning. The anger and embarrassment which had twisted Len's face into a grimace earlier was now replaced by blank fear. Baron Neill smiled at him grimly.

The bull's tail was stiff with the bones still in it, so the length of hide had been wound around the base of that tail like thread on a spindle. Baron Neill held the strop by the head end, one hand on the hairless muzzle and the other on the poll between the horns, each the length of a man's arm along the curve. He shook out the roll with a quick jerk that left the brush of the tail scratching on the boards at the head of the stall.

The Baron cautiously held the strop against his back with the clattering horns dangling down to his knees. The old man gave a little shudder as the leather touched his bare skin, but he knelt and leaned forward, tugging the strop upward until the muzzle flopped loosely in front of his face.

The Baron muttered something that started as a curse and blurred into nondescript syllables when he recalled the task he was about. He rested the palm of one hand on the floor, holding the receipt flat and in the light of the candle. With his free hand, he folded the muzzle and forehead of the bull back over the poll so that he could see.

"Make a circle around me," ordered the patriarch in a voice husky with its preparations for declaiming the spell.

He should have been ridiculous, a naked old man on all fours like a dog, his head and back crossed by a strip of bullhide several times longer than the human torso. The tension in the barn kept even the children of the clan from seeing humor in the situation, and the muzzled plowhorse froze to silence in her curtained stall.

The Neills shuffled into motion, none of them speaking. The man who held the infant's lips pinched shut handed the child back to its mother. It whimpered only minutely and showed no interest in the breast which she quickly offered it to suck.

Two of the grandsons joined hands. The notion caught like gunpowder burning, hands leaping into hands. In the physical union, the psychic pressure that weighted the barn seemed more bearable though also more intense.

"Remember," said the Baron as he felt his offspring merge behind him, two of them linking hands over the trailing strop, "Ye'll not hev another chance. En ye'll git no pity from me effen ye cain't foller my deaconin' en you're no better off thin ye are now."

"Go *on*, ol' man," Mary Beth demanded in a savage whisper as she looked down on Baron Neill and the candle on the floor between her and the patriarch.

Baron Neill cocked his head up to look at the woman. She met his eyes with a glare as fierce as his own. Turning back to the paper on the ground, the old man read, "Ek neckroo say mettapempomie."

The candle guttered at his words. The whole clan responded together, "Ek neckroo say mettapempomie," their merged voices hesitant but gaining strength and unity toward the last of the Greek syllables like the wind in advance of a rainstorm.

"Soy sowma moo didomie," read the Baron. His normal voice was high-pitched and unsteady, always on the verge of cracking. Now it had dropped an octave and had power enough to drive straw into motion on the floor a yard away.

"Soy sowma moo didomie," thundered the Neill clan. Sparrows, nested on the roof trusses, fluttered and peeped as they tried furiously to escape from the barn. In the darkness, they could not see the vents under the roof peaks by which they flew in and out during daylight.

Baron Neill read the remainder of the formula, line by line. The process was becoming easier, because the smoky candle had begun to burn with a flame as white as the noonday sun. The syllables which had been written on age-yellowed paper and a background of earlier words now stood out and shaped themselves to the patriarch's tongue.

At another time, the Baron would have recognized the power which his tongue released but could not control. This night the situation had already been driven over a precipice. Caution was lost in exhilaration at the approaching climax, and the last impulse to stop was stilled by the fear that stopping might already be impossible.

The shingles above shuddered as the clan repeated the lines, and the candleflame climbed with the icy purpose of a stalagmite reaching for completion with a cave roof. Jen kicked at her stall in blind panic, cracking through the old crossbar, but none of the humans heard the sound.

"Hellon moy," shouted Baron Neill in triumph. "Hellon moy! Hellon moy!"

Mary Beth suddenly broke the circle and twisted. "Hit's *hot!*" she cried as she tore the front of her dress from neckline to waist in a single hysterical effort.

The woman's breasts swung free, their nipples erect and longer than they would have seemed a moment before. She tried to scream, but the sound fluted off into silence as her body ran like wax in obedience to the formula she and her kin had intoned.

The circle of the Neill clan flowed toward its center, flesh and bone alike taking on the consistency of magma. Clothing dropped and quivered as the bodies it had covered runneled out of sleeves and through the weave of the fabrics.

The bullhide strop sagged also as Baron Neill's body melted beneath it. As the pink, roiling plasm surged toward the center of the circle, the horns lifted and bristles that had lain over the bull's spine in life sprang erect.

The human voices were stilled, but the sparrows piped a mad chorus and Jen's hooves crashed again onto the splintering crossbar.

There was a slurping, gurgling sound. The bull's tail stood upright, its brush waving like a flag, and from the seething mass that had been the Neill clan rose the mighty, massive form of a black bull.

Eldon Bowsmith lurched awake on the porch of the Neill house. He had dreamed of a bull's bellow so loud that it shook the world.

Fuddled but with eyes adapted to the light of the crescent moon, he looked around him. The house was still and dark.

Then, as he tried to stand with the help of the porch rail, the barn door flew apart with a shower of splinters. Spanish King, bellowing again with the fury of which only a bull is capable, burst from the enclosure and galloped off into the night.

Behind him whinnied a horse which, in the brief glance vouchsafed by motion and the light, looked a lot like Jen.

When Eldon Bowsmith reached the cabin, Old Nathan was currying his bull by the light of a burning pine knot thrust into the ground beside the porch. A horse was tethered to the rail with a makeshift neck halter of twine.

"Sir, is thet you?" the boy asked cautiously.

"Who en *blazes* d'ye think hit 'ud be?" the cunning man snapped.

"Don't know thet 'un," snorted Spanish King. His big head swung toward the visitor, and one horn dipped menacingly.

"Ye'd not *be* here, blast ye," said Old Nathan, slapping the bull along the jaw, " 'ceptin' fer him."

"Yessir," said Bowsmith. "I'm right sorry. Only, a lot uv what I seed t'night, I figgered must be thet I wuz drinkin'."

"Took long enough t' fetch me," rumbled the bull as he snuffled the night air. He made no comment about the blow, but the way he studiously ignored Bowsmith suggested that the reproof had sunk home. "Summer's nigh over."

He paused and turned his head again so that one brown eye focused squarely on the cunning man. "Where *wuz* I, anyhow? D'ye know?"

"Not yet," said Old Nathan, stroking the bull's sweat-matted shoulders fiercely with the curry comb.

"Pardon, sir?" said the boy, who had walked into the circle of torch-light, showing a well-justified care to keep Old Nathan between him and Spanish King. Then he blinked and rose up on his bare toes to peer over the bull's shoulder at the horse. "Why," he blurted, "thet's the spit en image uv my horse Jen, only thet this mare's too bony!"

"Thet's yer Jen, all right," said the cunning man. "There's sacked barley in the lean-to out back, effen ye want t' feed her some afore ye take her t' home. Been runnin' the woods, I reckon."

"We're goin' back home?" asked the horse, speaking for almost the first time since she had followed Spanish King rather than be alone in the night.

"Oh, my God, Jen!" said the boy, striding past Spanish King with never a thought for the horns. "I'm so *glad* t' see ye!" He threw his arms around the horse's neck while she whickered, nuzzling the boy in hopes of finding some of the barley Old Nathan had mentioned.

"Durn fool," muttered Spanish King; but then he stretched himself deliberately, extending one leg at a time until his deep chest was rubbing the sod. "Good t' be back, though," he said. "Won't say it ain't."

Eldon Bowsmith straightened abruptly and stepped away from his mare, though he kept his hand on her mane. "Sir," he said, "ye found my Jen, en ye brung her back. What do I owe ye?"

Old Nathan ran the fingers of his free hand along the bristly spine of his bull. "Other folk hev took care uv thet," the cunning man said as Spanish King rumbled in pleasure at his touch. "Cleared yer account, so t' speak."

The pine torch was burning fitfully, close to the ground, so that Bowsmith's grimace of puzzlement turned shadows into a devil's mask. "Somebody paid for me?" he asked. "Well, I niver. Friends, hit must hev been?"

Spanish King lifted himself and began to walk regally around the cabin to his pasture and the two cows who were his property.

"Reckon ye could say thet," replied Old Nathan. "They wuz ez nigh t' bein' yer friends ez anybody's but their own."

The cunning man paused and grinned like very Satan. "In the end," he said, "they warn't sich good friends t' themselves."

A gust of wind rattled the shingles, as if the night sky were remembering what it had heard at the Neill place. Then it was silent again.

I was so impressed with the first David Campton story I read that it became the first true reprint (although first North American appearance) I used in Whispers *magazine. I have since used more than half a dozen Campton tales, several of which found places in Year's Best books. The following is an unusual ghost story told by this talented English playwright.*

REPOSSESSION

by David Campton

The Johnson audit took longer than I anticipated, but I stayed working until it was finished, and was heading for home when a threatened wintery shower materialised. When I drove by the old Marlow factory I was concentrating on the wet road, so the light in the upper window barely registered and I was well past before the oddness struck me. What was a light doing on in a building that had been shut down for years? Was it vandals? Squatters? Should I do anything about possible trespassers?

I could have telephoned the police, but was sure nobody would thank me. With the place scheduled for demolition there was every possibility it might fall down before the bulldozers moved in; so if some benighted soul had found shelter in the ruin, who was I to interfere? Constructed on the forbidding lines of a Victorian workhouse the derelict works offered only marginally better comfort than an exposed doorway. Let whoever was up there stay there.

I continued to speculate on the light, though. Surely all services had been cut off when Marlow's went into liquidation, so the gleam could hardly have been electric. Could a candle so far away have caught my attention through a sleet-spattered windscreen? Not even a hurricane lamp could have been expected to do that, so why had I even considered it? Except that the light forced itself more and more on my attention.

I tried to shrug off the problem, yet found myself musing on alternatives, even with the car locked away and myself sinking into a reclining chair, keeping the chill at bay with a high-proof rum toddy.

In my mind's eye I could see that top window. Clearly now. No rain or sleet to obscure it. Harsh light streaming through. Who or what could be up there?

From the point of view of the waste ground in front of the building, its grim silhouette made even more forbidding by the glow of city lights in the sky behind it, that solitary rectangle, like a single bright eye high above, was almost fascinating enough to make one forget the freezing slush underfoot. Who? Or what?

I came to my senses when I dropped the toddy glass—fortunately empty by now. No, I was not shivering in the shadow of that monument to nineteenth-century economics. I was comfortably established in my own bachelor domain.

In which case why were my feet so cold? Why were my sodden slippers caked with sludge? And why was icy cloth clammy against my legs?

I was as wet as if I had been standing outside, exposed to the wintery weather. Impossible. But there were the dark stains. Had I been so engrossed that I had spilt the contents of my glass? No. Whatever was soaking into my clothes was not hot rum and lemon. I had not moved from my chair, and yet . . .

An accountant is expected to have a logical brain, and logically there was only one thing to be done—change into something warm and dry. The autopilot that guides us through daily routine took over while my thought processes slithered and foundered, trying to come to terms with the patently unbelievable.

If I had not left the house why did my reflection in the wardrobe mirror look as though I had been trudging through fallow fields? There were actually blades of coarse grass sticking to the mud. A dried leaf. A fragment of paper. On slippers that since the day they were bought had never stepped farther than the front door. Half of me wanted to scream "there is something wrong here," the other half laid out clean underwear, peeled off oozing socks and decided a shower was called for.

While not exactly washing my bewilderment away, the hot water was at least soothing. As circulation returned, my numbed mental powers recovered sufficiently for me to take stock of the situation. I had been sitting back indulging—as surely as a man is entitled to after a long day with ledgers—in idle reverie. Something to do with a light, wasn't it? In the old Marlow place. Yes, now I remembered the lighted window. At the top of . . . and the warm water was rinsing away fresh streaks of dirt from my feet.

Later, wrapped in my bathrobe, I took the rum bottle to my empty glass. Such refinements as lemon and hot water were dispensed with. My present state of nerves called for undiluted restorative. When I stopped shaking I tried to consider what might have happened.

Surely such things did *not* happen. A person cannot be here one minute

and somewhere quite different the next. Yet what could not have happened seemed to be connected in some way with . . . No! Don't think
about the light. That light was part of the—illusion?—delusion?—phenomenon. Comforting word—phenomenon. A word for papering over
cracks. Phenomenon can be applied to anything from young Miss Crum-
mles to a light that . . . No, not that light again! Even at the flicker of
memory a gust of night wind seemed to ruffle my hair. I must not think
about a light in an upper window.

How to keep at bay those insistent, intrusive images? The baleful hulk
of the factory . . . Take a swig of neat rum, fierce enough to concentrate
attention on tongue and throat . . . with the glowing rectangle . . .
More rum . . . like a signal . . . At this rate I should soon be tight, and
how much control would be left then? Another tot. The alcohol was
taking effect. Even if I happened to think of a lighted window, it would be
a blurred window because I was by now experiencing difficulty in focusing
on anything; and at last stopped caring about anything . . .

I woke with a head like an echo chamber and a mouth like a sweaty
sock. A thin ray of sunlight picked its way through a gap where the living
room curtains failed to overlap. I had passed the night in my reclining
chair and the empty bottle on my chest explained why. There are few
things to be said in favour of a hangover, but at least its demands take
precedence over other preoccupations. I was washed, dressed, aspirin-
dosed and half-way through my second black coffee before I recollected
the light and what had apparently followed.

Perhaps fully dressed in daylight I felt bolder; perhaps the ache behind
my eyes left me feeling that nothing worse could happen; at any rate I
tried to repeat last night's experience. Nothing happened.

Somehow I could not exactly picture the way the window had appeared
in the looming wall. Anyway, everything there would have been different
in the stir of morning. My feet remained firmly planted on the kitchen
floor. Whatever had (or had not) taken place was over now. Just something to look back on. "A funny thing once happened . . ." becoming
dimmed and distorted with time. The detail was blurred already. Ah,
well . . .

The day's work was something to be staggered through. Making allow-
ances for impaired concentration, by midday I was almost normal again.

Though I still could not face a meal. Ploughman's cheese-and-pickle at
the pub round the corner lacked appeal; as did the alternative little spa-
ghetti place. I suppose I could have worked through the lunch-hour on
more coffee, but I felt a need for fresh air. So I took a walk.

The weather had improved and a fitful sun struggled through thin clouds. There was no mysterious inner compulsion and I did not wander in a daze; but I ended my stroll outside the Marlow factory.

It had once been surrounded by rows of inadequate houses, built to accommodate mill-hands as cheaply as possible. Those streets had been swept away in the first stage of a massive slum-clearance project, but Local Authority had not yet raised finance for the second phase; and the inner-city area, flat as a highwayman's heath, had become an urban wilderness. Playground and natural hazard for stray animals and children, it stretched like an abandoned battlefield, strewn with discarded cans, bottles and waste paper, between a rusted chain-link fence and the grimy factory walls.

I had never been so close to the place before, hardly ever having paused to give the eyesore a glance. After all, on that stretch of road a motorist usually concentrates on rush-hour queue-jumpers and the traffic lights ahead. I felt no more than mild curiosity, but I had half an hour to play with before being due back at the office. So I stepped cautiously across a broken section of fencing, and picked my way through the rough grass and tough weeds that sprouted as mangy covering over the broken ground. Underfoot was still spongy after last night's wintery showers, though to a pedestrian mud was the least noxious of the hazards. By the time I reached the factory I needed the piece of sodden newspaper blown against the door for cleaning my shoes.

Wiping away as much of the mess as I could, I leaned against the door. It opened. I might have guessed the lock would have been smashed. Architectural derelicts tend to attract human counterparts.

Technically I suppose I was trespassing too; but there was no one to stop me—or even shout a word of warning. (Notices warding off intending intruders had long since been burned.) Having seen Marlow's monument from the outside, why pass up the chance to look inside? If anyone should ask, I was interested in industrial archeology. I stepped over the threshold and pulled the door shut behind me.

The entrance lobby was small with narrow stairs in one corner. When first built it must have constituted a natural fire hazard: so many employees jammed into so little space; but in old Marlow's heyday human lives were just so much raw material. Such paint as had not peeled off the walls was mostly obscured with dust, cobwebs and handprints. The floor was littered with torn packets and empty bottles—evidence of previous interlopers.

I called "Anyone there?" not so much expecting a reply as seeking the

reassurance of my own voice. Silence followed. Feeling bolder I mounted
the stairs.

Dim light filtered into the stairwell from above and below—half-way up
was particularly dreary—yet at no time did I feel any sense of foreboding.
This was merely an abandoned building that had served its purpose and
was waiting to be scrapped. At the first landing a corridor stretched to the
rear. On one side open doors revealed a work-room extending over most of
the first floor. Iron pillars at intervals supported the floor above. Rough
outlines indicated where machinery had once been fixed. There were
other indications of more recent occupation. I soon had my handkerchief
pressed to my nose: at least that kept out the worst of the stench.

It was probably this that drove me up to the top floor. Here the pattern
of the floors below was repeated: on one side of the corridor another work-
room (mercifully not yet used as a lavatory) and on the other side several
closed doors. I opened them one after the other, peering into rooms that
had been stores or offices. One still had shelving in place. But the last door
along the corridor would not open.

At first I assumed it had jammed. Stains down the walls suggested a
roof in need of attention, and damp could have caused the woodwork to
swell. However the door resisted all my pushing and after some wasted
effort I had to admit that it must be locked. Ridiculous. Why lock up one
room in a building as wide open as this?

Given time I could have doubtless thought of half a dozen explanations,
but there was no time for putting theories to the test. I had to be on my
way back to the office.

There were stairs at the end of this corridor, too. I hoped they might
lead down to the ground floor, avoiding the unpleasantness at the end of
the first floor work-room.

As I reached the last few steps I thought I heard a slight scuffle. Rats?
The notion brought me to a temporary halt. We all have our phobias, and
rodents happen to be one of mine. I silently swore for not taking the
possibility into account sooner, especially having seen those food wrap-
pings lying about. I froze while all the data I had ever encountered concerning attacks by vermin flickered through my brain. Did they really
make instinctively for the groin? Wasn't that why navvies tied the bot-
toms of their trousers with string?

But a move had to be made one way or the other. As quietly as possible
I peeped round the corner to make sure no grey furry beastie was lying in
wait for me. There was nothing.

Only a door almost opposite the stairs slowly edging shut.

Rats, no matter how intelligent, do not close doors with excessive caution. A surge of irritation now replaced my instinctive panic, almost reaching the point of equally irrational fury. I had just made a fool of myself and needed to blame somebody. I bounded forward and booted the door with all the force I could muster. The blow was violent enough to thrust the person on the other side across the room; while, thrown off balance by such feeble resistance, I executed a miniature pirouette before steadying myself. A girl, wide-eyed and open-mouthed, sagged against the wall opposite.

My first impression was of tatters and patches. Even her hair was a dirty yellow-and-brown skewbald—not deliberately so, but the result of inexpert dying half grown out. Her clothes were a jumble of rummage—jeans with one knee out, grubby jumper and torn anorak. She obviously belonged in the dump more than I did. I guessed her age as late teens. Young and frightened I suppose she ought to have aroused my sympathy, but affronted dignity crowds out finer feelings. I wasn't sure what sort of figure I was presenting, but I had a suspicion it must have been fairly ridiculous.

We stared at each other without a word. Until she snivelled and whimpered. At least that broke the ice, and I felt free to bawl, "What the hell are you doing here?"

"I ain't done nothing," she whined, like a rabbit appealing to the better nature of a stoat. Not that I ever thought of myself as a predator; but that please-don't-hit-me-when-I'm-down attitude inevitably provokes the opposite effect.

"You realise you're trespassing," I snapped; which was as near as I could ever get to putting the boot in.

"I ain't done nothing," she repeated forlornly.

A badly tied brown paper parcel lay in one corner. Near it on the dusty floor were an unopened can of fizzy drink and a packet of crisps. A half-eaten meat pie appeared to have been dropped when she was disturbed.

"Yours?" I asked unnecessarily.

"I ain't done nothing," she whispered. What else was there to say? She was lunching at home today. As far as she was concerned this bleak hole was home. Temporary accommodation, no doubt, but with the only alternative a doss under one of the nearby canal bridges, who was I to frighten her away?

"Have you been upstairs?"

She shook her head.

"Liar."

"I ain't done nothing." She slid down the wall and sat in an attitude of huddled resignation.

"I've just been upstairs," I said, and left the implication to register. She looked up at me dumbly. The grubby little creature wasn't even intelligent. Her only attraction lay in her vulnerability. Suddenly I wanted to get away without losing too much face.

"Oh, go to hell," I growled, turned abruptly and left her. I may only have imagined she cried, "I ain't done nothing."

Luckily I found a rear door, also unfastened, so I was spared the embarrassment of blundering about looking for an exit. I didn't even look back at the factory, and only hoped nobody spotted me recrossing the waste ground.

A fleeting memory of the girl came between me and my work a couple of times during the afternoon. In particular I recollected that pathetic half pie; but by then I was feeling hungry myself.

I stayed in town for a meal before going home, making up for my missed breakfast and lunch by indulging in a half carafe of plonk: so I passed the old Marlow factory about the same time as the night before.

It was all dark. At any rate there was now an explanation of yesterday's light. A girl on the premises could have been responsible for almost anything. It occurred to me that the window in question must have belonged to the locked room. More mystery? Whatever it was had nothing to do with me. By now I had convinced myself that whatever I may have imagined last night had been uneasily compounded of overwork, slight fever and rum. There would be no rum tonight. In the first place because there would be no need for it, and in the second place because there was none left at my place.

All the same I felt that early retirement was called for. Just an hour perhaps listening to music before a milky nightcap. There was a cassette already in the deck waiting for a press of the "play" button. Had I been listening to Allegri when . . . ? Did it matter? I could always find pleasure in Allegri. I pressed the button and sat back at ease.

The soaring treble of the "Miserere" usually has me feeling that the world is a better place than it is usually given credit for, and that I am probably a better person than I am generally given credit for. Self-indulgence maybe, but even an accountant needs some illusions.

Then, as the music took over, a picture began to form. Yes, I must have been listening to Allegri earlier, because the picture was as before—a lighted window high up on a dark wall. Only this time I seemed drawn towards the patch of brilliance. Then I was inside the upper room.

It was as bare as any I had seen in the factory that day, bare as a monk's cell: but unlike the others these bare boards had been spotlessly scrubbed and walls and ceiling freshly whitewashed. There was a man on his knees in the middle of the floor, his back towards me, his curling hair and broadcloth coat stark black against all that white. With head bowed he appeared to be praying.

Did music alone have the power to suggest all this?

What is more the figure seemed to be aware that I stood behind him. He raised his head and started to get up without looking round. He did not need to look round. Whoever he might be, he knew who I was.

Then a click as the music ended and the tape-deck switched itself off. Jerked back into my present surroundings I was staring at the mirror on the opposite side of my own room. Potent stuff the Allegri "Miserere" if it could conjure such impressions. I made no attempt to change the tape, but sat on, half under the spell. I did not want to move. I wanted a little time for contemplation.

Had the imagined room been part of the Marlow factory? However intangible, it had seemed more real than any of the others I had seen earlier in the day; just as the dreamed-up man had seemed more vital than the wretched girl I had actually encountered. The white room was the same size and shape as her miserable refuge. I found myself mentally comparing the two . . .

The girl's ground-floor squat for instance—so dimly lit that shapes could barely be made out in it. The slight effulgence from a frosty moon made its way through holes in corrugated sheeting fastened over the window space. The girl lay on the floor, using her paper parcel as a pillow. Her knees were drawn up and her hands tucked underneath her arms, no doubt for some slight protection against the cold. Was she asleep? She sniffed and then coughed. Automatically I stepped back, encountering the door with a slight thud. It must have been just off the latch, clicking as I pushed back.

The girl raised her head. "Who—?" she murmured. "Whosere?" She peered hazily in my direction, then suddenly sat up. I imagine she was about to scream, but I heard nothing.

Why should I? After all, I was sitting in my own chair. I had never left it. But if I had never left it, where had the thick smear of dust on the back of my hand and sleeve come from?

Although the rum was all gone the cupboard yielded the last of a bottle of gin and some abominably sweet sherry, bought long ago for a forgotten female guest.

Mixed in a tumbler they made a nauseating but necessary cocktail. Did I need the drink to help me to think—or to keep me from thinking? I wasted little time on such hair-splitting. I drank.

After a while my teeth stopped chattering and I tried to make connections. Nobody can be in two places at once, can he? Could I? Delirium! If I believed that, I'd soon have myself believing that I could bend forks. I was an accountant, not some fakir. I believed in facts. I had to. Flights of fancy could lead to trouble with the Inland Revenue Department. Normal people do not move across town instantaneously and unaided. So put aside the delusion that I had just returned to the factory.

Likewise the man in the Victorian frock-coat had been no more than a figment of the imagination. Of that I was certain. After all, it was my own imagination. What more natural than to suppose old Marlow had been such a person. Not so old either in the years when the factory had been turning out highly profitable goods for the Africa trade. Ruthless exploitation after a bright start made him a fortune by the time he was my age. About 1850 wasn't it? Hadn't I heard somewhere that skinning workers here and fleecing customers abroad had actually paid for the building of a Nonconformist chapel? How adroitly the solid citizens of that period manipulated their consciences, somehow contriving to serve both God and Mammon. In Marlow's case Mammon appeared to have been the more influential, because there was no trace left of the chapel, while at least the shell of the factory remained. But what part of its begetter lingered with it?

No doubt that had been Marlow kneeling in the bare white sanctum, locked against enquiring eyes. Praying perhaps to be spared the lusts of the flesh. Not so easy to curb animal instincts when one is master of several hundred souls—and the bodies that come with them. What did they say of him in the workshops? Why did some of the young minxes cock a speculative eye when he passed?

Not that such cattle offered temptation. More dangerous were the timid ones with frightened eyes, trying not to attract attention; because only token resistance was permissible in days when the rule was work or starve and dismissal meant the workhouse or the streets. With the door of the whitewashed room locked there had been prayers and prayers. Neither sort had been answered. Afterwards there had been occasional accidents (conveniently bestowed elsewhere) and even a suicide (believing the river better than a bastard). And inevitably agonies of remorse. Never again. Never, never—until the next time. He could no more resist than she— whoever may be next in the whitewashed room. In spite of all his prayers.

How could I be so certain? The man in the black coat turned to face me. It was like looking into the mirror again. His face was mine. There had been bastards, and after three generations who can be sure of his family tree?

I was certain. After all, an accountant ought to be aware of elementary mathematics. The Marlow factory was the lowest common denominator —for me, for him, for the girl. My grandfather had been conceived in that place where the spirit of old vice lingered.

Into which place that fool of a destitute girl had wandered. Whatever remained there wanted her. That helpless attitude, those familiar frightened eyes had roused him—it. Marlow had at least been a man: what was left was no longer human, and she was no more to it than tethered bait for a tiger. What justification did I have for reaching such a conclusion? An accountant is at least able to add up: even after a half-carafe of house wine and a gin-based concoction. There was enough of my great-grandfather's blood in me to know what he/it intended.

I felt I had to warn her. To explain. If absolutely necessary to pay for other lodgings for her. She must not stay where she was. I did not know what the thing in the black broadcloth might attempt, but I did know what it was still capable of. I had looked into its eyes and I knew. The time for prayers was past.

I stumbled out towards my car, even though I suspected I was in no condition to drive. As it happened I did not have to. I was thinking of the room with the blocked window. By now I should have known better . . .

The room was empty, but the door was open. There was a litter of newspaper on the floor. Perhaps she had been trying it as bedding. The paper-wrapped parcel had not been moved. I picked it up. It was very light. I wondered vaguely what she might keep in it. Then she was in the doorway, looking at me.

I found my voice first. "Get out of here," I said.

Her reply was a half-stifled wail. She shook her head, not so much saying "no" as in disbelief at my appearance.

"Get out," I repeated. "Now." Then in frustration at making no progress with the little idiot, shouted, "Get out!" I thrust her parcel towards her, intending her to take it and go. She must have misunderstood the gesture, because she backed into the corridor with a series of short moans. Then she turned and fled empty-handed.

She might so easily have found that rear exit. Instead she scampered up the stairs. I had no choice but to follow her. She had to be brought down. Upstairs in the Marlow factory was no place for her.

The staircase had been dim enough in daylight, by night I was climbing blind, feeling my way along the wall. I knew she was ahead of me by her frightened sobs. At the top of the stairs there was just enough of a grey glow for illumination. She was nowhere to be seen, but could only have ducked into one of the rooms off the corridor or into the empty work-space. As the door to the latter was flung wide I tried that opening first. I was right. She had stepped just inside, and stood with her back pressed against the wall, I suppose silently beseeching that I might not notice. When she saw me she gave a cry that echoed through the building and scuttled to the other end of the workroom.

I might have caught up with her then, but skidded on something repulsive underfoot. While I was recovering my balance she was on her way up the next flight of stairs.

It was then that I began to call to her. "Not up there. For God's sake, not up there." I doubt if my words made any sense to her. They were merely an alarming clamour that she answered with panic-stricken squeaks.

From the light into the dark, and into the light again. Always upwards. I was driving her towards the one place where she should not be; but what else could I have done? I had to catch up with her before she reached that upper room.

Its door was open now. The moonlight shining full on that side of the factory spilled from the room into the corridor.

As I emerged, panting at the head of the last flight of stairs, she was already half-way towards the open door. I had given up shouting. I needed the breath. Instead I made cooing and clucking noises as though trying to calm a terrified animal. I remembered with irrational clarity how when a boy I had once picked up a shrew and seen it die of fright on my hand. I think I murmured "There now. There now." But she backed away from me without a word.

Slowly, one step at a time, we edged towards the other end of the passage. Her eyes were wide and unblinking. She sniffed regularly, and the end of her tongue was constantly moistening her lips.

Desperately, I took one stride longer than the others.

"No," she whispered, and increased her backward shuffle.

Abandoning caution I lunged. She fled. She reached the open door seconds before I could, and it slammed in my face. Like a trap snapping shut, the light was cut off.

For one of those instants that stretch towards eternity I faced the dark panels. Then from inside the room came a feebly despairing wail.

Expecting to encounter the lock, I pushed furiously, but met no resistance and stumbled into his presence. The radiance of the full moon was reflected from the white walls, filling the room with an unearthly brilliance. Black from curling hair to immaculate boots, with only his face a pale oval, he contrasted starkly against the shining background.

She stood trembling between us, repeatedly looking from one to the other—apart from our clothes alike as twins. She was caught between devil and deep.

As he smiled, I realised this was no chance encounter. I had done what I had always been intended to do. Brought her to him.

At least he was on the far side of the room and I was the one between her and the way of escape. I cleared the way to the door and pointed. Words would not come, but at least she could see what I meant. So why didn't the spineless young fool take her chance? Why waver until history repeated itself?

As he moved, as silent and regardless of obstacles as a shadow, I stepped between them. From him I expected the rage of a patriarch denied, from her some final burst of activity. Neither reacted. It was like finding myself in the frozen frame of a film.

At last I seized her by the shoulders and tried to force her towards the door. She resisted me and began to scream. In desperation I began to shake her. Was I trying to shake some sense into her or merely trying to end those rasping shrieks? They stopped when her head flopped loosely from side to side like a rag doll's.

I realised I was supporting her full weight, and lowered her gently to the floor. As I leaned over her, my hands underneath her back, I realised that my arms were not covered by fawn lamb's-wool, but by black broadcloth . . .

Then here I was at my own kitchen door.

So what am I to do now? Tell the authorities what they are likely to find in the old Marlow factory? Why bother? Sooner or later she'll be found, if not by some prying vagrant then by the inevitable demolition crew. Will anything be found then that can be traced back to me?

Does it matter anyway? Something far more important weighs on my mind. You see, he has me too. He uses me. About the time of change in the moon is worst, when those old lusts rage again. There have been no more supernatural trips. No need because he is always with me, part of me.

F. Paul Wilson's writing skills allow him to travel equally well in fantasy, horror, or science fiction. He has won awards for the latter and his supernatural thriller The Keep *was made into a major motion picture. Through our meetings at conventions we found a shared interest in collecting first-edition books, an interest friend Paul thoughtfully remembered when he held on to the hardcover rights to his* The Tomb *and sold them to my* Whispers Press. *Shared interests like ours had a nice result, but I will let you be the judge as to whether the Commission's shared interests had as pleasing an end.*

THE YEARS THE MUSIC DIED

by F. Paul Wilson

Nantucket in November. Leave it to Bill to make a mockery of security. And of me.

The Atlantic looked mean today. I watched its gray, churning surface from behind the relative safety of the double-paned picture windows. I would have liked a few more panes between me and all that water. Would have liked a few *miles* between us, in fact.

Some people are afraid of snakes, some of spiders; with me, it's water. And the more water, the worse it is. I get this feeling it wants to suck me down. Been that way since I was a kid. Bill has known about the phobia for a good twenty years. So why did he do it? Bad enough to set up the meeting on this dinky little island; but to hold it on this narrow spit of land between the head of the harbor and an uneasy ocean with no more than a hundred yards between the two was outright cruel. And a nor'easter coming. If that awful ocean ever reared up . . .

I shuddered and turned away. But there *was* no turning away in this huge barn of a room with all these picture windows facing east, west, and north. Like a goddamn goldfish bowl. There weren't even curtains I could pull closed. I felt naked and exposed here in this open, pine-paneled space. Eight hours to go until dark blotted out the ocean. But then I'd still be able to *hear* it.

Why would my own son do something like this to me?

Security, Bill had said. A last-minute, off-season rental of an isolated house on a summer resort island in the chill of November. The Commission members could fly in, attend the meeting, and fly out again with no one ever knowing they were here. What could be more secure?

I'm a stickler for security, too, but this was ludicrous. This was—

Bill walked into the room, carefully not looking in my direction. I studied my son a moment: a good-looking man with dark hair and light blue eyes; just forty-four but looking ten years older. A real athlete until he started letting his weight go to hell. Now he had the beginnings of a hefty spare tire around his waist. I've got two dozen years on him and only half his belly.

Something was wrong with the way he was walking . . . a little unsteady. And then I realized.

Good lord, he's drunk!

I started to say something but Bill beat me to it.

"Nelson's here. He just called from the airport. I sent the car out for him. Harold is in the air."

I managed to say "Fine" without making it sound choked.

My son, half-lit at a Commission meeting, and me surrounded by water —this had a good chance of turning into a personal disaster. All my peers, the heads of all the major industries in the country, were downstairs at the buffet brunch. Rockefeller was on the island, and Vanderbilt was on his way; they would complete the Commission in its present composition. Soon they'd be up here to start the agenda. Only Joe Kennedy would be missing. Again. Too bad. I've always liked Joe. But with a son in the White House, we all had serious doubts about his objectivity. It had been a tough decision, but Joe had gracefully agreed to give up his seat on the Commission for the duration of Jack's presidency.

Good thing, too. I was glad he wouldn't be here to see how Bill had deteriorated.

His son's going down in history while mine is going down the drain.

What a contrast. And yet, on the surface, there was not a single reason why Bill couldn't be where Jack Kennedy was. Both came from good stock, both had good war records and plenty of money behind them. But Jack had gone for the gold ring and Bill had gone for the bottle.

I wasn't going to begrudge Joe his pride in his son. All of us on the Commission were proud of the job Jack was doing. I remember that inner glow I felt when I heard, "Ask not what your country can do for you, but what you can do for your country." That's *just* the way I feel. The way everybody on the Commission feels.

I heard ice rattle and turned to see Bill pouring himself a drink at the bar.

"Bill! It's not *noon* yet, for God's sake!"

Bill raised his glass mockingly.

"Happy anniversary, Dad."

I didn't know what to say to that. Today was nobody's anniversary.

"Have you completely pickled your brains?"

Bill's eyebrows rose. "How soon we forget. Six years ago today: November 8, 1957. Doesn't that ring a bell?"

"No!" I could feel my jaw clenching as I stepped toward him. "Give me that glass!"

"That was the day the Commission decided to 'do something' about rock 'n' roll."

"So what!"

"Which led to February 3, 1959."

That date definitely had a familiar ring.

"You *do* remember February 3, don't you, Dad? An airplane crash. Three singers. All dead."

I took a deep breath. "That again!"

"Not again. Still." He raised his glass. *"Salud."* Taking a long pull on his drink, he dropped into a chair.

I stood over him. The island, the drinking . . . this was what it was all about. I've always known the crash bothered him, but never realized how much until now. What anger he must have been carrying around these past few years! Anger and guilt.

"You mean to tell me you're still blaming yourself for that?" The softness of my voice surprised me.

"Why not? My idea, wasn't it?"

"The plane crash was *no*body's idea! How many times do we have to go over this?"

"There never seems to be a time when I *don't* go over it! And now it's November 8, 1963. Exactly six years to the day that I opened my big mouth at the Commission meeting."

"Yes, you did." *And how proud I was of you that day.* "You came up with a brilliant solution that resolved the entire crisis."

"Hah! Some crisis!"

A sudden burst of rain splattered against the north and east windows. The storm was here.

I sat down with my back to most of the windows and tried to catch Bill's eyes. "And you talk about how soon *I* forget! You had a crisis in your own home—Peter. Remember?"

Bill nodded absently.

I pressed on. Maybe I could break through this funk he was wallowing in, straighten him out before the meeting. "Peter is growing to be a fine man now and I'm proud to call him my grandson, but back in '57 he was only eleven and already thoroughly immersed in rock and roll—"

"Not 'rock *and* roll,' Dad. You've got to be the only one in the country who pronounces the 'and.' It's 'rock 'n' roll'—like one word."

"It's *three* words and I pronounce all three. But be that as it may, your house was a war zone, and you know it!"

That had been a wrenching time for the whole McCready clan, but especially for me. Peter was my only grandson then and I adored him. But he had taken to listening to those atrocious Little Richard records and combing his hair like Elvis Presley. Bill banned the music from the house but Peter was defying everyone, sneaking records home, listening to it on the radio, plunking his dimes into jukeboxes on the way home from school.

But Bill's house was hardly unique. The same thing was happening in millions of homes all over the country. Everyone but the kids seemed to have declared war on the music. Old line disc jockeys were calling it junk noise and were having rock and roll record-smashing parties on the air; television networks were refusing to broadcast Presley below the waist; church leaders were calling it the Devil's music, cultural leaders were calling it barbaric, and a lot of otherwise mild-mannered ordinary citizens were calling it nigger music.

They should have guessed what the result of such mass persecution would be: The popularity of rock and roll *soared*.

"But the strife in your home served a useful purpose. It opened my eyes. I say with no little pride that I was probably the only man in the country who saw the true significance of what rock and roll was doing to American society."

"You *thought* you saw significance, and you were very persuasive. But I don't buy it anymore. It was only music."

I leaned back and closed my eyes. *Only music* . . .

Bill was proving to be a bigger and bigger disappointment with each passing year. I'd had such high hopes for him. I'd even started bringing him to Commission meetings to prepare him to take my seat some day. But now I couldn't see him ever sitting on the Commission. He had no foresight, no vision for the future. He couldn't be trusted to participate in the decisions the Commission had to make. Nor could I see myself leaving my controlling interest in the family business to Bill.

I have a duty to the McCready newspaper chain: My dad started it with a measly little weekly local in Boston at the turn of the century and built it to a small string. I inherited that and sweated my butt to expand it into the publishing empire that spans the country today. There was no way I could leave the McCready Syndicate to Bill in good conscience. Maybe this was a signal to start paying more attention to Jimmy. He was a full decade younger than Bill but showing a *lot* more promise.

Bill showed promise in '57, though. I'll never forget the fall meeting of the Commission that year when Bill sat in as a nonvoting member. I was set to address the group on what I saw as an insidious threat to the country. I knew I was facing a tough audience, especially on the subject of music. I drew on every persuasive skill I had to pound home the fact that rock and roll was more than just music, more than just an untrained nasal voice singing banal lyrics to a clichéd melody backed by a bunch of guitar notes strung together over a drumbeat. *It had become a social force.* Music as a social force—I knew that concept was unheard of, but the age of mass communication was here and life in America was a new game. I saw that. I had to make the Commission see it. The Commission had to learn the rules of the new game if it wanted to remain a guiding force. In 1957, rock and roll was a pivotal piece in the game.

Irritating as it was, I knew the music itself was unimportant. Its status as a threat had been created by the hysterically negative reaction from the adult sector of society. As a result, untold millions of kids under eighteen came to see it as *their* music. Everyone born before World War II seemed to be trying to take it away from them. So they were closing ranks against all the older generations. That frightened me.

It did not, however, impress the other members of the Commission. So for weeks before our regular meeting, I hammered at them, throwing facts and figures at them, sending newspaper accounts of rock and roll riots, softening them up for my pitch.

And I was good that day. God, was I good! I can still remember my closing words:

"And, gentlemen, as you all know, the upcoming generation includes the postwar baby boom, making it the largest single generation in the nation's history. If that generation develops too much self-awareness, if it begins to think of itself as a group outside the mainstream, catastrophe could result.

"Consider, gentlemen: In ten years most of them will be able to vote. If the wrong people get their ear, the social and political continuity that this Commission has sworn to safeguard could be permanently disrupted.

"The popularity of the music continues to expand, gathering momentum all the time. If we don't act now, next year may be too late! We cannot *silence* this music, because that will only worsen the division. We must find a way to *temper* rock and roll . . . make it more palatable to the older generations . . . fuse it to the mainstream. Do that, and the baby boom generation will fall in line! Do nothing and I see only chaos ahead!"

But in the ensuing discussion, it became quite clear nobody, including myself, had the foggiest notion of how to change the music.

Then someone—I forget who—made a comment about how it was too bad all these rock 'n' roll singers couldn't give up their guitars and go into the religion business like Little Richard had just done.

Bill had piped up then: "Or the army. I'd love to see a military barber get ahold of Elvis Presley! Can't we get him drafted?"

The room suddenly fell silent as the Commission members—all of us—shared an epiphany:

Don't go after the music—go after the ones who *make* the music! Get rid of the raucous leaders and replace them with more placid, malleable types.

Brilliant! It might never have occurred to anyone without Bill's remark!

The tinkling of the ice in Bill's glass as he took another sip dragged me back to the present, to Nantucket and the storm. In what I hoped he would take as a friendly gesture, I slapped Bill on the knee.

"Don't you remember the excitement back then after the Commission meeting? You and I became *experts* on rock and roll. We listened to all those awful records, got to know all about the performers, and then we began to zero in on them."

Bill nodded. "But I had no idea where it was going to end."

"No one did. Remember making the list? We sat around for weeks, going through the entertainment papers and picking out the singers most closely associated with the music, the leaders, the trendsetters, the originals."

I still savor the memory of that time of closeness with Bill, working together with him, both of us tingling with the knowledge that we were doing something important.

Elvis was the prime target, of course. More than anyone else, he personified everything that was rock and roll. His sneers, his gyrations, everything he did on stage was a slap in the face to the older generations. And his too-faithful renditions of colored music getting airplay all over the country, the screaming, fainting girls at his concerts, the general hysteria. Elvis had to go first.

And he turned out to be the easiest to yank from sight, really. With the Commission's vast influence, all we had to do was pass the word. In a matter of weeks, a certain healthy twenty-two-year-old Memphis boy received his draft notice. And on March 24, 1958—a landmark date I'll never forget—Elvis Presley was inducted into the U.S. Army. But *not* to hang around Stateside and keep up his public profile. Oh no. Off to West Germany. Bye-bye, Elvis Pelvis.

Bill seemed to be reading my thoughts. He said, "Too bad we couldn't have taken care of everyone like that."

"I agree, son." Bill seemed to be perking up a little. I kept up the chatter, hoping to bring him out some more. "But someone would have smelled a rat. We had to move slowly, cautiously. That was why I rounded up some of our best reporters and had them start sniffing around. And as you know, it didn't take them long to come up with a few gems."

The singers weren't my only targets. I also wanted to strike at the ones who spread the music through the airwaves. That proved easy. We soon learned that a lot of the big-time rock and roll disc jockeys were getting regular payoffs from record companies to keep their new releases on the air. We made sure that choice bits of information got to congressmen looking to heighten their public profile, and we made sure they knew to go after Alan Freed.

Oh, how I wanted Freed off the air back then. The man had gone from small-time Cleveland DJ to big-time New York DJ and music show impressario. By 1959 he had appeared in a line of low-budget rock and roll movies out of Hollywood and was hosting a nationwide music television show. He had become "Mr. Rock 'n' Roll." His entire career was built on the music and he was its most vocal defender.

Alan Freed had to go. And payola was the key. We set the gears in motion and turned to other targets. And it was in May, only two months after Presley's induction, that the reporters turned up another spicy morsel.

"Remember, Bill? Remember when they told us that Jerry Lee Lewis had secretly married his third cousin in December of '57. Hardly a scandal in and of itself. But the girl was only thirteen. *Thirteen!* Oh, we made sure the McCready papers gave plenty of press to that, didn't we? Within days he was being booed off the stage. Yessir, Mr. Whole Lotta Shakin'/Great Balls of Fire was an instant has-been!"

I laughed, and even Bill smiled. But the smile didn't last.

"Don't stop now, Dad. Next comes 1959."

"Bill, I had nothing to do with that plane crash. I swear it."

"You told your operatives to 'get Valens and Holly off the tour.' I heard you myself."

"I don't deny that. But I meant 'off the tour'—not *dead!* We couldn't dig up anything worthwhile on them so I intended to create some sort of scandal. We discussed it, didn't we? We wanted to see them replaced by much safer types, by pseudo-crooners like Frankie Avalon and Fabian. I did *not* order any violence. The plane crash was pure coincidence."

Bill studied the ceiling. "Which just happened to lead to the replacement of Holly, Valens, and that other guy with the silly name—The Big Bopper—by Avalon, Fabian, and Paul Anka. Some coincidence!"

I said nothing. The crash *had* been an accident. The operatives had been instructed to do enough damage to the plane to keep it on the ground, forcing the three to miss their next show. Apparently they didn't do enough, and yet did too much. The plane got into the air, but never reached its destination. Tragic, unfortunate, but it all worked out for the best. I couldn't let Bill know that, though.

"I can understand why you lost your enthusiasm for the project then."

"But *you* didn't, did you, Dad? You kept right on going."

"There was a job to be done. An important one. And when one of our reporters discovered that Chuck Berry had brought that Apache minor across state lines to work in his club, I couldn't let it pass!"

Berry was one of the top names on my personal list. Strutting up there on stage, swinging his guitar around, camel-walking across back and forth, shouting out those staccato lyrics as he spread his legs and wiggled his hips, and all those white girls clapping and singing along as they gazed up at him. I tell you it made my hackles rise.

"The Mann Act conviction we got on him has crippled his career! And then later in '59 we finally spiked Alan Freed. When he refused to sign that affidavit saying he had never accepted payola, he was through! Fired from WNEW-TV, WABC-TV, and WABC radio—one right after the other!"

What a wonderful year!

"Did you stop there, Dad?"

"Yes." What was he getting at? "Yes, I believe so."

"You had nothing to do with that car crash in '60: Eddie Cochran killed, Gene Vincent crippled?"

"Absolutely not!" *Damn!* The booze certainly wasn't dulling Bill's memory! That crash had been another unfortunate, unintended mishap caused by an overly enthusiastic operative. "Anyway, it remains a fact that by the middle of 1960, rock and roll was dead."

"Oh, I don't know about that—"

"Dead as a *threat*. What had been a potent, devisive social force is now a tiny historical footnote, a brief, minor cultural aberration. Elvis was out of the service but he was certainly not the same wild man who went in. Little Richard was in the ministry, Chuck Berry was up to his ears in legal troubles, Jerry Lee Lewis was in limbo as a performer, Alan Freed was out of a job and appearing before House subcommittees."

Bill tossed off the rest of his drink and glared at me. "You forgot to mention that Buddy Holly, Richie Valens, and Eddie Cochran were dead!"

"Unfortunately and coincidentally, yes. But not by my doing. I say again: Rock and roll was dead then, and remains dead. Even Presley gave up on it after his discharge. He got sanitized and Hollywoodized and that's fine with me. More power to him. I bear him no ill will."

"There's still rock 'n' roll," Bill mumbled as he got up and stood by the bar, glass in hand.

"I disagree, son," I said quickly, hoping he wouldn't pour himself another. "I stay current on these things and I know. There's still popular music they *call* rock and roll, but it has none of the abrasive, irritating qualities of the original. Remember how some of those songs used to set your teeth on edge and make your skin crawl? That stuff is extinct."

"Some of it's still pretty bad."

"Not like it used to be. Its punch is gone. Dried up. Dead." I pointed to the radio at the end of the bar. "Turn that thing on and I'll show you."

Bill did. A newscast came on.

"Find some music."

He spun the dial until the sweet blend of a mixed duet singing "Hey, Paula" filled the room.

"Hear that? Big song. I can live with it. Find another so-called 'rock 'n' roll' station." He did and the instrumental "Telstar" came on. "Monotonous, but I can live with that, too. Try one more." A DJ announced The Number One Song in the Country as a twelve-string guitar opening led into "Walk Right In."

Bill nodded and turned the radio off. "I concede the point."

"Good. And you must also concede that the wartime and postwar generations are now firmly back in the fold. There are pockets of discontent, naturally, but, they are small and isolated. There is no clear-cut dividing line—*that's* what's important. Jack's doing his part in the White House. He's got them all hot for his social programs like the Peace Corps and such where their social impulses can be channeled and directed by the proper agencies. They see themselves as part of the mainstream, *involved* in the social continuum rather than separate from it.

"And we saved them, Bill—you, me, and the Commission."

Bill only stared at me. Finally, he said, "Maybe we did. But I never really understood about Buddy Holly—"

I felt like shouting, but controlled my voice. "Can't you drop that? I told you—"

"Oh, I don't mean the crash. I mean why he was so high on your list. He always struck me as an innocuous four-eyes who hiccuped his way through songs."

"Perhaps he was. But like Berry and Little Richard and Valens and Cochran, he had the potential to become a serious threat. He and the others originated the qualities that made the music so divisive. They wrote, played, and sang their own songs. That made me extremely uneasy."

Bill shook his head in bafflement. "I don't see . . ."

"All right: Let's suppose the Commission hadn't acted and had let things run their course. And now, here in '63, the wartime and postwar baby boom generation is aware of itself and a group, psychologically separate and forming its own subculture within ours. A lot of them are voting age now, and next year is an election year. Let's say one of these self-styled rock and roll singers who writes his own material gets it into his head to use his songs to influence the generation that idolizes him. Think of it: a thinly disguised political message being played over and over again, on radios, TVs, in homes, in jukeboxes, hummed, sung in the shower by all those voters. With their numbers, God knows what could happen at the polls!"

I paused for breath. It *was* a truly frightening thought.

"But that's all fantasy," I said. "The airwaves are once again full of safe, sane Tin Pan Alley tunes."

Bill smiled.

I asked, "What's so funny?"

"Just thinking. When I was in London last month I noticed that Britain seems to be going through the same kind of thing we did in '57. Lots of rock and roll bands and fans. There's one quartet of guys who wear their hair in bangs—can't remember the name now—that's selling records like crazy and packing the kids into the old music halls where they're screaming and fainting just like in Elvis Presley's heyday. And I understand they write and play and sing their own music, too."

I heard the windows at my back begin to rattle and jitter as hail mixed with the rain. I did not turn around to look.

"Forget Britain. England is already a lost cause."

"But what if their popularity spreads over here and the whole process gets going again?"

I laughed. That was a good one. "A bunch of Limeys singing rock and roll to American kids? That'll be the day!"

But I knew that if such a thing ever came to pass, the Commission would be there to take the necessary measures.

I, of course, was the first editor to discover the brilliance of Dennis Etch-ison, perhaps the finest short story writer we have. Strictly speaking, though, I guess several other perceptive editors beat me to the Etchison worlds, but I damned sure have used as much Etchison fiction as I could get him to produce. "The Woman in Black" is a brilliant tale from an issue of my Whispers *magazine and has since found reprinting overseas and in Karl Edward Wagner's* Year's Best Horror. *It is not a friendly piece!*

THE WOMAN IN BLACK

by Dennis Etchison

When they took his mother away he went to live in the big house.

There he discovered rooms within rooms, drapes like thick shrouds, a kitchen stove big enough to crawl into, overstuffed furniture that changed shape as he passed, a table with claw feet larger than his head, ancient carpets with designs too worn to read, floor heating grates that clanged when he walked on them, musty closets opening on blackness, shadowed hallways that had no end.

These things did not frighten him.

For soon he made friends with the boy across the street; his aunts and uncles came by to help with the meals; it was summer and the back yard stayed light forever.

Before long, however, after only a few days and nights, he found that he could think of but one thing: of the lot next door, beyond the fence, of the high wall that kept him from its bright and dark treasures.

He was in the grove behind the arbor, about to pluck a fig from a low-hanging branch, when someone opened the front gate.

The fig hung there among pale jigsaw leaves, swinging to and fro like a black teardrop. He looked over his shoulder, through luminous bunches of grapes clinging to the lattice. The air was still. At the end of the arbor a plum dropped from a tree, splitting its skin as it landed and spattering the grass below with glistening juice. A piece of heavy iron groaned on the other side of the fence, the same sound he heard at night when the blue lights began to flicker; he was thankful it was daytime now so that he could try to ignore it.

He turned his head in time to see his uncle striding toward him along the path, grinding fallen grapes into green stains on the gravel. The boy breathed again and returned his attention to the translucent leaves and the pendulous fruit swaying there.

"Hi, Uncle Ted."

"Willy." His uncle came up next to him and stood squinting sadly at the untended yard, at the scraggly weeds poking their way under the fence. "Have you talked to Grandma today?"

"When I got up. I made my own breakfast. I went into her room for a while. Then I went over to Vern's to play." He closed his fingers around the fig and pulled; the soft tissue bent and snapped and a milky drop of sap oozed out of the stem.

Uncle Ted shifted his weight and studied his shoes. "Do you like it, living here?"

"I like it fine. Uncle Ted, the Fair's coming to town next week. Vern says they have different rides this year. New animals, too. We're saving our money. Can I go?"

"We'll see, Willy, we'll see."

A breeze passed by, rustling the leaves. The tall iron that showed above the security fence groaned again but did not really move; that was only a tree throwing its shadow against the rusty bolts. On the next block a dog barked; Grandma's chickens clucked suspiciously in response. William peeled the fig and opened it like a flower in his hand. It was sweet and the tiny seeds popped in his teeth like soft sand.

"I know you miss your mother, Willy."

"Sure." He sucked the fleshy pulp until his tongue tingled, smearing his face, and wiped his mouth with his sleeve. He discarded the skin and glanced up. Uncle Ted was waiting for something. What was William supposed to say? "Is she coming home today?"

"We all miss her. Very much."

"Tomorrow?"

"I'm afraid not."

"Saturday? Maybe Aunt Emily and Aunt Grace could come over and we could make a special dinner for her. I can wash the dishes, and afterwards—"

Uncle Ted cleared his throat. He twisted his fingers together behind his back and pointed his chin at the sky and took a deep breath so that his chest puffed out, his tan shirt taut. He was looking toward the top of the iron crane towering above the fence, but that was not what he was thinking about. It must have been something a long way off, higher and farther than William could see.

"No," said Uncle Ted.

"Oh."

The man sighed. He unclenched his hands and ran them nervously over his head. William remembered the way his uncle had looked after his last tour of duty, his close-cropped hair and the sharp creases in his shirt. Since he got back he wore looser clothes and did not stand so rigidly, but his hair was still short and brushed slick.

Now Uncle Ted stood straight again, locking his knees till he was as tall as he could make himself. William almost expected him to salute.

"You haven't been trying to climb over the fence, have you?"

"No, Uncle Ted. Only—"

"Only what?" The man squinted again, and this time his brow furrowed with anger. He began opening and closing his eyes very rapidly. He set his jaw and glared down at the boy.

"N-nothing," said William.

"You got something to say, boy, say it!"

"Well—" What was his uncle so upset about? William was sure it could be nothing he had done. "Well, sometimes I wish I could see what's on the other side. Do you know what's over there, Uncle Ted?"

"Nothing for a child to worry about. It's private property and don't you forget it. From the fence down to the river it all belongs to the government. Only thing for a little boy to do over there is slip and fall and get hurt, get himself into a whole lot of trouble. But we'd better be glad it's there. And proud! We'd better be!"

"I believe you, Uncle Ted. I never tried to climb over. I wouldn't even go near it. I know I'm not supposed to—to—"

His voice broke and his eyes watered so that the branches wavered and his uncle's legs buckled as if they were made of jelly. He felt an ache in his chest and a numbness in his lips and cheeks; suddenly the air around him was unseasonably cold, a warning of some impending change in the weather. A hurting welled up in him that went far beyond this argument which was no argument at all and which seemed to make no sense.

A strong arm encircled his shoulders.

He opened his eyes wide. What he had seen a moment ago was true: now his uncle stood less tall, slumped as if the wind had been knocked out of him, his shoulders rounded under an oppressive weight. The man removed his arm self-consciously, put his hands together until his nails were white, and cracked his knuckles. The sound was painfully loud in the stillness, like bones breaking.

"I know, Willy," said his uncle, "I know." His eyes glazed with that same faraway look. He pinched his nose and massaged the furrow from his brow. William noted that the man's hand was shaking. "I'll take care of everything. From now on. We'll keep you safe and strong. We can do it. I know we can. Anything you need, you ask Aunt Emily or me and we'll do our best to . . ."

William said, "I think I'd like to visit my mother, if she's not coming home Saturday. I'd like to go soon. If that's all right."

The man shook his head, a decisive twitch. "They wouldn't let you in. Not even that. They never would."

William swallowed and cleared his head, trying to shake off the bad feeling. "Well," he said, "when *are* they going to let my mother out of the hospital?"

"When?" said Uncle Ted absently. "Wh . . ." And here his voice failed him for the first time. William wanted to do something to help him, to thump him on the back the way he did when Grandma got to coughing, but he could not reach that far. "I'm afraid," said the man, "that your mother's never coming back to Greenworth. You understand, don't you, boy? Do you understand what I'm telling you?"

The moment was frozen in time. William wanted badly to break and run. His eyes darted around the yard, desperate to find a way out, a secret passage, a doorway in the fence that he had not noticed before.

His uncle held him by the back of the neck. But it wasn't necessary. He couldn't run now.

For there, behind the screen of the back porch, half-hidden but visible in dark outline, was the figure of a woman. She was dressed in a flowing black garment. William could not make out her features, not even her eyes, but he knew that she was watching him as he stood in the garden.

He sat with his grandmother, rubbing the circulation back into her wrists, as the day came to an end.

"Oh, you must go, darling," she was saying. "Don't be afraid. There will be so many interesting things to see!"

"I don't want to," said William.

He knew his grandmother always let him have his way, even when it was not what was best for him, and he loved her for that. But now he had had a change of heart about going to the Fair and she would not understand. Had she turned against him at last?

It was as if she refused to acknowledge what had happened. She sat propped up in bed, looking out her bedroom window as usual, an expression of serene acceptance on her face. Didn't she notice that the back yard would soon be overgrown with stalky weeds like the ones near the fence? *My Grandma's getting old*, he realized, and then tried to force that thought from his mind.

She smiled and took his wrist in both of her hands. "I understand how you feel. It's only natural. But no one is ever quite ready for anything when it comes along. Besides, who knows what wonders you'll find waiting for you when you get there? It's not far at all."

She clasped his hands coolly and gazed outside again. A thin, blue twilight was rapidly descending, and already angular shadows had grown over the henhouse next to the fence, shading the tops of the machinery on the other side until the riveted joints and streaked I-beams became the jutting turrets of an iron fortress.

"Like what?" asked William without curiosity.

It would be no fun this time. How could it be? He had more important things to think about now, things he did not even know if he could make himself consider; things he felt certain he could not begin to understand. The Fair was too late this year, he knew, and his heart sank. From now on it would always be too late.

His grandmother drifted away from him, lost in the gray convolutions of the bed that marked the limits of her world now. Her eyelids closed halfway and her pupils thickened.

"Such wonders!" she said, her voice intense but growing fainter, her chest fluttering from the effort. "I've dreamed of them. Wings soft as clouds, doves with faces dearer than a baby's, all God's creatures come together at last . . . oh, darling, it will be so beautiful!"

"They have all that?" How could she know? The big trucks hadn't even crossed the city limits yet, he was sure. Only Vern seemed to know ahead of time, and that was because of his cousin who worked on the carnival crew. "Are you sure?"

"As sure as I've ever been of anything."

"Well," he said, "I still don't think I want to go."

"And why not?"

"I—it'd be too lonely."

"But you won't be alone!"

"Yes, I will," he said. He thought of Vern and the way his friend would behave around him now, cautious and polite, afraid to say the wrong things, so careful that they would have no fun at all. He remembered the way it was the day his father did not come home from the power plant, and for weeks after—the way everyone left him alone at school and did not ask him to play, as though he were fragile and might break if they came too close. Vern would walk apart from him all the way to the Fairgrounds, offering William too much of his candy and waiting for him to decide what they would do next, ride after ride the whole time. It was more than he could bear. He would feel different, special, and that would only make the day longer and sadder.

"Oh, darling, I wish I could go with you! Perhaps I shall," she added, patting his hand again. "One can never be sure . . ."

Of course he knew she didn't mean it. She couldn't.

"I wish my daddy could go with me," he whispered.

She beamed. "He's already there."

"What?"

Her eyes grew strange. "Don't you know that, child? You must try to believe. It will be so much easier for you."

William felt a knot in his stomach. Suddenly he was no longer sure of anything. He wondered if he and his grandmother were even talking about the same thing.

"What else do they have?" he said too loudly, testing her. "Do they have—" He groped for a word. "Do they have gorillas? From Africa?"

"They do."

"And elephants?" That was a good one. He knew the Fair was too small to have elephants.

"That, too."

He thought of the dream last week, after he had heard the groaning sound louder than ever from deep within the enclosure. "Do they have birds with wings you can see through?"

"Yes."

"And—and a talking pig? Do they have a pig that talks, Grandma? Do they really?"

"I'm sure of it. Anything the mind can imagine, and more."

He sat forward, making fists. "No, they don't. It's only a Fair, Grandma. A Fair!"

"What a lovely way of putting it. The Animal Fair! And all just there, on the other side. So close, and getting closer all the time. Soon there will be no barrier at all. The birds and the beasts . . . anything and everything, oh, yes!"

Anything? he thought. *If they have everything, do they have mothers there?*

He stood up in the close bedroom, his arms stiff at his sides, and stared defiantly at the old woman. But she only continued to peer out at the back yard as if it were a vision of the Promised Land, at the sea of weeds overrunning the grounds, the trees and vines that had grown gnarled and misshapen as her hands, the fruit that seemed to be illuminated by a cold light from within if you looked too closely in the night. Her eyes were filmed over; she could no longer see what had become of her home. Either that or she saw and embraced it all, and that possibility frightened him more than anything else.

"Don't you understand, Grandma? Don't you see? We—we've got to get away from here!"

Even after Daddy got sick they had stayed because of his work, and then when it was too late his mother refused to leave out of some kind of loyalty to his memory, and because her brothers lived here, because Greenworth was her home. But now in a blinding flash he knew that they were wrong. Their faith was a stubbornness that was killing them all.

"I want to leave, Grandma. Let's move away. I can go to another school. We can sell this house and—"

"And go where? Another house, another street, it's all the same. Child, it's everywhere . . ."

"Someplace else, then! If we go far enough away you'll get well and—and—"

Grandma's shoulders moved; she was laughing or crying, he couldn't tell which. "Don't you see, Willy? It's too late to run. This is the way it is now. For all of us. No use fighting it. It's growing up all around. The only answer left is to cross over . . ." Her weeping chuckle becomes a cough.

William moved reflexively to thump her between the shoulder blades and end the spasm. But this time he could not bring himself to strike her for fear that her frail body might not withstand the impact of his small hand. He touched the flannel of her nightgown and felt how unnaturally cool it was, saw the wan flesh of her neck above the ruffled collar. He yanked his hand away. His fingers were tingling. He looked at his palm. It was ashen, bloodless. Like her skin. *Does it rub off, Grandma?* he wondered in a panic. *Does it?*

He sprang away from the bed, bolted from the bedroom and ran out of the house without looking back.

She's dead, she's really dead. It hit him full force as he fled down the steps and into the garden. The stone path snaked out behind him, its tail eaten by the darkness gathering under the porch. Before him lay the remains of the back yard, a landscape that now seemed filled with skeletal trees and vines reaching impatiently toward the face of the rising moon. *My mother's dead.* He tore down the path, a chill piercing his heart. Branches like bony fingers tried to snare his arms. He zigzagged and caromed off a tree trunk, dislodging the last of the dark, testicular fruit drooping and shriveling there. *She's dead and she's never coming back, not ever!*

He hurried by the chicken coop, seeing the bobbing necks of the hens and roosters as they gawked with alarm at his passing. Their wings spread and beat out a flurry of feathers that were like snowflakes on the air. He could not escape their agate eyes. He paused long enough to open the pen and calm their squeaking. They assembled between his legs, covering his own ankles with their plumage.

"Shh," he told them, "it's all right, we're all all right," and did not believe it.

They observed him indifferently, the few remaining feathers on their scrawny bodies settling back into place.

His eyes filled with tears.

As he knelt one small chicken, his favorite, flew onto his knee. He stroked its piebald head and kissed its beak. The others tiptoed away to scratch at the hard dirt, and as the flock parted he saw a shape on the ground by the water trough.

It was the oldest and plumpest of the hens, lying on one side with her claws curled inward. Her feathers rippled and lifted.

He rose to a crouch and crept closer. He wondered how long she had been dead. It couldn't have been very long, but already an army of ants had established a supply trail in and out of the open mouth, where the tongue protruded like a pink arrow.

He extended his arm to touch her, and immediately snatched his hand away as if she were hot. Damp feathers fell aside. The wrinkled skin was teeming with maggots, busily transforming the carcass into something he did not want to see.

He gagged and hid his face.

Who would take care of her chicks now? He reached behind the perch and found her nest. This time there were no peeps, no tiny pecks at his fingers. That was good. She had left no little ones behind. He felt the polished roundness of an egg. Gently he lifted it out.

The egg was smooth as porcelain but oddly soft. And cold. He cupped it gingerly in his hand and raised it to the dying light.

The shell was full-sized but not all of it had hardened properly. Part of the surface was nearly transparent, little more than a stretched membrane.

He looked closer. Barely covered by the thin cellular wall was a distorted, malformed embryo. It was unlike any chick he had ever seen before, an error of nature mutated in vitro. Its congealed, elongated eye stared back at him through a delicate lace of veins.

William shuddered. Crying silently, he replaced the egg in the nest and covered it with straw. *There,* he thought, *you won't have anything to worry about now. Maybe it's better this way, after all.*

A cold wind blew through the trees. It whistled in from the front yard, catching and keening in the eaves of the house. Did something move there, just inside the screen porch? No, it couldn't be. Grandma never got out of bed anymore. If anyone else were inside there would be a light showing somewhere.

Could it be—?

No. There was nothing, nothing. He told himself that. He dug his nails into his hands until his palms bled. *What a baby you are. You're afraid of —of—*

There was a wailing sound. It blew in on the wind from the other side of the house.

He heard a commotion then, the dull clicking of heels on the sidewalk, and a scream. Somewhere a door slammed. The screaming did not stop.

He latched the chicken coop and hurried to the street.

At first nothing seemed out of place. The view from his gate was of the same houses, the roofs sagging under a dingy sky, the treetops jagged silhouettes against the horizon, their distended roots raising the pavement in uneven waves. There were the sunken boundary lines of cracked cement between the yards, only the reinforced security fence that began next door still tall and straight, porchlamps like the first stars of evening vibrating with oversized insects, Vern's house across the street leaking spikes of yellow light.

But wait. There was movement in the bushes by Vern's porch, a shaking out and a separating and then the stab of legs in the dimness.

Vern's mother was already at the corner, huddled under a streetlamp with her face in her hands. The shape of her body blended with the shadows so that she might have stood there for hours before William noticed her. But now Vern's older brother was running to bring her back to the house as the short bursts of screaming started again, tight and muffled by her knuckles.

William stepped off the curb.

The wailing at the end of the block became louder, rising and falling like a buzz saw, as a long car cut across the intersection and sped up the middle of the street. William jumped out of the way and saw that it was one of the dark military vehicles from the plant, like the one that had come to take his mother.

AMBULANCE, it said across the front.

It dipped and braked and three men in uniforms hopped down and raced to Vern's porch, a blur of equipment under their arms. The screen door flapped open. A moment later they reemerged carrying a litter, unfolded to support a bulky form. They were no longer in a hurry, and the sheet was drawn up all the way.

The screen door flapped again and Vern's family followed, heads low, their feet scraping the rough cement. There was Vern's sister Nan, two of the cousins from the next block, and Vern himself, so much shorter than the others. William looked for the stocky contour of Vern's father, the broad shoulders and thick waist, but no one like that came out except for the chunky mound under the sheet.

William called out and waved until Vern spotted him. His friend didn't wave back. His head was down between his shoulders and he was marching forward as though underwater.

Vern did not watch the men loading the gurney into the back of the van. The cousins waited solemnly a while longer, then went to help bring Vern's mother back. She did not want to come. Her screams became a whimpering. When Vern did not move, William started across the street.

"Vern? Hey, Vern! What happened? Are you all right?"

One more figure came out of the house. William did not know who she could be. By some trick of light and shade the door did not appear to swing open for her, and yet there she was, following Vern like a tall shadow. She glided down the walkway behind him, a breeze filling her draped black veil.

William stopped.

Vern finally raised his eyes, saw William, and his face relaxed slightly. But he did not come forward.

The woman drifted ahead, her flowing garment enfolding Vern and then passing him as though he were not there. She floated away from them all and into the street, heading for the house where William now lived. The wispy black material covered her completely, almost wrapping her legs and feet as it trailed out behind her, and yet she did not hesitate at the broken curb. As the veil blew against her face William thought he saw something familiar in the shape of her features, but he could not be sure. He turned to watch her cross the humped blacktop and alight on the other sidewalk.

Vern said something at last, but his words were lost on the wind.

The woman approached Grandma's house, only to bypass it in favor of the fenced-in area that began next door, not even slowing as she neared the high locked gate. Her face was still hidden by the veil, but William was sure that she was looking at him.

"No!"

Was Vern watching her, too? William looked back and saw his friend waving wildly, his arms raised in a railroader's highsign.

"No. Willy! Don't go in there . . . stay here! Don't . . . !"

It was too late. He had to know.

When William turned again she was already through the gate. The edge of her veil slipped through the metal links and disappeared inside the compound.

Drawn by a feeling he could not name, William ignored the ambulance as it pulled slowly away, its siren now silenced, and followed the woman in black.

The entrance was heavily chained and padlocked, as if no one had gone in or out for a very long time. He could not slip through or under. He could scale the fence and the wall behind it if he used the links in the gate for toeholds, but the barbed wire at the top would be a problem. He disregarded the old warning signs posted around the perimeter, hooked his fingers into the ragged metal, and started climbing.

The barbs were sharp but he squeezed his eyes shut on the pain, rolled over the top as quickly as possible, and dropped down on the other side.

It wasn't very far at all.

The sounds of life in the street, the tingling wind that blew across the town, the lights going out in the rest of the world were all distractions cut off from him now. The deepening darkness was inviting, a cushion that broke his fall and called him to enter it at last.

Where had she gone?

There was no path for him to follow. As his eyes adjusted he made out the struts and crossbeams of an old support scaffolding, the flaking treads of an abandoned earthmoving tractor, the corroded shell of an amphibious tank, a hydraulic scoop, the segments of a conveyor belt, a teetering stack of old tires shot through with twiggy, hybrid weeds. Somewhere behind the tires a flickering like cold fire shone between collapsed sidewalls.

He got up from his hands and knees and made his way through the debris.

He passed a junked truck and came out into a small clearing. The moon was high above bowed tiers of rotting lumber, but it was a different light that beckoned him now.

He paused to get his bearings. The wall to his right might have been the fence along his grandmother's yard, but how could he be sure? Serpentine foliage pressed up to the boards in an ever-expanding tide; soon the last property lines would disappear, swallowed by the unchecked growth. He padded on, placing one foot carefully in front of the other as unseen life forms scurried out of his way, large insects or small animals, rats, perhaps, or something like them.

He brushed a dented panel, releasing a shiver of rust and dirt that fell around him like heavy rain. It was the cab of an outsized reconnaissance vehicle, apparently designed to maneuver over rough terrain. The steel door creaked on its hinges and sent a reverberation through the rest of the machinery.

He covered his head. The driver's seat was empty; the giant shift and brake levers were locked at odd angles, like the seized-up hands of a primitive timing device. He imagined that the vehicle might yet be capable of moving, inching forward to lead an assault under cover of darkness and establish a beachhead in occupied territory. That would explain the groaning he heard, loudest in the dead of night when everyone else was asleep, as though iron and steel were drawing relentlessly closer to the flimsy, unguarded barrier.

The rain of rust stopped. A last echo rang out. In the distant riverbed a population of bullfrogs resumed their fitful chorus. He tried to set a course from their singing but it was no use. There were no landmarks in this place, no way to know that he would not end up where he started. Fear gripped him as a new sound began, a steady rhythm like the pounding of surf on a far shore. It was the beating of his own heart in his ears.

Help me, he thought, *please! Somebody—*

A shadow like the dark, gauzy hem of a long dress skipped over the blade of a forklift, backlighted for an instant by a soft flickering the color of static electricity, and vanished behind the gutted chassis.

Without hesitation he moved toward it.

There was a narrow passageway between piles of ancient brake drums and hubcaps. He pulled in his elbows and pushed through, and came out into the blue light.

At first it was like the pale glow of the phosphorescent stars he had pasted to his bedroom ceiling, only larger and brighter and spread out in a wide band like the Milky Way. Then he focused and saw a loose barricade of old canisters. They were taller and broader than oil drums and were marked with the same stenciled symbol he had seen on the signs outside, a circle divided into six wedges like a cut-up drawing of a pie. One of them had tumbled onto its side and probably leaked, because the lid was ajar and a heavy inner lining of chipped glass showed where the top had been. Directly in front of it the ground was bare and scorched, but behind the containers a tangle of skinny plants had taken root, and it was these that shimmered with a faint but unmistakable radiance.

On the ground before him, leading up to the cylinders and disappearing into the spray of shrubbery behind, was a series of elongated spots like ghostly footprints.

He placed his sneaker into one of them. The imprint was short and narrow but it fit him perfectly.

William started walking again.

His legs shook tall weeds, and a shower of pollenlike metallic dust settled on his skin. He looked at his hands, transfixed by their sparkling, and his toe thudded into one of the drums.

A few feet away, hidden only by the vegetation, there was an explosion of hysterical squealing and then a great thrashing, as if someone had taken a wrong step and plunged headlong into the darkness.

He swept the weeds aside.

There, sprawled on one side, was an enormous animal. It reminded him of the sows he had seen at the Fair in years past, and yet it was not one of their kind. It was much too large for any pen to hold, its snout thicker than his thigh, its huge underside rising and falling with peaceful regularity. It was black as coal from head to tail except for the immense belly, where now several smaller animals wriggled to regain position. Their fat shapes were stretched with translucent skin, their veins and capillaries aglow with a cold, unearthly light. Tiny silken hairs moved on their restless bodies, which were already pigmented in places with black spots that would soon toughen into a hide able to contain their new forms.

Does it talk? he wondered. *Does it, really?*

Awestruck, he stood and watched her suckling her hungry offspring. Then, stumbling desperately, he lunged forward into the glowing circle and flung himself at her teats, his hands feverishly pawing the air as he fought to gain a place there for himself.

On several occasions I have presumed upon my friendship with Bill Nolan to fill the pages of my Whispers *anthologies. He has, despite more pressing and better-paying assignments, come through each time with something for me, a piece totally different from the previous one. My latest plea resulted in this shocker.*

MY NAME IS DOLLY

by William F. Nolan

MONDAY—Today I met the witch—which is a good place to start this diary. (I had to look up how to spell it. First I spelled it dairy but that's a place you get milk and from this you're going to get blood—I hope—so it is plenty different.)

Let me tell you about Meg. She's maybe a thousand years old I guess. (A witch can live forever, right?) She's all gnarly like the bark of an oak tree, her skin I mean, and she has real big eyes. Like looking into deep dark caves and you don't know what's down there. Her nose is hooked and she has sharp teeth like a cat's are. When she smiles some of them are missing. Her hair is all wild and clumpy and she smells bad. Guess she hasn't had a shower for a real long time. Wears a long black dress with holes bit in it. By rats most likely. She lives in this old deserted cobwebby boathouse they don't use anymore on the lake—and it's full of fat gray rats. Meg doesn't seem to mind.

My name is Dolly. Short for Dorothy like in the Oz books. Only nobody ever calls me Dorothy. I'm still a kid and not very tall and I've got red hair and freckles. (I really *hate* freckles! When I was real little I tried to rub them off but you can't. They stick just like tattoos do.)

Reason I went out to the lake to see old Meg is because of how much I hate my father. Well, he's not really my father, since I'm adopted and I don't know my real father. Maybe he's a nice man and not like Mister Brubaker who adopted me. Mrs. Brubaker died of the flu last winter which is when Mister Brubaker began to molest me. (I looked up the word molest and it's the right one for what he keeps trying to do with me.) When I won't let him he gets really mad and slaps me and I run out of the house until he's all calmed down again. Then he'll get special nice and offer me cookies with chocolate chunks in them which are my very favorite kind. He wants me to like him so he can molest me later.

Last week I heard about the witch who lives by the lake. A friend at school told me. Some of the kids used to go down there to throw rocks at her until she put a spell on Lucy Akins and Lucy ran away and no one's seen her since. Probably she's dead. The kids leave old Meg alone now.

I thought maybe Meg could put a spell on Mister Brubaker for five dollars. (I saved up that much.) Which is why I went to see her. She said she couldn't because she can't put spells on people unless she can see them up close and look in their eyes like she did to Lucy Akins.

The lake was black and smelly with big gas bubbles breaking in it and the boathouse was cold and damp and the rats scared me but old Meg was the only way I knew to get even with Mister Brubaker. She kept my five dollars and told me she was going into town soon and would look around for something to use against Mister Brubaker. I promised to come see her on Friday after school.

We'll have his blood, she said.

FRIDAY NIGHT—I went to see old Meg again and she gave me the doll to take home. A real big one, as tall as I am, with freckles and red hair just like mine. And in a pretty pink dress with little black slippers with red bows on them. The doll's eyes open and close and she has a big metal key in her back where you wind her up. When you do she opens her big dark eyes and says hello, my name is Dolly. Same as mine. I asked Meg where she found Dolly and she said at Mister Carter's toy store. But I've been in there lots of times and I've never seen a doll like this for five dollars. Take her home, Meg told me, and she'll be your friend. I was real excited and ran off pulling Dolly behind me. She has a box with wheels on it you put her inside and pull along the sidewalk.

She's too big to carry.

MONDAY—Mister Brubaker doesn't like Dolly. He says she's damn strange. That's his words, damn strange. But she's my new friend so I don't care what he says about her. He wouldn't let me take her to school.

SATURDAY—I took some of Mister Brubaker's hair to old Meg today. She asked me to cut some off while he was asleep at night and it was really hard to do without waking him up but I got some and gave it to her. She wanted me to bring Dolly and I did and Meg said that Dolly was going to be her agent. That's the word. Agent. (I try to get all the words right.)

Dolly had opened her deep dark eyes and seen Mister Brubaker and old Meg said that was all she needed. She wrapped two of Mister Brubaker's hairs around the big metal key in Dolly's back and told me not to wind her up again until Sunday afternoon when Mister Brubaker was home watching his sports. He always does that on Sunday.

So I said okay.

SUNDAY NIGHT—This afternoon, like always, Mister Brubaker was watching a sports game on the television when I set Dolly right in front of him and did just what old Meg told me to do. I wound her up with the big key and then took the key out of her back and put it in her right hand. It was long and sharp and Dolly opened her eyes and said hello, my name is Dolly and stuck the metal key in Mister Brubaker's chest. There was a lot of blood. (I told you there would be.)

Mister Brubaker picked Dolly up and threw the front of her into the fire. I mean, that's how she landed, just the front of her at the edge of the fire. (It's winter now, and real cold in the house without a fire.) After he did that he fell down and didn't get up. He was dead so I called Doctor Thompson.

The police came with him and rescued Dolly out of the fire when I told them what happened. Her nice red hair was mostly burnt away and the whole left side of her face was burnt real bad and the paint had all peeled back and blistered. And one of her arms had burnt clear off and her pink dress was all char-colored and with big fire holes in it. The policeman who rescued her said that a toy doll couldn't kill anybody and that I must have stuck the key into Mister Brubaker's chest and blamed it on Dolly. They took me away to a home for bad children.

I didn't tell anybody about old Meg.

TUESDAY—It is a long time later and my hair is real pretty now and my face is almost healed. The lady who runs this house says there will always be big scars on the left side of my face but I was lucky not to lose my eye on that side. It is hard to eat and play with the other kids with just one arm but that's okay because I can still hear Mister Brubaker screaming and see all the blood coming out of his chest and that's nice.

I wish I could tell old Meg thank you. I forgot to—and you should always thank people for doing nice things for you.

This is Juleen Brantingham's first appearance in a Whispers *hardcover although I have been privileged to use her work in both my* Death *anthology and magazine, one story of hers therein gaining a place in one of Karl Edward Wagner's Year's Best books. Juleen recently moved from New York to Louisiana and tells me her attic has rats. I wonder if they can be better friends than Celia's home held?*

TOAD, SINGULAR

by Juleen Brantingham

When release finally came it was August and the dog was having her annual nervous breakdown. It was predictably perverse of him, leaving her to cope with the formalities of death while Vickie yapped a shrill, hysterical counterpoint.

All through those postdeath, prefuneral days she felt as if she trembled on the brink of disaster, with control of the situation just beyond her reach. The doctor came and went, leaving pills she didn't need. The lawyer and the staff of the funeral home must consult with her about arrangements. Neighbors appeared on her doorstep with gifts of food and unwanted sympathy. It was annoying to realize that all these people ascribed her condition to grief.

On this, the afternoon of the funeral, the day she most needed to feel calm and competent, there was a domestic crisis: a tattered, bloody rag on the balcony outside his room, a rag that turned out to be the remains of a squirrel, headless and dripping.

She first had to catch the dog. But Vickie, normally sweet and obedient, could not be coaxed or bribed with doggy treats. She was frantic, dashing madly up the stairs to bark at the balcony door, down again to scratch at front and back doors, snapping, snarling, and evading when Celia came near. Finally driven to desperate measures, Celia threw a sheet over her, caught her up in its folds, and carried her to the basement.

For this, too, she blamed Daddy. He'd driven the dog insane.

A bucket of water took care of the gouts of still-fresh blood and she buried the body in the garden. She wasted precious minutes combing through the grass below the balcony in search of the head. People would be stopping by to visit after the funeral and she could imagine the shock and disgust if one of them should find it, kick it, perhaps, while walking across the lawn to the door. A severed head with death-blinded eyes, rolling, leaking fluids over a pretty summer shoe. Celia shuddered. It was just the sort of grace note he would have arranged if he'd thought of it.

The cause of the squirrel's death was a puzzle. The dog promised genocide to the squirrels every August but the screen door was undamaged and there was no other way for her to reach the balcony. A stray cat then, but that would be unusual. They were seldom bothered by stray animals here, one of the fringe benefits of being her father's daughter.

She went to her bedroom to dress and heard the parade, interrupted by her activity, begin again. The dog muttered curses behind the basement door. Celia smiled.

Every August the hickory tree on the front lawn bore a crop of nuts. And every August the gray squirrels—"damn tree rats" Daddy called them —harvested that crop. They crossed the phone lines from woods to house, scrambled up over the roof, dropped to the railing on the balcony outside his room, then along the railing to leap from house to hickory tree. With green-hulled nuts wedged in their jaws, they reversed direction, stopping on the balcony sometimes to munch their prizes and, Celia suspected, deliberately to infuriate Vickie, always safely shut away behind glass and screen.

If it hadn't been for the mess of chewed-up hulls and shells that had to be swept up several times a day and the dog's noisy agony, Celia would have enjoyed the season. She liked to watch the squirrels hull the nuts, turning them round and round in their tiny paws, just like a person gnawing corn from a cob. She admired the daring leaps and even the pitter-patter as they crossed the roof was pleasant. She certainly didn't begrudge them the nuts. Just once Daddy had sent her out with a bushel basket to gather the ones the squirrels had dropped.

"We'll let these dry in the attic and in a couple months those old hulls will drop off by themselves," he told her. "Won't it be fun, come Christmas time, all our friends sitting around the fireplace, telling stories, cracking nuts from our very own hickory tree? Huh, CeeCee? Won't it be fun?"

Celia had been thirty-seven at the time, old enough to feel demeaned by the grubby chore. Daddy knew it, too. Why else would he have stood out on his balcony like a lord, looking down at her crawling on hands and knees in the grass? If she had been a slender woman, one less inclined to perspire and get red in the face, it might not have been so bad. But of course Daddy had taken that into account. He loved to scold her for having wisps of hair out of place or stains on her dress.

"There's one over there on your right, a nice fat one. No, you stupid cow! On your *right*. Your *right*."

That had been twenty years ago and Celia still felt humiliated when she thought of it.

When Daddy suggested that Christmas gathering, when he spoke of "our" friends, of course he meant his friends, his political pals, some elected officials but most too secure in their power to need titles and public acknowledgment. Her friends, if she could remember back that far, had been "little friends" as in, "Tell your little friends to run along now. Daddy's got business to discuss."

Decades of hushed conversations in that upstairs room, part bedroom, part office. Talk that stopped instantly when she appeared in answer to his summons, to play hostess with coffee cups, the aura of power plastered over with shallow smiles and clod-kicker gallantry.

Sometimes Celia thought Daddy had the fix in every place that counted.

But not, apparently, in nature's councils. His plans for the hickory nuts hadn't worked out, which suggested to Celia there might be some justice in the world after all. The hulls had clung to the shells as if glued. When, with the aid of hammers, nutcrackers, picks, and quickly bruised fingers they had gotten down to the tiny nutmeats it was to find, more often than not, a worm in residence. Celia thoughtfully substituted store-bought walnuts and the party had become cozy once more. Daddy, of course, never referred to the incident again.

Even after that, even when he must have known the nuts could be of no earthly use to him, Daddy hated the squirrels, called them thieves. What was his was *his,* by God. He bought a slingshot and left the balcony door open so he could take potshots when a squirrel appeared. Fortunately his aim was bad and he soon gave up.

The one thing Celia had ever done that won his wholehearted approval was to buy the dog six years ago. Daddy immediately recognized an ally for his August war. Vickie, a springer-cocker spaniel mix, was affectionate, energetic, and an unashamed coward. The appearance of mailmen and meter readers sent her scrambling under the nearest bed but squirrels were safe targets.

Celia had brought the dog home in July and by August Vickie knew her place in the natural scheme of things. The rest of the year she might be Celia's companion but in August she belonged to Daddy.

"Look at her go," he would laugh. "She'd rip them old squirrels to pieces if we let her out, wouldn't she?"

He encouraged the dog's frenzy, brought her up from the basement after Celia had coaxed her there to rest, egged her on with excited cries, and laughed at the show. Celia grew familiar with but never accustomed to the sound of Vickie's claws scrabbling at glass or screen, barking so shrilly it made Celia's nerves jump even if she was on the other side of the house. August was hell for Celia and probably for Vickie, but Daddy had loved it.

Once—just once—when Celia was out shopping, Daddy had let the dog out on the balcony to see what she would do when she met a squirrel nose to nose. The railing had no vertical bars to prevent things from falling through so naturally that's what Vickie had done. Lunging after a squirrel she had lost her balance and fallen to the ground. Miraculously, she broke only one leg. Daddy had never repeated that mistake. He must have thought the dog's noisy frustration more interesting than real conflict.

"You've got yourself a real brave watchdog, little toad. As long as nobody but a squirrel tries to break in we'll be safe, won't we?"

Toad. How she hated that name. No one had dared call her that since she passed out of the tricycle stage, no one but Daddy. She could have pointed out the strong family resemblance between them but it would only have made him laugh.

One of the many blessings of his death was that she would never again have to hear that name, pronounced in a mockery of affection.

Celia dressed carefully, as always, examining each article of clothing for stains, snags, or missing stitches. She applied the muted colors of her makeup without looking at the mirror, and sprayed her hair into rigid submission.

The car from the funeral home had not yet arrived. She walked through the house once more, assuring herself that every ashtray and window was polished, every cushion straight, no wisps of dog fur calling attention to the worn carpet. She knew she fussed too much but it had become unbreakable habit.

She paused at the foot of the stairs, her hand resting on the richly gleaming newel post. She hadn't thought to go up there again today but something—ridiculous. She felt as if she were being called.

The bed was *empty*. Of course it was. She hurried up the stairs.

There was a sharp, unpleasant smell in the room, a smell of old age and illness. *His* room, his office, his prison since he'd broken his hip a year ago and refused even to begin the therapy the doctor had ordered. His power had been unaffected by failing health. The men had still come at all hours, questioning, being instructed, begging for favors. Conversations she was not allowed to hear.

"Man talk, CeeCee. Run along."

Even if the political machine had discovered it could run without the cog labeled with Daddy's name, he would still have had Celia. Bound to him with chains she could neither break nor understand. There had been just the two of them for as long as she could remember. The sky would have fallen if she'd left home without his permission. Was that love or cowardice?

She laughed, loosening the knot of tension. He was gone. He was really gone.

She gazed around the room, taking pleasure in it for the first time. She had rearranged the furniture after he became bedridden. It looked strange now, the rolltop desk, the small filing cabinet with its locks, the guest chair with wobbly legs, bunched around the empty bed as if seeking comfort. A wheelchair stood alone in a corner on the other side of the room, outcast.

"What do I need one of them things for? Dammit, CeeCee, you're always spending my money on things we don't need."

"You don't want to spend the rest of your life in bed, do you?"

"Yes, why shouldn't I? I worked hard all my life. Now it's time for me to take a well-earned rest. Let someone else do the work for a change."

By someone else he meant her. All those personal chores, nasty ones if she let herself think about them. Keeping him clean. Lifting and carrying. Coaxing him into the wheelchair so she could push him out to the balcony to take some sun. Enduring his ever-worsening temper. Running up and down the stairs a hundred times a day. Never having a minute to herself. Not a minute.

It wasn't the lack of thanks that bothered her. She didn't expect gratitude from him. What goaded her almost past bearing was his attitude that *he* was doing *her* a favor.

"They'll give you your star in heaven, little toad." And he'd *laughed*. Laughed right in her face.

God, how she hated him.

This room would be hers now, the room she'd always coveted, secretly. Up so high she could see for miles, sheltered by the leafy green of the hickory tree. With the sliding glass doors taking up most of one wall, the room was a place for summer dreams, more like a treehouse than a part of the rest of the house. He had known how she felt. Of course he had. Only death could have made him relinquish ownership.

One of the first things she would do, she decided, would be to get rid of the scarred, ancient furniture and buy something pretty. Maybe she would have the room painted, or papered in a pretty floral print. Drapes to soften the look of the glass doors. Pastel carpeting in place of the stained brown rug.

It was very close in here. The room had been closed up since the day of her father's death. The smell seemed to come at her in waves, stronger, ever stronger, as if the old man still lay in the bed in the shadows, as if the whole thing were a hideous joke and soon he would throw back the covers and sit up with a triumphant cry and that wicked, chittering laughter, so much like the sound of the squirrels he loathed.

She would *not* turn to look at the bed. She would *not* peer into the shadows like some timid thing afraid to be alone.

With thoughts of the cleansing properties of fresh air and sunshine, she went to the glass doors where she received her second shock of the day. Two furry bodies were now smeared and scattered across the balcony floor.

She shuddered and blinked back sudden tears. It was almost too much. As if someone deliberately—

The room dipped and swayed around her. Was this the moment when she would lose control, *lose* to *him*, after successfully enduring his torments for nearly sixty years? No. Her mind rejected the idea firmly. If the pain of those years was to mean anything it must give her strength now. She collected herself, walked across the room, and closed the door behind her. No time to clean the balcony again. She would simply have to hope the blood spatters weren't visible from the lawn.

When the car arrived from the funeral home she was treated like a crown princess. There were two of them, a driver and a flunky assistant, entirely too solicitous for her taste. They took her arms as she approached the two wide steps to the walk and she shook them off angrily.

As she was getting into the car she happened to glance to the right. She saw a thin, spectacled face peering out at her from behind a bush. Little Frankie, the boy from next door. Without thinking she smiled at him, wiggled her fingers in a baby wave. The boy did not respond, perhaps awestricken by the gleaming, expensive car and the two solemn strangers. They had not seen the boy and they were, she realized, amused by her childish gesture. She sank back on the plush upholstery, feeling a blush stain her cheeks.

For this, too, the old man should rot in hell. Making her ashamed of a harmless friendship.

It had come about almost by accident, after Daddy's health had begun to fail. On nice days she had gotten into the habit of putting him into his chair and wheeling him out to the balcony—over his strong objections. She would go downstairs and out to the front of the house to work on her flower beds while he napped in the sun, daring her to think he enjoyed it.

One morning she was cutting pansies to press and use in the little pictures she arranged for her own amusement. She hadn't heard a sound but suddenly this boy, a stranger, was squatting in the grass beside her. Her first thought had been to send him away. She had had trouble with the neighborhood children before, grass and flower beds torn up, their excited cries at play disturbing her father and making him shorter-tempered than usual.

But there was something different about this child, something that made her delay her words of dismissal. Perhaps it was his stillness, his air of self-containment. Perhaps it was the large, black-framed glasses that kept slipping down his nose. Or perhaps it was simply a case of like calling to like. How did she know, she wondered, that this boy, too, perpetually stood on the edges of things, looking in?

He asked questions in a voice so soft it barely crossed the air between them. Not pestering questions but thoughtful ones.

It was flattering, she realized later when she had time for analysis. Frankie treated her as if she were someone whose opinions and knowledge were worthy of respect. A novel sensation. Another point that endeared him to her was that he seemed wary of the old man, never appearing until the bright, lizardlike eyes were hooded in sleep, darting away again only seconds before the old man woke and began to complain she was trying to kill him with heatstroke.

Frankie came to see her almost every day. They fell easily into a teacher-student relationship. It was a dangerous thing, snatched moments, right under Daddy's feet so he had only to open his eyes to catch them.

She began to look forward to Frankie's brief visits and to feel depressed when the weather prevented her outing or Frankie, for one reason or another, did not show up. Sometimes his questions astonished her and she had to spend the evening with her gardening books to refresh her memory. She squeezed pennies from Daddy's niggardly household budget to buy him little gifts: a packet of seeds, a trowel.

Secrets. Daddy lived and breathed secrets. He could see them, sense them in others. She should have known it couldn't last. Perhaps he hadn't been sleeping in the sun but only feigning sleep, peeping out from under lowered lids to spy on her.

He began to drop hints, to make sly remarks and she tried to tell herself he did not, could not possibly know about the little boy. But of course he did. One afternoon she came upstairs with the coffee tray to serve him and his guest, one of those sick old men nearly as evil as he was, and she heard—as she was intended to—she heard Daddy tell the man about her friendship with Frankie. Only, from his words, no one could have guessed the truth, that it was casual and harmless. No, he had to make it sound filthy. Her every word, every gesture to the boy made to seem twisted and sinful.

Her crime—her awful crime—had been to compose herself and serve the coffee as if she hadn't heard. Later she would drive the boy away with angry words and clods of dirt but that was only the final note of the betrayal. Denial of the one purely good thing in her life had been the first.

She put her hands to her face, not even caring that the men in the front seat would think the tears were for Daddy.

It had been foolish of her to think she could take revenge on him. She had hidden her rage, penned it up with blank looks and soft tones, encouraged it to grow in secret. But it was there. It existed. The old man seemed to wither and grow pale, as if her hidden hate sapped his strength and multiplied his years.

She plotted. He had spied on her, therefore she would do the same to him. Secrets were his treasure so she would hurt him by stealing some of those secrets. She wasn't sure what to do then. Innocently, perhaps, she thought it would be enough simply to possess a few of them, to casually betray her knowledge at a fitting time.

The meeting late at night. She waited until the three others had made their doddering way up the stairs. She heard the last one turn the key in the lock and she was certain then. There would be no call for refreshments this night. She crept, literally crept up the stairs, on hands and knees, taking ten whole minutes to reach the top, praying the occasional creak would be taken as the natural noises of a house settling itself on a cool night. She pressed her ear to the door panel and heard—

A quiet confusion. Voices but no words. A step. A rustle of clothing. Nothing certain, not what she had hoped to hear. She pressed her ear harder against the door, as if she would push it right through the thin panel.

She never heard the key being turned, or the knob. Suddenly the door was thrown open and she was upset, rolling into the room, her skirts and her dignity atangle around her knees. She had a dazed impression of overwhelming darkness and gleaming points of light. A scream. A roaring noise. For a moment she thought Vickie was in the room with them.

Then she realized the thing had too many legs for a dog, too few for a pair of them.

Someone hauled her to her feet. She blinked. The three others were sitting around Daddy's bed. The room was lit normally, no strange beasts lurked in shadows. She shook her head to clear away confusion.

He scolded her, shamed her like a child while his guests watched. He raved until spittle flew from his lips. He called her vile names. She stood there and took it, head hanging, for she knew no other way to act with him.

At last he screamed for her to get out and for emphasis, threw the heavy book lying next to his hand. It struck her on the shoulder, staggered her.

She wasn't sure what happened next. Perhaps something possessed her. Perhaps it was simply that a door had been opened somewhere and years of rage came boiling out. She blazed with it, felt it consuming her, was not even aware of what was happening until she heard horrified gasps, realized she had stepped close to the bed, teeth bared, fingers clawing.

She could have killed him if she hadn't heard those gasps. Could. Have. Torn him limb from limb, ripped into flesh with teeth and nails, gloried in the blood she shed. She could have.

But the gasps had stopped her, reminded her this was Daddy, a sick, helpless old man. A cold part of her mind wondered how, even now, she could find justice in *not* killing him. But it was so. The rage was gone, not as if she had calmed herself. Rather, the rage had seemed to cast her away, a useless vehicle for its expression.

She stumbled out of the room, down the stairs, wondering what had given her the impression Daddy and the others had been frightened even before she nearly attacked him. Were his secrets that precious? At the bottom of the stairs she noticed white, dusty marks on her skirt. She brushed them away.

Nearing the funeral home she saw the street was clogged with traffic. A crowd jostled along the walks and near the door. So many people come to pay their last respects, she mused. But was *respect* the right word? She was driven around to the back, handed out at the private entrance, her arm taken and even patted by a man in a blue suit, a man too accustomed to grief to recognize its absence. She wondered wryly how much longer she would be treated, mistakenly, as a power behind the throne now that the throne was unoccupied.

As she was escorted to the family alcove she saw the director of the home and the chief of police engaged in a quiet but seemingly heated conversation.

She felt a sudden stab of panic. But no, Daddy's death, strange as it was, had been called suicide—and not even at her suggestion. No one thought for a moment that she'd had anything to do with it. The doctor had even gone to some trouble to assure her Daddy had not been as helpless as he pretended, that he'd been quite capable when overcome by depression about his failing health, of crawling out to the balcony and throwing himself over the edge.

No one ever explained why, if this was so, there was a horrified expression on his face when she found his broken body in the flower bed the next morning. Perhaps few people saw that expression. The staff of this home was said to be skilled in covering the ravages of life and death.

No, if there were any doubts about the cause of death, someone would have told her so. Cat and mouse was Daddy's game.

Perhaps there were others as relieved as she was. Perhaps they only wanted to close the books on him.

She noticed the change as soon as she stepped into the room.

"Why is the casket closed?" she demanded of her escort. "It was open for calling hours last night and I left instructions it was to be open for the funeral. Why is it closed now?" She hadn't been happy about having to make that decision. Daddy hadn't been pleasant to look upon when he was alive. Death couldn't have improved his appearance. But some of the "mourners" wouldn't have believed the old bastard was dead unless they could see the cold body with their own eyes.

The man in the blue suit looked distressed. "I don't— Why, it must—"

"You *do* know," she snapped. "But you don't want to be the one to tell me. Tell the director I wish to speak to him."

She almost laughed to see the man scuttle away. No, the power wouldn't last. But she planned to enjoy the shreds of it that remained.

The director, in spite of his air of professionalism and his insulating poundage, looked almost as distressed as her escort had. The chief of police merely looked grim.

"Well, why did you close the casket?"

It took several minutes to get the story, pulling it almost word by word from the director's reluctant tongue. And she could not, even with her most Daddy-like expression, persuade him to be precise. Mutilation, he said. He was protecting her from some knowledge he feared would be too upsetting for her in her grief-stricken condition.

She allowed herself to be protected. She was certain Daddy was out of her life forever. Nothing else mattered.

"Someone must have broken in," the director said. "Someone with a grudge—"

"Nonsense," said the chief. "No sign of damage to any of the locks. It must have been one of your own people."

For a moment Celia thought there might be another death here and now. The director's face looked ghastly. Her words rode right over his stammered protests.

"All right. It happened and there's nothing to be done about it now. Is there any reason we can't get on with the funeral? Some of these people have come for miles to see that he's put where he belongs."

Her words startled the man, destroyed the last shreds of his composure. He began to wring his plump hands. "The minister should be—"

"You can go ahead with the funeral but we'll have to delay burial," the police chief said.

"Oh, now really—"

Celia's gaze locked with his. It was worse than she suspected, his expression told her. Much, much worse. There was a pain in her chest as if a hand had just squeezed every drop of blood from her heart. Then she called herself a fool and raised her chin, daring anyone to find a superstitious bone in her body. Dead men did not get up and walk. Not in *her* world.

The moment of panic passed and she was caught up in the solemnities. Outside the alcove the room began to fill but for the moment she was left in peace. There was something almost stately about her solitude, as if she were a queen in a private box. Semisheer drapery hanging across the arch separating the alcove from the main room veiled but did not entirely conceal her from the gaze of the curious.

If the occasion had not been what it was, if her feelings had not been so at odds with what she was supposed to be feeling, she might have been able to enjoy it more. The music, the flowers, the knowledge that she was the true center of attention and not that cold lump of flesh in the wooden box—these were all very pleasant. These things would be part of her new life, she promised herself, as different as possible from the bare existence she had endured as Daddy's handmaiden.

Twice while the minister droned through the ritual—Nailing him into his coffin with words, Celia thought—she felt a cold touch on that place between her shoulder blades where shivers began. She refused to think about it.

Parts of the proceedings were even amusing: the kind, pious lies of the eulogy, the phony concern for her expressed by those who came to the house afterward.

The women, quietly competent politicians' wives, could not do enough for her. These were the people who truly kept the machine running. In their wardrobes they would have the proper dress for every occasion, appropriate words, like appropriate accessories, organized and filed for instant use. They ushered her to the most comfortable chair in the living room and left her to hold court while they took over in the kitchen, knowing that the only way to get rid of a houseful of guests was to feed them.

The men, Daddy's friends, ran true to form. They hung back, allowed their wives to speak and act for them, while they made faces that were supposed to convey sympathy but only made them look like basset hounds with indigestion.

No one referred to the closed casket, the presence of the police chief at the funeral home, or the omission of the graveside portion of the service.

But they knew. The entire town and half the state must know. It would be the scandal of the decade.

"Keep busy, my dear. That's what you need now. Volunteer work—"

"A great man. A great, public-spirited man."

"—my advice is to sell this house. Too many memories—"

After an hour or so it was no longer amusing. She was tired of the pretense—but perhaps they thought they were being kind. Perhaps they thought she believed the things they were saying. They expected her to be shattered by his death. What else were they to think? She had spent her life caring for him, doing his bidding. She had never married, never spent a night outside her home. They must think she had built her life around him because that was the way she wanted it.

They were wrong but they would never know.

She felt strange—detached. Her body was in the chair but her mind seemed to be hovering in one of the upper corners of the room. The funeral and the gathering afterward were forms to be followed, a punctuation mark at the end of a life. But something more was needed. Another kind of mark to signal the beginning of—whatever. She wished she knew what that something was.

Finally the last guests were gone. She closed the door behind them and leaned against it, listening to the peace of the house that was now hers alone. She searched her soul for the sense of victory she should have felt but found nothing.

There was a scrabbling noise from the roof. A thump. Vickie, in her basement prison, began to yip hysterically and Celia smiled. The squirrels must have hidden in the woods while all these people were about but they were back now, to claim what was rightfully theirs.

The squirrels. The balcony. The upstairs room. Of course. Where better to begin her new life than in his bedroom, his eagle's nest. She ran up the stairs, giggling, feeling about twelve years old.

Day was melting into dusk, that time when the sky still seems bright but hasn't the strength to hold back encroaching shadows. In-between-time, neither one thing nor the other. A time when senses can be fooled, when the threat of oncoming night excites childhood fears denied in daylight.

She opened the door, her mind engrossed in what she was about to do, her feet hurrying in a preplanned track. Shadows in the room were thick, stifling, almost like Daddy's presence.

She was halfway to the glass doors before she heard the faint noise and saw the—something. A white gleam. A shape crouched on the floor of the balcony. An impression of a face turned impossibly far to look at her over a shoulder. A grin shaped by bloodstained lips.

A movement and the thing was gone before eyes and brain could agree on the truth of what it had been.

She staggered, put a hand to her chest. Too big, too pale for a squirrel. It must have been a cat. Yes, of course. What else could have flashed so quickly from floor to railing to roof? Of course it had been a cat.

That sound. Lapping, memory insisted.

"You're a silly old woman," she told herself, but indulgently.

She opened the door and the screen as far as they would go, heard squirrels scrambling in the tree for better hiding places as she stepped outside. She refused to acknowledge the superstitious chill that went over her, refused to look above and behind to the roof. There were now three torn bodies on the balcony. She kicked them off, too excited to be fastidious.

The filing cabinet with its shiny locks was first. She tipped it over on its side, slid it across the room, and off the edge. It hit the ground with a satisfying crash, exploding papers over the lawn. She giggled, thinking of the news going out, sweat and panic in the back rooms and the walnut-paneled studies. Damning secrets blown about by the night wind.

The rolltop desk followed, its dessicated wood splintering, releasing more papers, like a soul rising from a dead body. The dresser, the mattress and springs, the bed frame, the rug, even towels, toothbrush, and shaving things fell after the desk in quick succession. Contaminated by his evil. So much garbage now.

She gasped for air, heart pounding, laughing. She couldn't stop laughing.

How he would have screamed if he could have seen her. He never gave up anything that belonged to him.

Last of all she pushed the wheelchair over the edge of the balcony. It landed on one wheel, wobbled, then righted itself as if an unseen occupant had brought it under control at the last moment.

The wind must be rising. There was a low moaning from somewhere behind her, in the woods, perhaps.

She braced her hands on the railing like a conqueror, threw her head back for a deep, cleansing breath. Hers now.

As her breathing slowed and her pulse stopped thundering in her ears, she became aware of a quiet stirring up and down the street. Doors opening. A child being called in from play. Footsteps. Curtains lifted at a window. Celia's face grew warm. Her neighbors were out there watching, thinking the thing they expected—and perhaps hoped for—had come to pass, her grief had deranged her.

Let them, she thought tiredly.

The job was not finished, of course. Her habits would not let her rest until she'd done something about the mess on the front lawn. She would not touch the papers but the fragments of furniture would have to be dragged down to the curb or the trash collectors would not trouble themselves.

She was on the front lawn, struggling with the stubbornly limp mattress, when she realized she had a helper. It was little Frankie from next door. He said nothing until they were almost done.

"If you don't want that anymore can I have it?" He pointed to the wheelchair.

"What on earth for?"

He shrugged. "Oh, *things.* Have races in it. Take it apart so I can build stuff. Just things."

She smiled and nodded. The boy's parents would probably think it was a gruesome thing to give a child but she would worry about that later. It was the perfect solution, even better than having it hauled away with the rest of the trash. Daddy had hated children.

Frankie took a few minutes to examine his prize. Celia stood with him in companionable silence. She was thinking she should go inside and fix herself a hot meal, or at least a cup of tea. But for the moment it was pleasant to breathe the night air and to feel the warm ache of fatigue.

"I never noticed before that you had one of those things," he said, glancing up at the house.

"One of what things?"

"A goggle."

Her mind was not entirely on what the boy had said but her instinct was aroused. Perhaps if things had been different she could have been a teacher. She found so much enjoyment in instructing Frankie.

"Like swimming goggles, you mean? You forgot the *s*, dear. Goggles is one of those funny words, like trousers. It ends in *s* but it's not really plural. Do you know what I mean?"

He stared at her, uncomprehending, simply waiting for the words to end.

"You can't have one goggle because if you have half a pair, you have nothing at all."

Still nothing.

"Anyway, we don't have any goggles. My father and I never cared for swimming." How delightful it was to use that expression, my father and I, knowing it would soon drop from her vocabulary. My father and I, like ham and eggs or death and taxes.

Frankie shook his head, pointed to the roof line of the house. "No, I mean a goggle. Up there."

She looked up and stared and when she did not respond to his questions or to tugs on her sleeve, he gave up and went away, pushing the wheelchair. One wheel had developed a squeak, a sound almost like that of a cricket. When it faded away the night was still.

But for Celia it was full of the thunder of destruction and ruin.

Up there above the door where Vickie stood to scream at the squirrels. Up there above the room where he used to make deals with everyone who could be bought. Up there above the place where squirrels had begun to die so strangely.

The thing the boy had seen scuttled along the edge of the roof, gleaming fish-belly white in the dying light. Impossibly tiny limbs, huge head. It chittered angrily—and was it only in her mind that it began to call?

Stupid boy didn't know how to pronounce gargoyle.

Come to me, my little toad.

When I recently received a manuscript submission from one Richard Wilson, my thoughts turned to a giant woman on a Richard Powers cover for a 1950s' Ballantine book, The Girls from Planet Five. *It was authored by a Richard Wilson, but I did not expect this to be from the same man. I was delightfully wrong. And "Sleeping Booty" exhibits the same good fun Dick's earlier fiction had.*

SLEEPING BOOTY

by Richard Wilson

Harry Protagonist thought up the device one evening as he lay in a warm bath. How wonderful it would be, he mused drowsily, to design a watertight sleeping bag in which a person could lie comfortably in warm water and doze off to sleep. What a boon to insomniacs!

Harry soon had a working model. Not choosing to test it himself, he placed a small classified ad. It said: "Wanted: male insomniac for scientific experiment. Easy work."

Late that night a heavyset but impoverished-looking man rang Harry Protagonist's doorbell. He gave his name as George Grimes and said he had seen the ad in a discarded newspaper. "Misfortune has reduced me to the pitiful state in which you now observe me," he told Harry. "Once I was president of a large corporation. I chose a high cash salary instead of retirement benefits and tax-avoiding emoluments. Then, after a merger, I was dismissed. Inflation has eaten all my cash."

Harry Protagonist murmured sympathetically as he led Mr. Grimes to his workshop. "You have trouble getting to sleep?"

"I haven't had a full night's sleep since the merger. I would gladly pay, although I have very little, if your experiment could help me."

"Nay, sir," Harry told him. "Our agreement is that I will pay you. What time do you customarily retire?"

"At about 11 P.M., although it is useless as I toss and turn for hours before dropping off."

"It is now 11 P.M. precisely," Harry noted. "We shall begin at once. If you will go behind that screen, disrobe and put on this pajama-style wet suit . . ."

The bath-bed lay atop a folding cot, awaiting its occupant. It was ingeniously simple and probably could retail for $99.99 (value $149.99), giving its inventor a profit of $89.99, or maybe even $90, per bag.

Harry Protagonist had filled a tank with comfortably warm water, which was to flow into the bag enclosing Mr. Grimes. The man looked even more corpulent when he came from behind the screen dressed only in the wet suit.

"Ready, sir?" Harry asked.

At Mr. Grimes's nod he closed the watertight zipper and arranged the watertight air cushion comfortably around the subject's neck. He connected a tube from the vat to the bag and turned a valve to let the warm water flow around Mr. Grimes's body. "Not too hot, is it, sir?"

"Just right."

When the bag was filled, Harry Protagonist disconnected the tube. He inserted the wall plug, explaining, "There is a small heating element and thermostat which will keep the water at a comfortable temperature all night. How do you feel now?"

"Deliciously sleepy," Mr. Grimes said. "Oh, bless you, sir."

"Then I will leave you. I will be working in the next room. You have but to call and I will be at your side."

Mr. Grimes's languid good night was barely audible. He seemed already on the verge of slumber.

But when Harry came back at 2 A.M. to check on the experiment, Mr. Grimes was beyond the verge. As a matter of fact he had been cooked like a lobster. Something had gone wrong with the thermostat.

Harry was annoyed. Still, the man probably hadn't suffered. The water temperature must have risen slowly or Mr. Grimes would have called out. Harry was fairly sure of this—hadn't he read in a couple of books by gourmet chefs that this was the humane way to prepare lobsters? The temperature rose gradually, soothingly, and the lobster died drowsily. What was true for a lobster must have been true for Mr. Grimes.

Harry, never one to despair when an experiment encountered a setback, carried on.

Unplugging the cord, he rolled out a big copper-lined box to put Mr. Grimes into while he considered his next step. As he moved the body he thought, "Good Lord, how heavy he is! You'd think some of the fat would have boiled off him."

It was then that Harry Protagonist had the inspiration that was to make him one of his many fortunes. He remembered a friend from one of the emerging countries in the Southwest Pacific—the son of a defrocked missionary whose mother was the daughter of a cannibal chief. The friend was in the United States on an exchange scholarship to the Northeastern Academy of Culinary Arts.

His friend was also a member of the United Nations delegation of the Republic of Newer Georgia, one of several countries created when Australia relinquished its trusteeship in the area.

A quick telephone call brought Ngala Mbwani to Harry's laboratory. Ngala had several ideas of his own and the two men talked for hours.

After they had shaken hands on their agreement, it was but the work of a few days to purchase the assets of a bankrupt canning factory in Brooklyn and convert it to their purposes.

Ngala conferred with Newer Georgia's consul general in New York, who was his first cousin, and the enterprise was created. Within a month the Newer Georgia Gourmet Foods Specialty Co. was a going concern, set up in the basement of the diplomatically immune mission of the Republic of Newer Georgia.

The honor of being the first of the new company's specialty products, however, did not fall to Mr. Grimes. He'd spoiled and had to be discarded.

Fortunately many other applicants answered Harry Protagonist's ads for insomniacs. A goodly number of them were profitably fat.

Jerry Williamson and I hit it off from his very first phone call. We discussed fantasy-horror fiction, his books, and his projected anthologies. I have given him referrals to some authors from whom he was able to get stories where I had failed. In partial repayment for this largesse, I suppose, he gave me first crack at "Privacy Rights," a psychological thriller in touch with the best fiction around today.

PRIVACY RIGHTS

by J. N. Williamson

"All right, damn you, I'm coming, I'm coming!"

Irritably, Ann lifted her head to answer the children's collective complaints, and punched out her cigarette. She'd tried to keep the irascibility out of her voice, knowing she should really be used to it by now. Nearly four years of being a single parent ought to have taught her to expect a clamor or two before the four of them drifted off. But she'd wanted to leaf quietly through her scrapbook tonight—*needed* to—and tonight's round of demands for glasses of water and accusations leveled at one another was just too much.

What had made her swear at them was recognizing her latest failure and hearing her own irascible tone only two words into her reply.

One last time before standing, Ann glanced down at the yellowing newspaper clipping at the front of her scrapbook. Her hand trembled when she smoothed the page with her palm. "Gang Rape in Hollywood Hills," the headline screamed.

She heard Trudy cry "Ouch!"—or was it little Patrick?—and she was on her feet even before Cal or Lori could call "Mah-ummmm." *Mom is a one-syllable word,* she thought for the umpteenth time, fists doubled in frustration as she headed toward the bedroom. *I'm going to change my name to Louise, or—or Oscar!*

Little Patrick—Ann was sure, this time, it was the baby—began to sob. Loudly. It was his wounded-pride cry, easily differentiated from his familiar shriek of real pain. It was closely followed by the noise of a small hand slapping flesh, and a yelp, and a round of cautionary *"Shhhs."* Lori declared, in a great stage whisper, "I won't shut up, I *am* gonna tell." Then —it was clearly Cal's turn—"Mahh-ummmm!"

Then she thought she heard something shatter.

Ann stopped stock-still in the dimly lit hallway of the small house, midway between the front room and the children's room. Ann's room was straight across the hall, where she could always hear them if they needed her. If they ever *really* needed her. Right now, she could have cared less.

"I wish this old dump would go up in flames," she said at a pitch no greater than a whisper. "I just wish I'd wake up in the morning and find all four brats ashes—incinerated!"

Ann opened her eyes wide, unaware that they'd been tightly squeezed together, horrified by what she'd said. For one instant the narrow hallway seemed to close in on her, to pinch and elongate her and send her unfit mother's head and shoulders soaring up through the ceiling like Alice when she'd tasted a forbidden biscuit and turned Wonderland into Hell House. She felt huge and exposed, her unmotherly culpability naked before all of Los Angeles County.

"My *poor*, fatherless babies," she breathed, and rushed the rest of the way to their bedroom.

Tranquil, it was tranquil inside with them. The pair of double-decker bunk beds might have almost been empty, or the kids sound asleep, as Ann passed quietly through the nine-by-twelve darkness. How did children know the very *moment* you were going to enter their world; how could they subdue their anxiety or wounds, return so soundlessly to their individual beds, without a mother ever catching them in the act?

But, *what matters is that they are peaceful now*, Ann assured herself, stooping slightly to caress a soft and hairless cheek, then to reach on tiptoe to give a rough, good-humored shake to a tiny foot squirmed out from under the covers. *Maybe their fathers never will come to see them*, Ann mused, rumpling a third head. *But I'll always put them ahead of everything else.*

"What is it, Lori?" she inquired, response to a sleepy, nearly inaudible query. "Is Daddy coming for Christmas?" Tears welled, unbidden. "I don't know his plans, sweet princess, I'm sorry." Slowly, gracefully, she turned in an agonized circle, a mother's pirouette, to include all four of them in her explanation. "Honestly, I don't know if any of your fathers will be here for the holidays." Ann bit her lip.

Soft stirrings like angel's wings murmured from one of the lower bunks. Wanting to be cheerful, optimistic, Ann dropped to a perch on the mattress edge. "Darling little Patrick! You must be courageous, like your big brother Cal. I'm certain each of your fathers thinks of you quite often and loves you enormously! They are simply . . . busy . . ."

Busy with any women they could find! Suddenly she had to be away from there, from all the reminders they meant. And she was in the bedroom door in an infant's gasp, glad she had not switched on the overhead light. To steady herself, she lit a cigarette, inhaled deeply. "The Sleepytime Express is coming and you mustn't be late! Have your tickets ready— all 'board!'" She could not see their faces at all clearly in the gloom but knew each doleful expression better than she knew her own. "I try to be . . . enough . . . for you," she told them. "I wish that was all you needed. I'll *always* be here for you."

Ann eased the door shut behind her. Not all the way—both Trudy and little Patrick liked it left ajar because, like Ann, they were afraid of shadows and more terrified by the prospect of being alone. She'd tiptoed two or three paces away from their room when she heard Cal, brash Cal— second oldest—giggle. "You twerps," he sneered to the others. "They ain't ever comin' to see us. We're stuck with ol' Mom forever."

He's just like Mr. Washington, Ann thought furiously. *Each is just like the father, whether it's Mr. Ranzino, Mr. Uhl or Mr. Medford.* The word seemed to rise from the ripped wallpaper: *Ashes,* it came persistently. *Wish all of them were incinerated.*

Ann fled to her chair in the front room before the hallway walls began to squeeze and expose her again.

"Gang Rape," her eyes again scanned the headline. By now, she heard the horrifying words, the stigma, the accusation, as much as she read it. And the rest on that page: "Four Men Attack Pregnant Mother."

The type was so huge it had filled up most of the white page in the inexpensive paperbound scrapbook Ann had brought home from the drugstore. Pretending it was merely a newspaper story in the morning paper, a report about people she'd never met—humming tunelessly—Ann turned to the next page.

The remainder of the report was Scotch-taped over the two facing pages. *If,* Ann reflected, again, *I can ultimately read it as if it were fresh in the paper, I'll be fine, I'll be okay again.* Eyebrows intentionally arched in mock, offhand curiosity, she began afresh to read the faded words:

"Andrew Parkhill, 22, husband of the rape victim, apparently attempted to grapple with the four alleged perpetrators. His remains were found, partly mutilated, at the foot of a hill near Mulholland Drive and—"

"Dear me, dear me," Ann clucked, pretending to be mildly shocked. "Whatever is this old world coming to?"

While she continued to read, her fingers slipped beneath the page on the right side, ready to turn it—or to slam the scrapbook shut as she'd done so many times in the past. But her hand shook so violently she could no longer read the clippings and she withdrew it from the slender volume as calmly and nonchalantly as possible and went on reading.

"According to early reports from a reliable but anonymous source," the four-year-old article continued, "Mrs. Parkhill, 20, was on a maternity leave from her job. The Parkhill family doctor feared the consequences of an experimental fertility drug privately procured for the Parkhills by a medical technician of their acquaintance. Our source reported that the rape victim and her murdered husband are childless after two years of marriage. Mrs. Parkhill was enroute to—"

"Mahhhh-*uummmmmmm!*"

Startled, Ann jumped and the scrapbook flew from her lap and fell to the uncarpeted floor. Her temper flared at once. *Wake up . . . find them all incinerated . . .*

Spasming, furious at them and at herself, she didn't dare go back into that room then; not that minute. She heard another child's voice summoning her. Her head shot up and tears broke the dam of her full eyelashes. "Stop it—*now!" I will not scream or curse them, I won't.* "Do you *hear me,* Calvin? Lori? Stop that idiotic laughing and *talking* this *instant* before I *come in there and burnnnnnn!"*

Ann's hands raised to her mouth like winged, colorless birds scattering. She had to stifle the dreadful, horrible, unfor*gi*vable thing she'd almost shrieked at them. Afoot, she saw the front room begin to spin before she knew her eyes were once more open. When she braced herself on a three-legged table beside the couch, nearly knocking away the tower of old books that kept it and the crack-based lamp upright, her vision involuntarily *zoomed* in on all the defects around her—cruelly picked out and focused narrowly upon layers of dust cloaking most of the objects in the room, the broken-down lawn chair substituting for a genuine easy chair, an empty used record cabinet, the black-and-white ten-inch TV that no longer operated, even the contents of the front closet which Ann could see because its door gaped wide—her threadbare Good Will–acquired coat and nothing else . . . *nothing* else, not so much as *one* hat or coat for *any* of the four kids; and sure, this was L.A., certainly, it didn't get very cold—but winter was coming, sometimes it *was* chilly on the way home from school, she had to *do* something before—

Ann's frantic gaze dropped to the scrapbook open at her feet. It was as if the words in the old newspaper clippings rose to her by some terrible deceit of bitter dark magic: "She was enroute to Memorial General for tests to determine if a multiple birth was actually expected. Mrs. Parkhill was beaten and subsequently unable to answer questions—"

Ann shook her head, stared toward the front door, trying to remember when she'd last locked it. There was more in the clipping, not from that day's banner story but another in the ongoing nightmare of newspaper reportage. On the next page. Now Ann was undecided whether the children were truly going to sleep at last, if she dared to resume her reading, her therapy. "That's it, it's my therapy," Ann said aloud, nodding, beginning to bend down to retrieve her scrapbook.

"Ohhhhh! That *hurt,* Cal—that hurt real *bad!"*

Patrick, little Patrick—scarcely getting the moaning words out of his mouth. Only a mother might have understood them, he sounded in such agony. This was not the baby's wounded-pride cry, it was a real wail of pain!

"I'm coming, darling, Mom's coming," Ann shouted, spinning away from the one functioning chair and propped-up end table, lurching past the dilapidated couch and lawn chair and the TV with the unwatchful eye and into the hideous darkness of the corridor that separated her from her children.

But, *ashes,* something whispered as she left the front room; hot, smoldering, fleshy *ashes.* Ann halted, glanced desperately from left to right, shockingly cold now. Ahead, she saw, the hallway narrowed alarmingly; to her right, to her left, the peeling walls pulsed in a satirical impersonation of life. *Mom,* Patrick called abruptly, shockingly, the one word the most distinctly enunciated and peremptory Ann had ever heard. "I'm coming, baby," she shouted, and edged forward.

Then Cal snickered. A deep, surprising tenor, unlike the boy's customary treble giggle; it was filled with little-boy adenoids and snot, edged by some strain of anomalous maturity so remorselessly *purposive* that Ann staggered back a step. *All four of them,* the wall voice cooed, and Ann instinctively groped in her pocket for cigarettes and her lighter. "I smoke too damn much," she said aloud, once more heading forward into the shadowed corridor.

"Mom!" Patrick again. With great urgency. And the bedroom ahead, to her left, was otherwise silent, the door to it scarcely visible now because of the odd way the hallway had narrowed. *I can't get* inside, *Patrick,* Ann sent her thoughts out, growing frantic; *it's too small.* But she took a step—

Over here, gorgeous, Cal called, urging her forward. But when he swore and snickered a second time, Ann knew it wasn't Cal, her Cal. And the one who barked "Mom!"—that wasn't little Patrick, either! *Oh God*, Ann groaned in her anguish, *what's happening to my girls?*

Incinerated, answered the walls, and squeezed the woman violently between them. Before she was popped back into the room at the front of the house, before she understood it was too late, that it had always been too late for the children and for her, Ann saw the smoke curling from under the kids' door like something sentient, covert, *uncoiling* . . .

"Must go *help* them," Ann mumbled, finding her scrapbook in her lap, too dazed to know how it had gotten there. Turning her head, she saw the tumorous, tumbling smoke begin to roll into the front room with her. *I need a cigarette*, she thought, pawing the pockets of her dress—

Remembering that she'd left them in the children's bedroom.

"It's Definite: Rape Victim Expecting Multiple Birth," wailed the headline on the lefthand page of Ann's scrapbook. Accompanying the story was a grainy newspaper photograph of a very young, quite pregnant woman staring into the camera from a hospital bed. The eyes in the picture said she had no idea who or where she was, but they spoke of other, darker knowledge, they spoke for her affronted flesh. Behind Ann's chair now, lusty smoke shrouded the make-do furniture and fire that trickled on the floor like bloodied urination ran all over it, staining Ann's remnant world with flame.

Somewhere, the whooping of fire engines and yodels of police vehicles sounded, but Ann thought it was little Patrick, weeping, or maybe that clever Cal was merely trying to prolong the time when he must surely, inevitably sleep.

The old newspaper story on the right-hand page of the scrapbook was shorter. It read: "Pregnant Rape Victim Aborts Multiple Birth." There was a subheadline: "Ann Unable to Bear It." And another: "Four Healthy Fetuses Reported."

"—Mahhhhhhhhhmmmmmmmm! . . ."

"Be there in a moment, darlings." She snuggled deeper into her chair, absorbed by her clippings. "You know your mom will always be there for you."

At the end of the hallway, four children's beds burned quietly. Apart from the blankets, nothing, and no one, lay upon the charring white sheets. No one ever had.

There was time enough for Ann to turn to the last page and read the final clipping before flame nipped at a corner of the scrapbook and liked the taste:

LOS ANGELES—The Board of Supervisors Tuesday voted to bury 16,500 fetuses in a private mortuary, ending a three-year court battle between antiabortion and prochoice factions.

The fetuses were discovered in 1982 in a storage bin at the Woodland Hills home of a former medical laboratory director. The fetuses originally were to be turned over to the Catholic League for burial and ceremonies.

The American Civil Liberties Union filed suit to stop the burial and asked that incineration be performed to protect the privacy rights of mothers of the fetuses.

The ACLU won in the U.S. Supreme Court, and—

(Author's note: The final four paragraphs of this story were printed in Los Angeles newspapers, in fact. Courtesy of the Bee News Service.—JNW)

Although I purchased David's second story sale, by the time I got it into print he had almost had a career! That story (which waited four years in my files) appears below and was selected for one of Karl Edward Wagner's Year's Best books. David is the author of The Outer Limits: The Official Companion *as well as* The Kill Riff, *a lead horror title from Tor Books. He has also received* The Twilight Zone's *1985 Dimension Award for "Coming Soon to a Theatre near You."*

ONE FOR THE HORRORS

by David J. Schow

He recalled a half-column article that had said Stanley Kubrick postedited *A Clockwork Orange* by something like two-and-a-half minutes, mostly to deter jaded MPAA types from slapping it with an "X" rating, that probably would have murdered the film in 1971. It might have been consigned to art houses for eternity. Inconceivable.

Clay Colvin strolled through the theatre waiting-room with its yellowing posters of *Maitresse* and Fellini's *8-1/2*. Wobbly borax tables were laden with graying copies of *Film Quarterly* and *Variety* and *Take One* amid a scatter of the local *nouveau*-undergrounds—which, Clay thought, weren't really undergrounds anymore but "alternative press publications." More respectable; less daring, less innovative. Victims of progress in the same way this theatre differed from the big, hyperthyroid single-play houses with their $4.50 admissions.

Predictably, the wall was strewn with dog-eared lobby cards, one-sheets, and film schedules citing such theme-oriented programs as Utopian Directors, Oh-Cult and Modern Sex Impressionism. The front exit was a high-school-gym reject that had been painted over a dozen times or so, the color finally settling on a fingerprinty fire-engine red that also marred the tiny box window set into the door's center. Outside, worn stone-and-tile stairs spiraled beneath a pale metal canopy, down to the street and back into the world-proper.

Clay's wife of twenty-one years, Marissa, had died on October 17, 1976, about seventeen hours before his promotion to Western Division Sales Manager finally came through. It would have been the upward bump that would embellish their life together. Her reassurances that the position would be awarded to him "sometime soon" were devoted and unflagging; her belief in him was never half-hearted, not even when her hospital bills had become astronomical. Clay dined on soups and kept a stiff upper.

Guilt at her passing was the last thing Clay would allow himself, for Marissa would not have permitted it. What surprised him was the way he settled into a regimen during the next six months: 8-to-5 with overtime on each end, mail stop, and then filling the several hours hitherto devoted to the hospital stop. As substitutes, Clay either took work home, or went to a movie, or a bar, or tried a bit of television or a dollop of reading matter *(damned if you can't make fifty pages a night, old man,* he chided himself) prior to slumber in a bed realistically too big for a single person the likes of Clay Francis Colvin, Jr.

A birthday and a half later saw more impressive sales rosters and salary hikes for Clay. A bit more hair and vision lost. Unlike Marissa, his checking account had bounced back robustly. His new gold wire-rims were respectably costly. Comparatively frugal since Marissa's death, he splurged on a Mercedes and fought the cliché of a widower faced with the steep side of late middle age. Although he looked a bit rheumy-eyed in the mirror, he eventually concluded that he had been dealt to fairly.

It had been an unusually productive Wednesday, and upon spotting a Xerox place during his drive home, Clay pulled over to duplicate some documents he'd forgotten to copy at the office. From his cater-cornered viewpoint, the block consisted of the Xerox shop, flanked by a pair of health-food restaurants, a hole-in-the-wall tenspeed store, a pizzeria and a place called Just Another Bijou—it seemed that the business establishments on the periphery of the university district were the only places open after six o'clock. In the Xerox shop, a thumbtacked flyer caught Clay's eye. He scanned a list of features and discovered the theatre he had seen was referred to as J. A. Bijou's. The bill for the night highlighted Fredric March in *Death Takes A Holiday* and *Anthony Adverse,* the latter Clay knew to feature a neat Korngold score. He knew both films—of course—and the jump from Xerox shop and dull evening to the lobby of J. A. Bijou's was a short, easy one.

Clay enjoyed himself. More importantly, he came back to the theatre, and without his vested business suit.

What there was: Theatre-darkness and old cinema chairs of varied lineage and age, in wobbly rows, and comfortably broken-in. Loose floor boltings. The mustiness of old cushions; not offensive, but rather the enticing odor of a library well-stocked with worthwhile classics. Double-billed tidbits like *Casablanca* and *The Maltese Falcon* together, for once, or the semiannual Chaplin and Marx orgies. Clay favored Abbott and Costello; J. A. Bijou's obliged him. Homage programs to directors, to stars, and on one occasion to a composer (Bernard Herrmann). Also cartoon fests, reissues, incomprehensible foreign bits and the inevitable oddball sex-art flicks, which Clay avoided. But the oldies he loved and the better recent items insured his attendance. It was a crime not to plunk down two bucks—or $1.50 before six P.M.—to escape and enjoy, as Clay had done frequently in the five months between *Anthony Adverse* and tonight's offering, Kubrick, who had wound up in an art house, censors or no. Clay enjoyed himself—it was all he required of J. A. Bijou's. He never expected that anything would be required of him, nor did he expect to be blown away in quite the fashion everyone was during the following week.

Clay had an affection for Dwight Frye's bit parts, and Fritz in *Frankenstein* was one of his best. After Renfield, of course. It was opening night of a week's worth of Horror Classics, and Clay was in enthusiastic attendance. He, like most of the audience, would cop to a bit of overfamiliarization due to used-car screenings on the tube after midnight.

There were some unadvertised Fleischer Betty Boops and the normal profusion of trailers before the shadow-show commenced. *Frankenstein* had been the *Exorcist* of its heyday, evoking nausea and fainting and prompting bold warnings on screen and ominous lobby posters. Many houses in the 1930s offered battle-ready ambulances and cadres of medics with epsoms primed. Then came the obsessed censors, cleavers raised and hair-triggered to hack out nastiness . . . quite an uproar.

Soon after Colin Clive's historic crescendo of *"It's alive!"* filtered into J. A. Bijou's dusty green curtains, Clay's eyelids began a reluctant, semaphoric flutter. His late hours and his full workload were tolling expertly, and he soon dozed off during the film, snapping back to wakefulness at intervals. His memory filled in the brief gaps in plot as he roller-coastered from the blackness to the screen and back. It was a vaguely pleasing sensation, like accomplishing several tasks at once. Incredibly, he managed to sleep through the din of the torture scene and the Monster's leavetaking from the castle. He was wakened by a child's voice instead of noise and spectacle.

"Will you play with me?"

The voice of the girl—little Maria—chimed as she addressed the mute, lumbering Karloff. She handed him a daisy, then a bunch, and demonstrated that they floated on the surface of the pond by which they both sat.

"See how mine floats!"

Together the pair tossed blooms into the water, and for the first time a smile creased the Monster's face. Having expended all his daisies, he gestures and the girl walks innocently into his embrace. He hefts her by the arms and lofts her high and wide into the water. Her scream is interrupted by sickly bubbling.

Clay was fully awake now, jolted back in his seat by an image that was the essence of horror—the Monster groping confusedly toward the pond as it rippled heavily with death. There was something odd about the scene as well; the entire audience around Clay, veterans all, shifted uneasily. A more familiar tableau would soon have the girl's corpse outraging the stock villagers, but for now there was only the Monster and the horrible pond, on which the daisies still floated.

The scene shifted to Elizabeth in her wedding gown, and the crowd murmured. It had been a premiere, of sorts.

Clay dreamt peacefully. He became aware of impending consciousness as per his usual waking-up manner, a rush of images coming faster and faster and why not a pretty girl?

And up he sat. For the first time, he thought of the drowning scene in *Frankenstein*. Clay shook his head and rolled out of bed into the real world.

Next on the roster was *King Kong*.

The college kid who vended Clay's ticket that evening after work was gangly and bearded, his forehead mottled, as though by a pox. Five years ago, Clay would have dismissed him as a hippie; ten years, a queer. Now hippies did not exist and he regarded the gay community with a detached, laissez-faire attitude. He queued before the cramped snackbar to provision himself.

He had taken a dim view of the uninspired "remake" of the 1933 RKO Studio's *King Kong*—in fact, had avoided an opportunity to see it for free. The chance to again relish the original on a big screen was pleasant; in this one, unlike the new version, the only profiteering fame-grubbers were the characters on the screen.

Clay conjured various other joys of the original while conversing with the lobby-smokers: the glass-painted forests, the delightfully anachronistic dinosaurs of Skull Island. He was told that this was not a "butchered" print, that is, not lacking scenes previously excised by some overzealous moralist in a position of petty authority—shots of Kong jawing a squirming man in tight closeup, picking at Fay Wray's garments with the simian equivalent of eroticism, and a shot of Kong dropping a woman several stories to her death were all intact.

This time around, Clay was more palpably disturbed. He clearly recalled reading an article on *King Kong* concerning scenes that had never made it to the screen in the *first* place—not outtakes, or restorative footage, or Band-Aids over some editor's butchery—and among those were bits that were *now* streaming out of J. A. Bijou's projection booth.

Carl Denham's film crew was perched precariously atop a log bridge being shaken by an enraged King Kong. One by one, the marooned explorers plummeted, howling, into a crevasse and were set upon greedily by grotesque, truck-sized spiders. *It stopped the show,* the film's original producer had claimed, over forty-five years ago. It was enough justification to excerpt the whole scene; no audience had ever seen it, because it would have stopped the show.

It certainly does, thought an astonished Clay, as he watched the men crash to the slimy floor of the pit. Those who survived the killing fall confronted the fantastic black horrors; not only giant spiders but shuffling reptiles and chitinous scorpions the size of Bengal tigers. The audience sat, mouths agape.

New wonders of Skull Island manifested themselves: A triceratops with a brood of young, plodding along via stop-motion animation, and a bulky-horned mammal Clay later looked up in a paleontology text and found out it was an Arsinoittherium. Incredible.

"Where did you come across this print?" he questioned the bearded kid, with genuine awe. He was not alone. Fans, buffs, and *experts* had been drilling him since the beginning of the week, and the only answer he or the other staff could offer against the clamor was that they had nothing to do with it. The films came from the normal distribution houses, the secretaries of which were unable to fathom what the J. A. Bijou employees were babbling about, when they phoned long-distance—an expense just recently affordable. Word of mouth drew crowds faster than Free Booze or Meet Jesus signs, and the theatre's limited capacity was starting to show the strain of good business. No one else had ever seen these films. In all of history.

And instead of acting then, when he should have, Clay was content to sit, and be submissively amazed by the miracle.

Recently, two 1950s' science-fiction flicks had been shunted into a two-and-a-half hour timeslot on Sunday afternoon television. A quick check of a paperback TV-film book revealed their total running time to be 160 minutes. The local independent station not only edited the films to accommodate the inadequate time allotment, but shaved further in order to squeeze in another twenty minutes of used-car, rock-and-roll, pimple-killing, free-offer, furniture-warehouse, Veg-o-Matic madness per feature. Viewers were naturally pissed, but not pissed enough to lift their telephones. The following week boasted the singularly acrobatic feat of Tod Browning's *Dracula* corking a one-hour gap preceding a "Wild Kingdom" rerun.

Edited-for-Television notices always grated Clay's nerves when they intruded in video white across the bottom of his 24-inch screen. The J. A. Bijou wonderfulness was a kind of vengeance realized against the growly box; a warm, full-belly feeling. No one seemed to realize that the J. A. Bijou prints were also of first-rate, sterling caliber and clarity, lacking even a single ill-timed splice. They were all too stunned by the new footage. Justifiably.

Clay sat and viewed Fredric March again, but this time as Dr. Jekyll, mutating for the first time into the chunky fiend Hyde *without* the crucial potion—a scene never released, along with another sequence where Jekyll witnesses the bloody mauling of a songbird by a cat, a scene that serves as the catalyst for another gruesome transformation.

He watched a print of Murnau's premier vampire movie, *Nosferatu*— not the remake—clearly not from the 1922 pirate negatives; in short, an impossibility. Bram Stoker's widow had recognized Murnau's film as an unabashed plagiarism of her husband's novel, *Dracula,* and won the right in court to have all extant prints and negatives of *Nosferatu* destroyed. The film survived only because film pirates had already hoarded illegal prints, and it was from these less-than-perfect "originals" that all subsequent prints came. Yet what Clay watched was a crystal-sharp, first-generation original, right down to the title cards.

He saw Lon Chaney, Jr., as Lawrence Stewart Talbot, wrestling a cathedral-sized grizzly bear in *The Wolf Man.* Not the remake. He watched a version of *Invasion of the Body Snatchers* a full five minutes longer than normal. Not the remake.

He saw Janet Leigh's naked breasts bob wetly as she cowered through her butcher-knife finish in an incarnation of Hitchcock's *Psycho* that was one whole reel more complete. He wondered idly when they would get around to grinding out a tacky remake of *this* classic as well, before he actually thought about it and realized that second-rate producers had been trying and failing for years.

The blanket denials by the film outlet that had shipped the entire festival as a package deal were amusing to hear, as related by J. A. Bijou's staff. The most the tinny voices from LA would concede was that *maybe* the films had come out of the wrong vault. That other phone calls were being made to them, along with lengthy and excited letters, was undeniable.

This expanding miracle had hefted an unspoken weight from Clay's shoulders. It was overjoy, giddiness, a smattering of cotton-candied jubilation, a reappearance of fun in his life, sheer and undeniable. A shrink would delve so far beyond this simple idea that Clay would become certifiable; so, no shrinks. Accept the fun, the favor.

The "favor" of J. A. Bijou's was, Clay reasoned, repayment to him, personally, for his basic faith in the films—a faith that endured the years, and that he allowed to resurface when given an opportunity. This made sense to him, though he did not totally comprehend the *why*, yet. He did toy with the phrasing, concocting impressive verbiage to explain away the phenomena, but he always looped back around to the simplicity of his love for the films. He was one with the loose, intimate brotherhood that would remain forever unintroduced, but who would engage any handy stranger in a friendly swap of film trivia.

He felt that, despite his happiness, the picture was still incomplete. The miracle of the films he was viewing was a kind of given. *Given A, B then follows* . . . He discussed his idea with other (unintroduced) J. A. Bijou regulars. Had anyone the power to inform him of the turn of events to follow, Clay would have thought them as whacko as his imaginary psychiatrist would have diagnosed him. If he had told anyone. He didn't.

The projection booth of J. A. Bijou's was a cluttered, hot closet tightly housing two gargantuan, floor-mounted 35 mm. projectors and a smaller 16mm. rig, along with an editing/winding table and a refugee barstool. Knickknacks of film equipment were jumbled together on tiers of floor-to-ceiling shelving. Homemade egg-carton soundproofing coated the interior walls, throwing soft green shadows under a dim work light. The windows were opaqued with paint and the floors were grimy. A large cardboard box squatted to receive refuse film just beneath a rack on which hung the horribly over-used Coming Attractions strips that got spliced hundreds of times per month, it seemed.

J. A. Bijou's air-conditioning system was almost as old as the vintage brownstone that housed the theatre. The first time it gave up the ghost was during the mid-Thursday afternoon showing of *Psycho*, just as Vera Miles began poking about the infamous Bates mansion. There was a hideous shriek as metal chewed rudely into metal, followed by a sharp spinning that wound down with a broken wagon-wheel clunk. The audience nearly went through the ceiling, and afterward everyone laughed about the occurrence as things were makeshifted back to order.

The insulation on the cooler's motor held out until Friday night, for the benefit of the overflow audience. The years of humidity and coppery, wet decay had been inexorable. The engine sparked and shorted out, fuses blew, and as the blades spun down a second time, the theatre filled up with acrid electrical smoke, from the vents.

Gray smoke wafted dreamily around near the ceiling as the exits were flung open. A few moved toward the fresher air, but most kept stubbornly to their prize seats, waiting.

In the darkness of the booth, the projectionist had concluded that a melted hunk of old film might be jamming the film gate, and was leaning over to inspect it when the lights went out. Sitting in the dark, he groped out for his Cinzano ashtray and butted his Camel as a precaution against mishaps in the dark.

It did not do any good.

When the cardboard film bin later puffed into flames, the projectionist had temporarily abandoned the booth in search of a flashlight. The preview strips quickly blackened, curled, and finally ignited, snaking fire up to the low ceiling of the booth. The egg cartons blossomed a dry orange. The wooden shelves became fat kindling as the roomful of celluloid and plastic flared and caused weird patterns of light to coruscate through the painted glass. It took less than thirty seconds for the people sitting in front of the booth to notice it, dismiss it, and finally check again to verify.

The projectionist raced back. When he yanked open the door, the heat blew him flatly on his ass. People were already panicking toward exits; Clay rose from his seat and saw.

The bearded kid had already scurried to the pizzeria to trip the local fire alarm. Nobody helped the projectionist. The sudden chaos of the entire scene remained as a snapshot image in Clay's mind as he rapidly located a fire extinguisher, tore it from its wall-mount, and hurried to the booth. A crackerbox window blew outward and fire licked out of the opening, charring the wall and lighting up the auditorium.

Only slightly dazed, the projectionist was up and had one foot wedged over the threshold of the booth entrance, but the sheer heat buffeted him back as he exhausted his own tiny CO_2 canister. He yelled something unintelligible into the fire, then he stepped back, fire-blind and nose-to-nose with Clay, shouting for him to get out.

Clay haltingly approached the gaping doorway and nozzled his larger extinguisher into the conflagrant oven. A better inferno could not have been precipitated if the Monster himself had tipped an ancient oil-lamp into dry straw. Clay's effort reduced the doorway to smoke and sizzle, and he stepped up in order to get a better aim on the first projector, which was swathed in flames. He took another excruciating step inside.

The Monster, having tried his misunderstood best, always got immolated by the final reel. Friday night's screening of *Psycho* keynoted the close of the horror classics festival at J. A. Bijou's. Clay understood, as he moved closer to the flaming equipment and films. It would not hurt much.

Above the booth, a termite-ridden beam exploded into hot splinters and smashed down through the ceiling of the booth, showering barbecue sparks and splitting the tiny room open like a peach crate. It was a support beam, huge, weighty and as old as the brownstone, and it impacted heavily, crushing the barstool, collapsing the metal film racks and wiping out the doorway of the booth.

It was a perfect in-character finish, complemented by the welling sound of approaching sirens.

One of the health food places threatened a lawsuit after the fire marshal had done *his* job—J. A. Bijou's had been unsafe all along, etcetera. Negligence, they claimed.

The festival package of films was gone, gone to scorched shipment cans and puddles of ugly black plasma. When the projection booth died, so did they, even though they were being stored at the theatre manager's house for safekeeping. They had been, after all, perfect prints, and the door-locks at J. A. Bijou's had not yet been updated against a particular kind of desperate collector.

Now the new sprinkler and air-conditioning systems were in. The new projection booth was painted and inspected; the new equipment, spotless and smelling of lubricant. J. A. Bijou's insurance, plus the quick upsurge in income, sparked financial backing sufficient to cause its rebirth in time for the following semester at the university.

With the new goods in place and all tempers balmed, the projectionist's somewhat passionate tale of an unidentified customer supposed to have died in the blaze was quickly forgotten or attributed to his excited state during the crisis. He steadfastly insisted that he had witnessed a death, and maintained his original story without deviation despite the fact that no corpse or suggestion of a corpse had ever been uncovered in the wreckage. No one had turned up tearfully seeking dead relatives.

But no one could explain about the films, either. And from opening night onward, none of the J. A. Bijou staffers bothered to consider why, on full-house nights (weekends, for the college crowd), the ticket count always came up two seats short. Nor could they give a solid, rational reason explaining why J. A. Bijou's was the sole theatre—in the universe, apparently—that regularly featured peculiar, never-before-seen cinema gems. The phone voices still had no answers.

The bearded kid suggested that J. A. Bijou's had a guardian spirit.

Clay relished the cool anonymity of the darkened theatre. As always, the crowds were friendly, but unintroduced. The film bond held them together satisfactorily without commitment. He had been cussing/discussing the so-called *auteur* theory with a trio of engineering majors seated behind him, when the house lights dimmed. You never learned their names.

The first feature was *The Man Who Would Be King*, starring Humphrey Bogart and Clark Gable. Clay had not decided what the second feature would be, yet.

Marissa returned, with the popcorn, as the trailers commenced.

I gained Lucius Shepard's friendship via the equivalent of an Androcles and the Lion story. Suffice it to say my lion is one of the fantasy and science fiction field's major "new" talents. I have to thank my friendship with the Jewish lion, Jack Dann, for bringing this stark haunting my way.

THE BLACK CLAY BOY

by Lucius Shepard

They'd robbed her of her life, sucked out the middles of her joy like marrow-eating ghouls. Memories she had, but they'd drained them of juice and left the husks stuck in her head like dead flies in a web. Left her bitter and dotty, an old cracked hag fit for taunting by the neighborhood children.

Take those Kandell boys.

Always traipsing across her lawn and peeing their initials in the snow-crust, shaking their tiny pale things at her as if the sight would do an injury. There they were now, sneaking up to the house, clumping onto the porch. A piece of notebook paper scrawled with a kid's crooked letters was slipped under the door. Hanging onto the knob for balance, teetering, Willa picked it up and read: "Old lady Selkie is a fuking bitch!"

She snatched open the door and saw them humping toward the fence, two blue-coated, wool-hatted dwarfs sinking to their knees in the snow. "You got that right," she squalled. "Fucking with a C!" Yelling took the wind out of her, and she stood trembling, her breath steaming in ragged white puffs, her eyes tearing.

The Kandells stopped at the fence-line, and one gave her the finger.

"I see you back there," she shrilled, "I'll go down in my cellar and make me a Black Clay Boy. Jab pins in its eyes, and prick you blind!"

Now where the hell had she gotten that idea? A Black Clay Boy? Some senile trick of broken thoughts happening right for once. Well, maybe she *could* hex 'em. Maybe she'd shriveled up that pure and mean.

She shut the door, leaned against it, her heart faltering. The next second, a snowball splintered one of the side windows, spraying sparkles of glass and ice over her new sofa. She was too weak to shout again.

Smelly little shits!

A Black Clay Boy might be just the ticket, she thought. Might scare 'em. They'd run to their mommy, their father would come over to have a serious talk. She'd pretend to be a tired and desperate old woman, scared to death of his vicious brood.

No need to pretend, Willa.

Muttering under her breath, she hobbled down to the cellar, and with popping joints and many a gasp, she troweled a bucketful of the rich black bottomland that did for a floor. Then she lugged the bucket upstairs to the kitchen and set it on the table. The kitchen whined, buzzed and hummed with the workings of small appliances and the electric motor inside the cold box . . . or could be the hum was the sound of her mind winding tight, getting ready to spew out shattered gears and sprung coils.

The wall clock ticked loud and hollow like someone clucking her tongue over and over.

Willa made the Boy's torso first, patting a lump of clay into a fat black lozenge. She added tubular arms and legs, rolling them into shape between her palms the way she did with dough before flattening it into a crust. Finally she added a featureless oval head. The whole thing was about two and a half feet long, and it reminded her of those shapes left by frightened men crashing through doors in the Saturday morning cartoons. Black crumbs of it were scattered like dead bugs on the white Formica. She reached into her apron pocket for a pincushion and . . . Steam vented from the teakettle with a shriek, stopping Willa's heart for a dizzy split-second.

Oh, God! Now she'd have to get up again.

It took her three tries to heave out of the chair. Sweat broke on her forehead, and she stood panting for almost a minute. Once she'd regained her breath, she crossed to the stove and shut off the flame. She kept a hand on the stove, stretched out the other hand to catch the edge of the table for balance, and hauled herself back across. She dropped heavily into the chair and nearly slipped off the edge.

One day soon she'd do that and fracture her damn spine.

She plucked a pin from the pincushion, and, hoping to hear a distant scream, she shoved it into the Boy's face. Pressed it home until the pinhead was flush with the clay, a tiny silver eye. It shimmered and seemed to expand. She blinked, denying the sight. It expanded again. Somehow it didn't resemble an eye any longer. More of a silver droplet, a silver bead. Her memories would be that way, she thought. Hardened into pearls. The bead melted at the edges, puddling outward like mercury (*Don't tell me I need glasses!*), and a memory began to unfold.

It was rich, clear, and full of juice.

"Oh, God!" she said. "It's a miracle."

The recollection rolled out from fifty years ago, during her marriage to Eden McClaren, the wealthiest citizen of Lyman, Ohio. She hadn't wanted to marry him. He was old, fiftyish, and even older in spirit, a dried-up coupon-counter. But her father had persuaded her. *Man's so rich he builds his house on the finest piece of bottomland in the state,* he'd said. *You won't do any better than a man who can afford to waste land like that. Marry him, marry him, marry him.* And her mother, who'd had her doubts, what with Eden being an atheist, had eventually chimed in, *Marry him, marry him, marry him.*

What was an eighteen-year-old girl to do?

Eden courted her in a manner both civil and distant. He'd sit on the opposite end of the porch swing, as far from her as possible, gazing out at the hedge, and say, "I'm quite taken with you, girl."

She would stare at her clasped hands, watching her fingers strain and twist, wishing he'd blow away in a puff of smoke. "Thank you," she'd say.

After their wedding supper of overdone beef and potatoes and stale bread pudding, he sat her down and informed her that she would have to perform her wifely duty once a week. More would fray the moral fiber, and less would be unsalubrious. Then he took her upstairs and deflowered her in a perfunctory fashion, propping himself above her, thrusting in and out, maintaining a rhythm of one, two, one, two, regular as a metronome, until he sighed and gave a quiver and rolled off, leaving her with a fair degree of pain and no pleasure, wondering why people made such a fuss over sex.

But she knew why.

Knew it in her heart, her loins.

She wanted a lover like lightning who'd split her wide open and leave her smoldering. And if Eden couldn't give her that pleasure, she'd pleasure herself. She'd done it a few times before, despite her mother's depiction of the horrid consequences. She didn't care about the consequences. But she had been frightened by having so much pleasure without someone to hold onto afterward, and so she decided to do it in front of the full-length mirror in her bedroom. That way at least she'd have her reflection for company.

She stripped and posed before the mirror. She was a beauty, though she'd never understand how beautiful. Red hair, green eyes, milky skin. Pretty breasts tipped with pink candy, and long legs columning up to that curly red patch a shade lighter than the hair on her head. She cupped the undersides of her breasts, thumbed the nipples hard, and ran her palms down her hips, her flanks. Then she touched the place, already slippery and open to its hooded secret. Her knees buckled, weakness spread through her, and she hung onto the corner post of the mirror stand to keep her feet. Her eyelids fluttered down, her breath came harsh. She forced herself to hold her eyes wide, wanting to see what happened to her face when the pleasure started to take. Her cries fogged the mirror, and her mouth twisted, and her eyes tried to close, tried to squeeze in all that good feeling, and . . .

"Slut!" Eden shouted from the door. "Bitch!"

Despite his rage, he seemed to have enjoyed her show. His face was flushed, his crotch tented.

"I'll not have it!" he said. "I'll not have you trailing your slime . . . your filth. Fouling my house!"

For the next three days he railed at her, and on the afternoon of the third day he suffered a coronary, and was confined to bed by Dr. Malloy, who tsk-tsked, and warned her to prepare for the worst.

"Curse you!" Eden said when she went into his room. As weak as he was, he warped his mouth into a frown and spat out, "Curse you!"

She wondered then what sort of curse a godless man could lay, but later she concluded it must have been one of rules and joyless limits.

They buried Eden in a corner of the bottomland. In a dream she saw his bones floating in blackness like the strange money of a savage isle. And from that dream she knew him more than she ever had. She followed the track of his blue-faced primitive ancestors with their bone knives and their terrified little gods hiding in the treetops, and she trod the rain-slick stones of Glasgow town, where black-suited Calvinists screwed their souls into twists, and she crossed the great water with a prissy man of God and his widow-to-be, watched their children breed the bloodline thin and down to this miserable cramped sputter of a soul, this mysteryless little man, sad birthright of the clan.

Scratch one McClaren, sound the horn.

Willa wanted to sell the bottomland and move to the city. She wanted to live free, to kick up her heels, to have life take her in its arms and then to a nice restaurant and maybe afterward to a hotel. What harm could come of that? Twenty-two, and she'd never had any fun.

Sell the bottomland? her family said. *That'd be like selling Plymouth*

Rock! Bottomland's something you hang on to, something you cherish. We won't let you do it.

And they didn't.

She did Eden widow's service for a year, and for a year after that she hardly set foot off the land. One day her high school friend Ellie Shane came to visit and said, "Willa, there's gonna be a party Friday at the old Hoskins place." She glanced left and right as if to defeat the wiles of eavesdroppers. "Gonna be college men and coupla businessmen from Chicago . . . and every one's a looker. You gotta come."

Willa couldn't say no.

This was in October, the air crisp, the leaves full turned. Bright lights sprayed from the windows of the old house, outshining the moon, and inside couples danced and groped and sought out empty rooms. Willa's man was lean and dark. He had a sharp chin and the Devil's toothy white grin, and he carried a silver pint flask that he kept forcing on her. She saw his thoughts working . . . He'd get this townie ripped, slip it to her quick and leave her spinning. But Willa passed on the liquor. He'd read law at Michigan, he said, but had left school to run his father's *nationwide* trucking firm. He tried all night to impress her with his money, never knowing he didn't have to try, that it wasn't his money she wanted. He guided her out onto the porch. A blond man was sitting with a girl on a bottomed-out sofa there, his hand hunching up under her skirt, a rat-sized creature looking for its burrow. Willa stood by the porch rail, gazing at the moon-dappled woods. Her man hemmed her in against the rail, moved in for a kiss. Willa slipped away and went halfway down the steps.

"My kisses are for my husband," she said. "But all the rest is yours." And with that she skipped down from the steps and ran into the woods.

She found an old oak with gnarly bark and a lightning scar, and leaned against it. Moonlight streamed through the webbed branches, illuminating the red and yellow leaves . . . Wind seethed through them, and they looked to be shaking in separate dances, red and yellow spearpoints of flame. She undid the top two buttons of her blouse and touched the slope of her right breast. God! The chill of that touch went through her like something sharp and silver. She undid a third button. The wind coiled inside the blouse, fondling her. She lifted her skirt, skinned down her panties and flung them behind the oak. She could feel herself moist and open. The man's footsteps crunched in the dead leaves. He peered into the shadows, his mouth set grim. Probably angry at her, thinking her a tease. He spotted her and came forward at a slow pace. Dark head, gleaming eyes. When he saw that she had unbuttoned the blouse, he walked faster. Stopped and tipped back the flask. His Adam's apple bobbed twice. He tossed the flask away and reached inside her blouse. His hands moved over her breasts, squeezing, molding, knowing their white rounds from every angle. "Christ," he said. "Oh, Christ." She closed her eyes and arched to his pressure. Moonlight penetrated her lids. After a few seconds she pushed him off and hiked up her skirt.

The man swallowed hard at the sight, made a soft noise deep in his throat. He tore at his buckle, ripped down his zipper, sprung out at her, a needle seeking its pole. He lifted her the necessary inch, settled into place and plunged into her. She threw her arms back around the oak trunk, dug in with her fingers. Rough bark scraped her buttocks, but even the pain was good. He battered at her. The leaves hissed, the limbs shook, and a vibration went through the oak, as if what was going on between Willa and the man were threatening to uproot it. "Go slow," she said, the words pushed out hoarse by a thrust. "Slow, slow." That made him treat her too gently, and she told him how she needed it to build, guiding his moves. "There," she said. "There . . . like that." And even before her pleasure came, she cried out just for the joy of finally having a man hot and urgent inside her.

Afterward she went back to the party and paid no attention to him. He couldn't understand her, and his lack of understanding anointed her a mystery. He trailed her around, saying he had to see her again, he'd fly her to Chicago. Willa could have owned him, married him and secured her future. But she had lights dancing in the miles of her eyes, and she wasn't worried about the future.

More's the pity, Willa.

Ah, God, Willa thought. Why hadn't they let her live? That part of her, that need, it was nothing sinful. How could they have wanted to be with her and not accept her all in all? She shook her head, ruing the wasted years, then glanced at the Black Clay Boy.

Was it her imagination, or was he quivering a little, as if he'd been trying to roll himself off the table?

Calm yourself, Willa . . . that's just the trembling of your head on its feeble stalk of a neck.

The Boy's silver dot eye stared up at her. Hmm, Willa said to herself. Wonder what'd happen if I give him another. She plucked out a second pin and rammed it home.

The pinhead shimmered, began to expand into a memory.

"Lord Almighty," said Willa. "I can do magic."

After that night at the Hoskins place, Willa cut a wild track through the tame fields of Ohio possibility. Roadhouses knew her, hotels took messages for her, and midnight dirt roads where nobody drove echoed to her backseat music. Rumors smoked up from her footprints, and the word went around that while she wouldn't kiss you, you just hadn't lived till Willa McClaren doctored your Charlie. The people of Lyman scandalized her name. That Willa, they said, she wasn't never nothin' more than hips and a hole, and I hear it was her evil needs what put ol' Eden in the ground. Willa didn't care what they said. She was having her life in sweet spasms, and for now that was enough. When the time was right, she'd settle down.

Tom Selkie, a supervisor at the seat-belt factory over in Danton, knew Willa's reputation and asked her out to get himself a sample of that real fine Charlie-doctoring. That was all Willa'd had mind, but in the back of Tom's Packard they experienced one of those intoxicating mistakes that people often confuse for love, and Willa let him kiss her. His tongue darted into her mouth, and though she liked how that felt, it startled her more than some.

"What's the matter?" Tom asked, and Willa blushed and said, "Me and Eden never did it with tongues."

Well, knowing this innocence in her made Tom feel twice a man, and he asked her straight off to marry. "Yes," said Willa, confident that fate had finally done her a turn by giving her both a good man and the Power of True Romance. But True Romance lasted a matter of weeks. Tom kissed better than he tickled, so to speak, and was more interested in drinking with the boys after work than in getting prone and lowdown with Willa. When she tried to awaken his interest, he rejected her; his rejections grew more and more blunt, until at last he suggested that something must be wrong with her, that her needs were unnatural. Bored with marriage and having little else to engage her, she got pregnant with her firstborn, Annie. The year after Annie, she bore a son. Tom, Too, his proud dad called him. The kids grew, Tom's belly sagged, and life just dragged along.

It was at the age of thirty-six that Willa next had Big Fun. She left the kids with Tom and caught the train to Cleveland to talk with a broker about some stock Eden had hidden under the fireplace bricks. On the train she struck up a conversation with Alvah Medly, a pricey hooker with silkburns on her hips and fingers prone to breaking under the weight of her many diamonds. She was a big sleepy cat of a woman, her languid gestures leading Willa to believe she had syrup instead of marrow in her bones. Voluptuous to the point that it seemed an ounce more weight would cause everything to slump and decay. She had long black hair and big chest problems and a rear end just made for easy motion. But she was no finer a looker than Willa, who had held on to beauty and could still pass for her twenty-two-year old self.

Willa was curious about Alvah's fancyhouse life and asked dozens of questions, and Alvah, perhaps sensing something more than mere curiosity, said, "Honey, if you wanna know all about it, whyn't you give it a whirl?"

Willa was flabbergasted. "Uh," she said, "well . . ." And then, finding refuge in the dull majority of her life, added, "I'm married."

"Married!" Alvah said the word like it was something you'd scrape off your shoe. "Everybody's been married." She inhaled from a slim black cigar and blew a smoke ring that floated up to the corner of the compartment and spelled out a lie. "The life ain't nothin' but one long lazy lack of limitations."

The train rattled as it went over a crossing, and everything inside Willa's head rattled. Could what Alvah was saying be true? The whole vital world was barreling east, shaking side to side, and blasting out its warning to the sexless villages of the heartland.

"You come on over to Mrs. Gacey's tonight," said Alvah, "and I bet she'll give you a try."

"I don't know," said Willa distractedly.

" 'Course you don't, honey," said Alvah. "How you gonna know 'less you explore the potentials?" She chuckled, "And believe you me, there's some mighty big potentials come through the door of Mrs. Gacey's."

Willa couldn't think of anything to say. Her mind was miles ahead in Cleveland, in a room with a dark and faceless stranger.

"You come on over," said Alvah. "Mrs. Gacey'll fix you up with a room and a trick or two."

"Well," said Willa hesitantly. "Maybe . . . maybe just one."

That night she lay amid perfume and shadow on a harem bed draped in filmy curtains, wearing a scrap of silk and a few of Alvah's spare jewels. The door opened, and a gray-haired monument of a man walked in. His face had a craggy nobility that looked as if it should be printed on money. Willa was tense, but when she saw how the man stared . . . Oh, she could almost see how she appeared to him. A red-haired, green-eyed bewitchment with her silk pushed up to reveal a hint of that down-pointed curly patch of fire between her thighs. The man parted the curtain and sat on the edge of the bed, drinking her in.

"Good evenin'," he said.

"Evenin'," said Willa, a little confused. She hadn't thought she'd have to talk.

"Now where in the world did Mrs. Gacey find a girl like you?" asked the man.

"Lyman," said Willa.

"Lyman." The man loosened his tie and seemed to be trying to locate the place in some interior atlas.

"It's near Danton . . . that's the Winton County seat."

"Ah, yes. I carried Winton three to one."

"Whatcha mean you carried it?"

The man looked at her askance. "You don't recognize me?"

"No," said Willa. "You famous or somethin'?"

"I'm the governor," said the man, unbuttoning his shirt.

"You *are?* I voted for you!"

The man unbuckled his belt and smiled a warm professional smile. "I trust your enthusiasm for my candidacy has remained undimmed."

Willa enjoyed her evening with the governor. It gave her a chance to try some things that Eden and Tom had considered either unnatural or unmanning. But there was a distance to this kind of passion that didn't appeal to her, and when Alvah came in to find out how things had gone, she told her she didn't think she had the stuff it took for the life.

"Oh, you got what it takes, honey," said Alvah, sitting beside her. "You just don't know it."

Her robe had fallen partway open, and the globes of her breasts were visible, marble-white and moon-smooth. Looking at them, Willa suddenly perceived in Alvah a kind of sad blankness, as if a greater sadness had been erased or paved over, and she felt a wave of affection for this sculpture of a woman. And maybe her affection washed across the space between them, because Alvah put a hand on Willa's stomach and caressed its curve, resting it on her upper thigh. One of her fingertips brushed the margin of Willa's curly hair.

"You're so beautiful," said Alvah, her voice a tongue of shadow in that perfumed place.

There was a squirmy feeling in Willa's stomach, and she was a bit scared . . . but not scared enough to ask Alvah to take her hand away. "You're prettier than me," she said meekly, entranced by the desire in Alvah's face and by an anticipation of forbidden fruit.

Alvah eased her hand an inch south and down between. "No, honey," she said. "It's you, it's you."

Willa tried not to respond, but she could feel her pulse tapping out the message, "Yes, I will," against Alvah's fingertip.

"Please," whispered Alvah, and that word was a little wind that went everywhere through Willa, that told her a thousand things no one had ever troubled to tell her, that elevated her to something perfect and needed, that showed Alvah's need to be as strong and unalloyed as her own. *Please, please.* The word lowered over her like a veil, like the veil of Alvah's black hair fanning across her stomach, curtaining her off from the moral precincts of Lyman and her marriage. Willa wouldn't have believed a woman could make her burn, and true, it felt strange to be loved and not have a body covering her upper half, but Alvah's kisses and touches gave a tenderness to pleasure that she had never known from a man's rough bark. And though Willa had dreaded the idea of doing to Alvah what Alvah had done for her, though she set to it out of duty not desire, she came to desire. It seemed she had entered some Arab kingdom of musk and honey, some secret temple where a new god basked in its own heat, and when Alvah's white stomach quaked and her thighs clamped tight, Willa knew for the first time what it was to have the power and pleasure of a man.

For six years thereafter Willa guest-starred at Mrs. Gacey's and passed the idle hours in Alvah's arms. Eden's stocks had proved worthless, but Willa's one-trick-stands gave her the profit required to justify her Cleveland weekends to Tom, and she let him think that the stocks were the source of this extra money. Her relationship to Alvah was the closest thing to love she had ever known, soft and slow and undemanding, and she would have told far greater lies to maintain it. But all good things must come to an end, or such was the regulation of Eden's curse. When Tom got fired from the seat-belt factory *(Woman, don't you even think 'bout sellin' that bottomland!)*, Willa was forced to take a job, and her weekends were no longer her own.

The memory evaporated, and Willa pinched up a nose from the Black Clay Boy's face. His chest rose and fell rapidly, and breath whined through his tiny nostrils. But no new memory breathed from him. She gouged out a mouth and listened hard. Heard a noise that brought to mind those lumps of sadness often disgorged from her own chest. But maybe that was his first word, because the noise opened just like the widening of a silver eye into a world as fresh as yesterday.

"What's happening?" Willa asked, becoming terrified now of magic and miracles.

The kitchen ticked and buzzed, and the Black Clay Boy lay silent. But Willa thought this absence was an answer all the same.

Willa waited tables at O. V. Lindley's Dirtline Cafe, its name deriving from the line of dirt that showed on the wrists of the farm boys who ate there when they took off their work gloves. They would come in drunk and sit swaying at the counter, pawing and teasing Willa, plugging the leaks in their souls with quarters'-worths of country and western philosophy from the glowing sage of the jukebox. She searched among them for a lover, but found no one of the proper measure. Sometimes she would go into the john on her break, skin down her panties, sit on the toilet, and remember Alvah, her hand moving between her legs. Sweat would pour off her, and she would bite back her cry. But even so they caught her on occasion and would offer to help scratch her itch.

"What I got right here," she'd say, holding up her hand, "can do the job a damn sight better than any one of you."

And because she was still beautiful, they worried that she might be right.

Three years of this.

Time seemed to speed up, to turn a corner on an entire era and accelerate into an unfamiliar country, a place without hope or virtue. Before Willa knew it, she was wrapped in a web of trouble so intricate and thick that her own needs were suffocated. First, Annie—herself a redhead and possessing a streak of Willa's wildness—got pregnant by an unknown agency, her teen-age stomach stretched by a baby boy who weighed fourteen pounds on delivery, and whom she was dissuaded from naming Nomad. Bruce, her second choice, was deemed acceptable. Willa went through Annie's high school yearbook, looking for Bruces. Found two. One deceased, one long departed. After giving birth, Annie took to her room and would pass the days listening to vapid love songs on the radio and gazing out the window, leaving Willa to care for the infant. She spooned jar after jar of purée into its mouth, watching it pale and fatten under the harsh kitchen lights, wondering if this monster child might not be the ultimate credential of the efficacy of Eden's curse. She had begun to believe in the curse, that Eden had breathed some vileness out with the words that enveloped her like an aura and restricted her life—all her pleasures seemed to run a minimal course and span that accorded with Eden's notions of moderation.

Tom developed cancer *(Don't sell the bottomland)*, and Tom, Too took something that caused him to vomit blood and avoid mirrors for almost a month. Not long thereafter he ran away from home. Willa found a note on his pillow confessing that he was Bruce's father. From his bed of pain, Tom shouted that all this was the fault of Willa's abnormal sexual urges, and while she did not accept his reasoning, she knew it was her fault in that she had not entered motherhood with love but out of boredom. Four years after his departure, Tom, Too returned, a convert to that mean, squinty-eyed form of Christianty that everywhere spies out its enemies. He begged forgiveness and received his father's blessing. The two of them would go bowling on Wednesday nights and walk home along the river, discussing philosophy (his brush with cancer had provided Tom with the insight that We Are Everyone of Us All Alone) and real estate (Tom, Too's chosen profession). Annie had moved with Bruce into a newly built garage apartment, and Tom, Too would visit them frequently, proclaiming that the boy needed a dad. One night Willa saw him coming down Annie's stairs long after the lights had been switched off. Two weeks later, following a whirlwind courtship, Annie married a fishing-tackle salesman and moved to Akron, vowing never to set foot in Lyman again.

Willa turned fifty-one.

Amazingly she looked to be in her early thirties, an age not without a hint of maturity yet nonetheless appealing. However, there was no one in sight who might respond to her appeal, and hoping to subsume her desires in spiritual pursuits, she began attending church with Tom and Tom, Too. And, lo, her faith was rewarded. The new pastor, the Reverend Robert Meister, was a ruggedly handsome man of thirty-five, with piercing blue eyes and a virile physique. A heavenly hunk. But his most attractive feature was his bachelorhood. Willa noticed the tension that flooded his face when he talked to the young girls after services, when they stuck out their gloved hands for him to shake. The poor man, she thought, imagining his solitary bouts of guilt-ridden self-abuse in a dark rectory bedroom. He didn't look at her the way he looked at the young girls, but she determined that one day soon he would.

With a fervor that even drew grudging praise from Tom, Too, who had become the family's spiritual drill sergeant, Willa threw herself into church work. Nothing was too inconsequential for her attentions. She served on the Ladies' Auxiliary, she taught Sunday School, she organized fund raisers and baked truckloads of cakes and cookies, all the while carrying on a flirtation with the Reverend, contriving to brush against him, touching his hand in conversation, gradually making him aware of her fundamental charms. And when the Reverend timorously suggested that she accompany him to a church conference on famine in New York, Willa knew that paydirt was near.

But two days passed at the conference, and the Reverend had yet to make his play. At last Willa contrived a trap. She ordered from room service, went to take a shower, and called out to the Reverend—who had at least been sufficiently bold to reserve adjoining rooms—asking him to answer her door when her order arrived. Then when she heard the waiter close the door behind him, heard the Reverend wrestling with the food cart, she walked buff naked into the room, affecting surprise that he was still there. The Reverend's jaw went slack, his eyes bugged, and turning back to the bathroom, Willa gave him a full view of her pert breasts, her long legs, and thighs undimpled by cellulite.

That evening over dinner, though nothing was said, Willa was, as ever, familiar with the Reverend, touching him often, letting him know that she was not displeased by the afternoon's event. But again he made no move to deepen their relationship. Desperate now, that night Willa disrobed and waited beside the connecting door until the Reverend's light was dimmed. She pressed her ear to the crack, and when she heard the beginning of heavy breathing, of creaking bedsprings, she threw open the door and walked in. The Reverend tried to conceal his actions, pretending to be wrestling with the bedclothes. But Willa was not to be denied. She flung back the covers, exposing the limp yet still tumescent evidence, and then with all the wiles she had learned while in Mrs. Gacey's employ, she proceeded to restore it to its former fisted grandeur.

The Reverend Meister proved Willa's equal in need, and together they explored the realm of Position, tying complex knots of heat and sinew that often took hours to unravel. Once Position had been exhausted, they began a study of Location. There was a scarcely a place in Lyman that did not know their clandestine passion, and each grunting thrust, each stifled cry, was a godsend to Willa after those long and joyless years. She came half to believe that the Christian God had truly blessed her. "Hallelujah," she whispered as they lay in sweet congregation beneath the church's midnight altar. "Thank you, Jesus," she sighed as she stood pressed into a corner of the closet below the choir stalls, her skirts lifted high and the Reverend kneeling down to take communion. "Praise the Lord," she breathed, bending over a projector in the darkened Sunday School basement, while the Reverend mounted her from behind, and a dozen children sat in front, munching cookies and ice cream, their eyes fixed on a slide show of the Holy Land *sans* narration.

Willa lived in a green world again, in world where hope and possibility conjoined. Her relationship with the Reverend was that rarest of commodities—they were friends who could make love and not allow their carnality to lead away from friendship. And in their lovemaking . . . well, let it suffice to say that the depth of Willa's devotion and the extent of the Reverend's commitment to excellence were compatible in every extreme.

But, lo, this too shall pass.

One night at the suggestion of Tom, Too, they had the Reverend over for dinner, and after the dessert dishes had been cleared away, Tom, Too displayed a packet of photographs he had taken, their subject being Willa and the Reverend. "Now this here," he said, handing one around, "it'll blow up real nice for the church newsletter. And this here"—he handed over another displaying a complex tangle of flesh, half of which comprised an illegality in the state of Ohio—"I was figurin' to do up some eight-by-ten glossies."

The Reverend lowered his eyes, and Willa shut hers.

"This has really got to stop," said Tom, Too. "Right, Dad?"

Tom was trembling, apoplectic, squeezing the arms of his chair.

Tom, Too held up yet another photograph that showed the lovers beneath the altar, the moonlit shadow of the cross thrown across them. "This one's got dandy symbolic value. Oughta raise a few eyebrows in the bishop's office." He searched among the remaining photographs. "Hey, Dad," he said breezily, picking one and sliding it over. "Check that out . . . Never woulda thought Mom was so limber."

Despite his choler, Tom looked broken, frail, on the verge of passing out, and two weeks later, he suffered a stroke that left him paralyzed and requiring constant nursing.

"Wouldn't sell the bottomland if I were you," Tom, Too advised Willa, reminding her of the leverage of his photographs. "I been considerin' puttin' up a shoppin' mall . . . after it's mine legal, of course. I 'spect the state'll take care of Dad if you can't."

That tore it for Willa. She crumbled all at once. It was as if her beauty had been its own self, had been hanging on for hope of some lasting appreciation, and now had just given up. By the time she reached the age of sixty, she looked it. At seventy, she looked a spry seventy-five, and at seventy-eight, morticians would perk up when she passed, clasp their hands and say, "How you feelin' today, Mrs. Selkie," in a tone that made clear they really wanted to know.

Tom died nine years after the disclosure of the photographs, having never spoken another word, and after the funeral, the Reverend Meister dropped over to see Willa. He had married a mousy little woman, and had written a book that everyone said was going to make him famous. Willa had never expected him to stay alone and didn't resent his marriage. In truth, she rarely thought about him anymore, being already a little distracted, halfway to dotty. But she was pleased about his book, and even more pleased when he told her that she was partly responsible for his writing it.

"Me?" she said. "What'd I do?"

"It was your intensity," he said. "When you made love, it was pure, an expression of something that had to come out. It was all of life you were taking in your arms. And if you'd been allowed to express it fully, it would have taken other forms as well. You made me want to find a way to express my own truth, to equal that intensity."

She often thought she might have done something with her life, but was glad to hear it from somebody else. "That's the second nicest thing anybody ever said to me," she told him.

"What was the nicest?"

" 'Please,' " she said, remembering.

He didn't press for clarification, and for a while they talked about trivial matters.

"How's it being married?" she asked.

"I don't love her," he said. "I just . . ."

"I know," she said. "What's it like?"

He thought a second or two. "It's like being sick . . . nothing serious. Like being in mild constant pain, and having a nurse and air conditioning."

For some reason that started her crying. Maybe it was because having him near made her notice her old-lady smell. Because he still looked young and she looked like death warmed over. He put an arm around her, but she shrugged it off. "Leave me be," she said.

"Willa . . ."

"You can't help me," she said. "I'm crazy."

"You're not crazy."

"Not now," she said. "But the minute you go, I'm gonna be wanderin' around the house, talking to myself, thinking all kinds of crazy thoughts. Now you get outa here and leave me to it."

He got to his feet, pulled on his coat, looking helpless and grim. "God bless you, Willa," he said.

"Ain't no such thing as God," she told him. "And don't argue with me 'bout it, 'cause I can feel the place where he ain't."

"Maybe you can at that," he said glumly.

When he closed the door, she had the idea that he stood outside for a long time . . . or could be he'd just left a thought leaning against the door, a wish for her, like an umbrella he had forgotten.

Night had fallen. Out the window, bare trees cast blue shadows on the rippled snow, and the air was so crystal clear it seemed you might be able to reach out and break off a chunk with a star inside it and put it in the fridge to save for Christmas. Oh, God . . . but it was a lonely clarity. And oh, God, there was life in the old girl yet, and wouldn't she love to move her hips again, and wouldn't it be more than love to know that sweet feeling of being filled, of being needed, instead of sitting here with liver spots a plague on her hands, with her son a Christian villain, and her daughter estranged, and her grandchild a hulking teen-age monster who visited once a year and stole money from her purse. With no future and all her memories played, all her lovers dead . . .

Not all, whispered the Black Clay Boy.

Yes, all! Even the Reverend Meister gone, a victim of that new disease taking the gay boys. Who'd have thought it? If she'd have stayed with him, she'd bet he wouldn't have strayed that far from heaven.

The Black Clay Boy seemed to smile at that.

"Quit makin' fun of me!" she said. "You're worse than them Kandell brats."

Much worse, Willa.

Lewd little bastard! I hear that sly tone, I know what you want!

And what's wrong with that? It's what you want, too.

She made a disparaging noise. "A runt like you couldn't give me a tickle."

You might be surprised, Willa.

Willa studied him. With his silver eyes and gouged mouth, he looked like a surreal Little Black Sambo. And, she realized, he favored Eden some. Eden had had that same unfinished look. She could, she supposed, give him hands and feet. But then he'd be traipsing his footprints all over her nice carpet, strewing black crumbs everywhere.

Crazy old bat, she thought.

But he *did* look unfinished.

And of course she knew just what he needed.

What we both need, Willa.

"Do you really think . . ."

I'm absolutely sure.

"I don't know, I . . ."

How you gonna know 'less you explore the potentials?

"Well," she said hesitantly. "Maybe just once."

More would be unsalubrious," said the Black Clay Boy.

She came to her feet effortlessly, as if the idea was a power, and she went rummaging through the kitchen drawer until she found the perfect accessory, long and sharp and silver. She wedged the handle into the crotch of the Black Clay Boy, jammed it in, and tried to wiggle it . . . It held firm. She'd always hated the bottomland for the hold it exerted, but now she was grateful for this quality.

God! She felt twenty-two again, all heart and hip, all nudge softness and clever muscle.

She picked up the Black Clay Boy, held him at arm's length and went whirling into the living room, each whirl bringing her hot thoughts closer to a boil. Oh, she was mad, mad as the pattern on the wallpaper, mad as the wind shaping her name from the eaves, saying *Willa, Willa, Willa,* with each and every spin, mad and whirling among the dark armoires and the huge iron-colored sideboard and the Victorian mahoganies. The shadows watched her, and the furniture was leaning together, gossiping, and in the folds of the drapes were cores of indigo that she recognized to be the cores of ghosts waiting to live their wispy lives once she had done.

"Won't be a minute," she told them gaily, and went whirling into the bedroom where the Black Clay Boy would have her once and silent, where love would once more be red and biting. She lifted him high. His silvery member was God's measure of a man, flashing with moonlight, tipped with pure charge . . . and the measure, too, of Eden's curse. She knew that clear, now. Knew that Eden's bones and dry flesh and even drier spirit infused this little devil she held in her hands. She could smell his meager scent of talcum powder and stale sweat, could sense his spirit hovering inside this loamy shell, and she knew she could expect only an Eden's worth of pleasure from his embrace, but that was so much more than she had for years, well . . . She not fell but floated down onto the bed, sinking into its bridal deep, and oh, she was eager, and oh, she could scarcely wait.

"Love," she said.

You never had it, Willa, whispered the Black Clay Boy.

"Love!" she cried. "Love, love, love."

Forever, said the Black Clay Boy, his voice acquiring a male sternness, a tone of command.

Forever, she thought she said, the word soft as a pillow. *Love forever,*

*Love for now, pin me deep and darling into the bottomland. Split me wide,
and take me where the pleasure lies.*

Lies, echoed the Black Clay Boy.

He quivered in her hands, wanting her, but she held him off, tasting the
delicious anticipation of the pure silver moment of going inside.

Now, Willa, now!

"When I'm ready," she said, laughing, teasing. "When I'm ready and
not a moment before."

Now!

"Yes!" she said, arching toward him, her eyelids fluttering down. "Yes,
now!"

With the powerful thrust of a man, with all the violent sweet force of a
man's need, she pulled him to her hard, and there was pain, yes, there was
pain, but it was filling and deep and real, and if she'd had the strength, she
would have plucked him out and pulled him in again and again and again.

Forever.

The perfect companion of that perfect gentleman, that perfect lover,
the Black Clay Boy.

His strange blank face was inches away, his eyes appeared to widen.
Maybe, she thought, this was the beginning of another memory.

Not hardly.

"Oh," she said sadly, and she could see the word come white from her
lips like a spirit, like the white poor thing of her life, her need, her sorrow-
ful ending. Like a blown kiss.

Better luck next time, he told her.

"Next time?" she said, hopeful. "You mean . . ."

Just kidding, Willa, said the Black Clay Boy as he winked shut first one
silver eye and then the other.

I deeply regret that this is Manly Wade Wellman's last story. He promised it to me about eighteen months before he died and our mutual good friend, Karl Edward Wagner, delivered it to me shortly after his death. The field's deep feeling for Manly was shown by the many thousands of dollars it raised to pay his medical bills and save his home. We will all miss him and his friend John.

WHERE DID SHE WANDER?

by Manly Wade Wellman

That gravelly old road ran betwixt high rocks and twiny-branched trees. I tramped with my pack and silver-strung guitar past a big old dornick rock, wide as a bureau, with words chopped in with a chisel:

> THIS GRAVE DUG FOR
> BECKY TIL HOPPARD
> HUNG BY THE TRUDO FOLKS
> AUG THE 12 18 & 49
> WE WILL REMEMBER YOU

And flowers piled round. Blue chicory and mountain mint and turtle-head, fresh as that morning. I wondered about them and walked on, three-four miles to the old county seat named Trudo, where I'd be picking and singing at their festival that night.

The town square had three-four stores and some cabin-built houses, a six-room auto court, a jail and courthouse and all like that. At the auto court stood Luns Lamar, the banjo man who was running the festival, in white shirt and string tie. His bristly hair was still soot-black, and he wore no glasses. Didn't need them, for all his long years.

"I knew you far down the street, John," he hailed me. "Long, tall, with the wide hat and jeans and your guitar. All that come tonight will have heard tell of you. And they'll want you to sing songs they recollect—'Vandy, Vandy,' 'Dream True,' those ones."

"Sure enough, Mr. Luns," I said. "Look, what do you know about Becky Til Hoppard's grave back yonder?"

He squinted, slanty-eyed. "Come into this room I took for us, and I'll tell you what I know of the tale."

Inside, he fetched out a fruit jar of blockade whiskey and we each of us had a whet. "Surprised you don't know about her," said Mr. Luns. "She was the second woman to get hung in this state, and it wasn't the true law did it. It was folks thought life in prison wasn't the right call on her. They strung her up in the square yonder, where we'll sing tonight."

We sipped and he talked. Becky Til Hoppard was a beauty of a girl with strange, dark ways. Junius Worral went up to her cabin to court her and didn't come back, and the law found his teeth and belt buckle in her fireplace ashes; and when the judge said just prison for life, a bunch of the folks busted into the jail and took her out and strung her to a white oak tree. When she started to say something, her daddy was there and he hollered, "Die with your secret, Becky!" and she hushed and died with it, whatever it was.

"How came her to be buried right yonder?" I asked him.

"That Hoppard set was strange-wayed," said Mr. Luns. "Her father and mother and brothers put her there. They had dug the hole during the trial and set up the rock and cut the words into it, then set out for other places. Isaiah Hoppard, the father, died when he was cutting a tree and it fell onto him. The mother was bit by a mountain rattler and died screaming. Her brother Harrison went to Kentucky and got killed stealing hogs. Otway, the youngest brother, fell at Chancellorsville in the Civil War."

"Then the family was wiped out."

"No," and he shook his head again. "Otway had married and had children, who grew up and had children, too. I reckon Hoppards live hereabouts in this day and time. Have you heard the Becky Til Hoppard song?"

"No, but I'd sure enough like to."

He sang some verses, and I picked along on my silver strings and sang along with him. It was a lonesome tune, sounded like old-country bagpipes.

"I doubt if many folks know that song today," he said at last. "It's reckoned to be unlucky. Let's go eat some supper and then start the show."

They'd set up bleachers in the courthouse square for maybe a couple thousand. Mr. Luns announced act after act. Obray Ramsey was there with near about the best banjo-picking in the known world, and Tom Hunter with near about the best country fiddling. The audience clapped after the different numbers, especially for a dance team that seemed to have wings on their shoes. Likewise for a gold-haired girl named Rilla something, who picked pretty on a zither, something you don't often hear in these mountains.

When it came my turn, I did the songs Mr. Luns had named, and the people clapped so loud for more that I decided to try the Becky Til Hoppard song. So I struck a chord and began:

> "Becky Til Hoppard, as sweet as a dove,
> Where did she wander, and who did she love?

Right off, the crowd went still as death. I sang:

> "Becky Til Hoppard, and where can she be?
> Rope round her neck, swung up high on the tree.

And that deathly silence continued as I did the rest of it:

> "On Monday she was charged, on Tuesday she was tried,
> By the laws of her country she had to abide.
> If I knew where she lay, to her side I would go,
> Round sweet Becky's grave pretty flowers I would strow . . ."

When I was done, not a clap, not a voice. I went off the little stage, wondering to myself about it. After the show, Rilla, the zither girl, came to my room to talk.

"Folks here think it's unlucky to sing that Becky Hoppard song, John," she said. "Even to hark at it."

"I seem to have done wrong," I said. "I didn't know."

"Well, those Hoppards are a right odd lot. Barely come into town except to buy supplies. And they take pay for curing sickness and making spells to win court cases. They're strong on that kind of thing."

"Who made the song?" I asked.

"They say it was sung back yonder by some man who was crazy for Becky Til Hoppard, and she never even looked his way. None of the Hoppard blood likes it, nor either the Worral blood. I know, because I'm Worral blood myself."

"Can you tell me the tale?" I inquired. "Have some of this blockade. Mr. Luns left it in here, and it's good."

"I do thank you." She took a ladylike sip. "All I know is what my oldest folks told me. Becky Hoppard was a witch-girl, the pure quill of the article. Did all sorts of spells. Junius Worral reckoned to win her with a love charm."

"What love charm?" I asked, because such things interest me.

"I've heard tell she let him have her handkerchief, and he did something with it. Went to the Hoppard cabin, and that's the last was seen of him alive. Or dead, either—he was all burnt up except his buckle and teeth."

"The song's about flowers at her grave," I said. "I saw some there."

"Folks do that, to turn bad luck away."

I tweaked my silver guitar strings. "Where's the Hoppard place?"

"Uphill, right near the grave. A broken-off locust tree there points to the path. I hope I've told you things that'll keep you from going there."

"You've told me things that make me to want to go."

"Don't, John," she begged me. "Recollect what happened to Junius Worral."

"I'll recollect," I said, "but I'll go." And we said goodnight.

I woke right soon in the morning and went to the dining room to eat me a good breakfast with Mr. Luns. Then I bade him good day and set out of Trudo the same way I'd come in, on the gravelly road.

Rilla had said danger was at the Hoppard place, but my guitar's silver strings had been a help against evil time and time again. Likewise in my pocket was a buckeye, given me one time by an Ozark fellow, and that's supposed to guard you, too—not just against rheumatics but all kinds of dangers. No man's ever found dead with a buckeye in his pocket, folks allow. So I was glad I had it as I tramped along with my pack and my guitar.

As I got near to the grave rock, I picked me some mountain laurel flowers. As I put those around the stone, I noticed more flowers there, besides the ones I'd seen the day before. Beyond was the broken-off locust, and a way uphill above it.

That path went through brush, so steep I had to lean forward to climb it. Trees crowded close at the sides. They near about leaned on me, and their leaves bunched into unchancey green faces. I heard a rain crow make its rattly call, and I spied out its white vest and blotchy tail. It was supposed to warn of a storm, but the patch of sky above was clear; maybe the rain crow warned of something else than rain. I kept on, climbed a good quarter mile to where there was a cabin amongst hemlocks.

That cabin was of old, old logs chinked with clay. It must have been built before the last four wars. The roof's split shakes were cracked and curly. A lean-to was tacked on at the left. There were two smudgy windows and a cleated plank door, and on the door-log sat a man, watching me as I climbed into his sight.

He was dressed sharp, better than me in my jeans and old hat. Good-fitting pants as brown as coffee and a bright-flowered shirt. He was soft-pudgy, and I'd reckon more or less fifty years old. His cheeks bunched out. His bald brow was low and narrow. He had a shallow chin and green eyes like grape pulps. His face had the look of a mean snake.

"We been a-waiting for you," he said when I got there.

"How come you to know I'd come, Mr. Hoppard?" I asked him.

He did a creaky laugh. "You know my name, and I don't know yours yet," he said, "but we been a-waiting on you. We know when they come." He grinned, with mossy-green teeth. "What name might I call you?"

"John."

We were being watched. Two heads at one of the windows. A toss-haired woman, a skinny man. When I looked at them they drifted back, then drifted up again.

"You'll be the John we hear tell about," said Hoppard. "A-sticking your nose in here to find out a tale."

"The tale of Becky Til Hoppard," I agreed.

"Poor Becky. They hung her up and cut her down."

"And buried her below here," I added on.

"No, not exactly," he said. "That stone down yonder just satisfies folks away from the truth. They don't ask questions. But you do—ask questions about my great-great aunt Becky." He turned his ugly head to the house. "All right, yoins," he bawled, "come out here and meet John."

Those two came. The young man was tall, near about my height, but so gaunt he looked ready to bust in two. He wore good pants and shirt, but rumpled and grubby. His eyes were green, too. The girl's frock looked to be made of flowered curtain cloth, and it was down off one rounded bare shoulder. Her tousled hair was as red as if it had been dipped in a mountain sunset. And she looked on me with shiny green eyes, like Hoppard's, like the young man's.

"These is my son and daughter," said Hoppard, a-smirking. "I fetched them up after my fashion, taught them what counts and how to tell it from what doesn't count. She's Tullai. I call the boy Herod."

"Hidy," I told the two of them.

Hoppard got up from the door-log, on crooked legs like a toad's. "Come on in the house," he said, and we went in, all four.

The front room was big, with a puncheon floor worn down with God alone knows how many years, and hooked rag rugs on it. The furniture was homemade. I saw a long sofa woven of juniper branches at back and seat, and two stools and an armchair made of tree chunks, and a table of old planks and trestles. At the back, a sort of statue stood on a little homemade stand. It looked to be chipped from dark rock, maybe three feet high, and it had a grinning head with horns on it. Its eyes were shiny green stones, a kind I didn't know, but the color of Hoppard's eyes.

"Is that a god?" I inquired of Hoppard.

"Yes, and it's been worshipped here for I can't tell how many generations," he said. "Walk all round the room and them eyes keep a-looking on you. Try it."

I tried it. Sure enough, the eyes followed me into every corner. But I'd seen the same thing to happen with a picture of George Washington in a museum, and a photograph of a woman called Mona Lisa. "You all pray to that idol?" I asked.

"We do, and he answers our prayers," said the girl Tullai, soft-voiced. "He sent you to us."

"Pa," said the boy Herod, "you should ought to tell John about us."

"Sit down," said Hoppard, and we sat here and there while he told the tale. Tullai sat next to me.

Hoppard allowed that his folks had always been conjure folks. Way back yonder, Becky Til Hoppard had been foremost at it. Some things she'd done was good—cures for sick folks, spells to make rain fall, all like that. But about Junius Worral, he said, what I'd heard wasn't rightly so.

"They told you he'd had a charm to win Becky?" said Hoppard. "It was more the other way round. She charmed him to fetch him here."

"What for?" I asked.

"He was needed here," said Hoppard; and Tullai repeated, "Needed here," and her green eyes looked at me sidelong, the way a kitten looks at a bowl of milk.

"To help Becky to a long life," Hoppard went on. "The hanging nair truly killed her, so her folks just set her head back on its neckbone and fetched her home." He nodded to a door that led to the lean-to shed. "She's in yonder now."

"You a-telling me she's alive?" I asked him.

"Her folks did things that fetched her back. In yonder she waits, for you to talk to her."

"John's got him a guitar," spoke up Tullai all of a sudden, her green eyes still cut at me. "Can't we maybe hear him pick it?"

"Sure enough, if you all want to hark at me," I said.

I did some tuning, then I sang something I'd been thinking up:

> "Long is the road on which I fare,
> Over the world afar,

The mountains here and the valleys there,
Me and this old guitar.

"The places I've been were places, yes,
The things that I've seen were things,
With this old guitar my soul to bless
By the sound of its silver strings."

"Hey, you're good!" squeaked out Tullai, and clapped her hands. "Go on, sing the rest."

"That's all the song so far," I said. "Maybe more later."

"But meanwhile," said Hoppard, "Becky's a-waiting on you in yonder." He looked me up and down. "Unless you're scared to go see."

"I got over being scared some while back," I said, and hoped that was more or less a fact. "I came here to find out about her."

Herod stomped over to the inside door and opened it, and I picked up my pack and guitar and went over and into the lean-to room. The door shut behind me. I heard a click, and knew I was locked in.

The room was a big one. It was walled, front and sides, with up-and-down split slabs, with bark and knots, and as old as the day hell was laid out. The rear wall was a rock face, gray and smooth, with a fireplace cut in it and a blaze on the hearth, with wood stacked to the side. Next to the hearth, a dark-aged wooden armchair, with above it the biggest pair of deer horns I'd ever seen, and in the chair somebody watching me.

A woman, I saw right off, tucked from chin to toes in a robe as red as blood, and round her neck a blue scarf, tight as a bandage. Her face was soft-pale, her slanty Hoppard green eyes under brows as thin as pencil marks. Her lips were redder than her red robe. They smiled, with white teeth.

"So you're John," and her voice was like flowing water. "Come round where I can look on you."

"How do you know my name?"

"Say a little bird told me." She mocked me with her smile. "A bird with teeth in its beak and poison in its claws, that tells me what I need to know. We waited for you here, John."

"You know my name, and I know yours, Miss Becky Til Hoppard. Why aren't you in your grave down by the road, Miss Becky?"

"They told you. I nair went in it. I was toted off here and my folks said some words and burnt some plants, and here I am. They left that grave for a blind. My old folks and my brothers died in right odd ways, but I do fine with these new kinfolks."

Blood-red-lipped, she smiled.

"What next?" I inquired.

"You," and she kept her smile. "You're next, John. Every few years I find somebody like you, somebody with strong life in him, to keep my life going. This won't be like poor Junius Worral, my first helper—he was traced here. Nobody knows you came. But why don't you play on your pretty guitar?"

I swept my hands on the silver strings. I sang:

"Becky Til Hoppard, as sweet as a dove,
Where did she wander, and who did she love? . . ."

All the way through, and she smiled and harked at me. "You sang that in town last night. I could hear you. I'm able to hear and see things."

"You've got you a set of talents."

"So have you. When you sang that song, I did spells to fetch you here."

"I don't aim to stay," I said.

"You'll stay," she allowed, "and give me life."

I grinned down at her, with my guitar across me. "I see," I nodded to her. "You took Junius Worral's life into you to keep you young. And others . . ."

"Several," she said. "I made them glad to give me their years."

"Glad?" I repeated, my hand on the silver strings.

"Because they loved me. You'll love me, John."

"Not me, I'm sorry. I love another."

"Another what?" She laughed at her own joke. "John, you'll burn up for love of me. Look."

The fire blazed up. I saw a chunk of wood drop in on the blaze.

She quartered me with her gleamy green eyes. "I could call out just one word, and there's two Hoppard men out yonder would come in here and bust your guitar for you."

"I've seen those two men," I said, "and neither of them looks hard for me to handle."

"There'd be two of them . . ."

"I'd hit them two hard licks," I said. "Nobody puts a hand on my guitar but just me myself."

"Then take it with you, yonder to the fire. Go to the fire, John."

One hand pointed a finger at me, the other pointed to the fire. It blazed high up the chimney. Wood had come into it, without a hand to move it there. It shot up long, fierce, bright tongues of flame. The floor of hell was what it looked like.

"Look on it," Becky Til Hoppard bade me again. "I can send you into it. I made my wish before," and her voice half-sang. "I make it now. I nair saw the day that the wish I made was not true."

That was a kind of spell. I had a sense that hands pushed me. I couldn't see them, but I could feel them. I made another step into the hot, hot air of the hearth. I was come right next to her, with her bright green eyes watching me.

"Yes," she sang. "Yes, yes."

"Yes," I said after her, and pushed the silver strings of my guitar at her face.

She screamed once, shrill and sharp as a bat, and her head fell over to the side, all the way over and hung there, and she went slack where she sat.

For I'd guessed right about her. Her neck was broken; her head wasn't fast there, it just balanced there. And she sank lower, and the flames of the fire came pouring out at us like red-hot water. I fairly scuttled away toward the door, the locked door, and the door sprang itself open.

I was caught behind the door as Hoppard and his son Herod came a-shammocking in, and after them his daughter Tullai. As they came, that fire jumped right out of its hearth into the room, onto the floor, all round where Becky Til Hoppard sunk in her chair.

"Becky!" one of them yelled, or all of them. And by then I was through the door. I grabbed up my pack as I headed out into the open. Behind me, something sounded like a blast of powder. I reached the head of the trail going down, and gave a look back, and the cabin was spitting smoke from the door and the windows.

That was it. Becky Til Hoppard ruled the fire. When her rule came to an end, the fire ran wild. I scrambled down, down from that height.

I wondered if they all burned up in that fire. I nair went back to see. And I don't hear that anybody by the Hoppard name has been seen or heard tell of thereabouts.

ABOUT THE EDITOR

Stuart David Schiff is the editor and publisher of *Whispers* magazine and the Whispers Press. Dr. Schiff has won four World Fantasy Awards while stories from his *Whispers* magazine and *Whispers* anthologies have also garnered four World Fantasy Awards. Other honors that have been accumulated by Dr. Schiff include the British Fantasy Award, two Hugo Award nominations, the Small Press Writers and Artists Organization Award, and two grants from the National Endowment for the Arts. His press has published original hardcover editions by authors such as Isaac Asimov, Stephen King, Fritz Leiber, F. Paul Wilson, and Robert Bloch. The *Whispers* anthologies published by Doubleday have received wide acclaim: *Publishers Weekly* has said, "*Whispers* is fertile ground for the imagination, a field in which nightmares graze"; *Library Journal* has stated that ". . . Schiff's *Whispers* has established itself as the leading anthology for Gothic and fantasy literature today . . . Highly recommended."